Pat Gillespie

GIVEN A
SECOND CHANCE

A Dream Worth Waiting For

iUniverse, Inc.
Bloomington

Given a Second Chance
A Dream Worth Waiting For

Copyright © 2011 Pat Gillespie

This is a work of fiction. All of the characters, names, incidents, organizations, and dialogue in this novel are either the products of the author's imagination or are used fictitiously.

iUniverse books may be ordered through booksellers or by contacting:

iUniverse
1663 Liberty Drive
Bloomington, IN 47403
www.iuniverse.com
1-800-Authors (1-800-288-4677)

ISBN: 978-1-4620-6233-1 (sc)
ISBN: 978-1-4620-6235-5 (hc)
ISBN: 978-1-4620-6234-8 (e)

Printed in the United States of America

iUniverse rev. date: 10/27/2011

CHAPTER ONE

ONE MONTH AFTER THE SHOOTING, Detective Jarred Stanton, the nephew and partner to one of Crawfordsfield County Police Department's toughest Detectives, Detective Alex Storm, found himself having to lay low in his own house, while recuperating from a gunshot wound to the chest.

"How are we doing about finding Delgado?" he asked his uncle, upon walking back into the living room from getting them both some coffee.

"No sign of him yet. Ted's been pounding the pavement ever since it happened. What about you?"

"Me?"

"Yes! Since you've been held up out here, anything happen?"

"No, not much of anything with those bloodhounds the Commander assigned me."

"Just try to hang in there. We'll find him."

"In the meantime, how's our happy couple?"

"Still on their honeymoon, so I hear," the tall, forty-nine year old, graying hair Detective grinned, while thinking about his other nephew, Craig, as the two went on talking.

"And Beth?" the tall, handsome, now, brown haired, bearded Detective asked, grinning.

"Detective training," he replied, recalling his red headed rookie officer and the feelings the two had once shared, before their relationship had to come to a sad, yet, sudden end due to departmental rules.

"She was sure one special lady," he laughed then at his uncle's expression.

"Yeah, she sure was," *and always will be,* he continued to himself, as his nephew turned away to stare out the front window, while thinking of a someone he was once so in love with, and still is after all this time, if only it hadn't been for her grandmother getting in the way.

Meanwhile, not far from there, staring off into space, in her office of Jodi's Antiques, Jodi's friend walked in to interrupt her thoughts. "Hey, there, why so quiet?" Karen asked the tall slender brunette, stirring her, now, cold coffee.

The look in Jodi Tate's blue-green eyes looked troubled, while standing at her coffee maker. "W…what?" she asked in a startled thirty-eight year old voice, when looking up to see her friend standing in the doorway, shaking her head.

"Do you want to talk about it?" she asked, walking on in with her own cup of coffee in hand.

Looking back at the pile of bills and other papers stacked high on her desk, she shook her head, sadly. "What is there to talk about? I've been having these disturbing dreams about a man who's been shot in his home!"

"Just like your cousin?"

"Yes," she sighed, "just like her."

Worried about her friend, the forty-three year old brunette asked, "Did you tell Jessi about it?"

"Yes, just before she left on her honeymoon."

"Oh my!"

"What?" she asked, seeing the look of puzzlement on her face.

"Oh, just thinking! Wasn't that how she met her husband, through a dream?"

Before giving her friend an answer, she poured herself another cup, and thought back to the conversation she had had with her a few days before she had gotten married. At that time, a warm smile came to her partially full lips, as she looked over at Karen and grinned. "Indeed it was! You might even say; we have a lot in common!"

"You can say that again!" she laughed, before turning solemn, thinking about how they had both lost their first love in tragic automobile accidents, and had married men who couldn't stay faithful. "And now you had both been raising two teenage daughters on your own."

"Yes," she returned numbly, when sitting the coffee pot down, to take a cautious sip from her cup. "Mmmm... I just wish I could have made it to her wedding, though. Why did Alison have to go and die on me when she did? I wouldn't have had to go up there, and missed my cousin's wedding, when I did. If only things could have gone the way they thought it was supposed to, none of this would have happened!"

"You never know about these things, and she was pretty old."

"Not really! She was around mom's age, but the cancer made her look older."

"Yes, but still your mom couldn't have made the trip without you being there for her. Didn't you say the woman was like an aunt to you, when you were pretty little?"

"Yes, and she also wanted me to have her doll collection, when she past. Man, and those dolls are really old, too."

"What did you end up doing with them?"

"The girls have one each, setting out on their dressers. The rest are setting out on my dresser and bookshelves."

"That reminds me, the girls are off staying with your folks for awhile aren't they?"

"Yes, but only for a few weeks, while I go and get granny's old antiques back."

"Boy, sounds like you're going to be busy for awhile, aren't you?"

"Yes, it does, doesn't it?"

"Well, it'll go by fast enough. With the way business has been going, the time will just fly by. Which also reminds me," she said, thinking of business. "Not meaning to change the subject, but were you able to get everything on your trip to Charlottesville the other day?"

"No, but he did say I would be able to get the rest of her things this weekend. Can you handle the shop alone, while I'm out?"

"Sure! But you know we're expecting another bad storm to come rolling in at anytime."

"Oh?" she stated, heading out to the showroom to get things setup for the day. "I hope not like the one I barely missed the other day!"

"Well..." her friend started, when Jodi stopped at one of the front picture windows to look out.

Noticing the clouds hadn't looked any more threatening than they did when she started out to Charlottesville the previous day, at that moment, she felt certain she would be all right going back over to pick up the rest of her granny's things. "I'm sorry, what were you saying?" She turned back to give her friend her undivided attention.

"Well, it was a pretty bad storm. Not to mention, I was plenty worried about your driving home in it."

"Yes, well, I was pretty scared." She shivered, recalling how she had come so close to being hit by a large utility pole, when a bolt of lightning struck it. "Oh… yes," she laughed nervously. "Definitely scared."

"Well, before you decide to head back out, you might want to double check the weather report, to be certain it will hold out for you, until you get back."

"You're right, I had better. I don't want any of her things getting ruined."

"Are you taking your cousin's truck again?"

"Yes, and I don't want to forget that Mr. Murphy said he was finally able to get her hutch and china cabinet in, too!"

"Great! I bet you're delighted about that!" she smiled, knowing Jodi had been after those particular pieces for some time.

"You bet I am!" she smiled. "And I have just the perfect spot for them, too!"

"In your granny's old dining room?"

"Yep! Just where I remembered it, while growing up."

"How is the house coming, anyway?"

"Slow, but she left me with enough money to make all the necessary repairs, and still have enough to buy back some of her old things."

"That must have been hard for her to have to go and sell them off, just to repair this plate glass window, when those kids broke it out years ago."

"It was. And I was here when she found the mess they had left after breaking in."

Thinking back, Jodi remembered when her grandmother had to call the police. The officer who had taken the call was just a few years older than herself, and looked really handsome in his uniform. Not to mention, his beautiful deep blue eyes and brown hair.

Then suddenly, remembering something, she went back into the office to reach into one of the side drawers of her desk. Pulling out a white handkerchief, on it, were his initials 'J. S.' stitched in one of the corners.

"What do you have there?" Karen asked, walking in behind her.

"His handkerchief!" she smiled. "He had given it to me when I began to cry. But for some reason I don't remember his name! Besides, it's been quite some time ago when the shop had been broken into."

"Do you still have a copy of the police report, mixed in with all your granny's things?"

"I should have! I took a bunch of her old papers home with me the other night, meaning to go through them."

"Well, you'll just have to find it, and…"

"And what…?"

"Well…!"

"Karen, he's probably married, and has some kids by now."

"You don't know that!" she grinned sheepishly, while turning at that time, to go back out to the showroom, to finish getting things setup for the day.

"No, but…"

"But nothing!" she said, stopping just outside the office door. "If he isn't…"

"Call him, I presume!" she finished, when coming back out.

"Yes!"

"Girl, do you know how long it's been since I've seen him? I was just a teenager, when all this had taken place."

"So! Have you seen him since then?"

"No…! Well, at least…" She stopped to think back to one particular day.

"Well…?"

"Well, then again, maybe, or, maybe not."

"Which is it? Yes, you did, or no, you didn't?"

"Well…" she returned, thinking a moment longer, "a couple of times I thought I had, but he acted as though I didn't exist!"

"Yeah, well, that was then. Now you are all grown up, and have a good running business that you had inherited off your grandmother."

"Speaking of which," she turned back, "I had better be getting my butt in gear, and get those doors open, so we can make some money. Those bills in there aren't going to pay themselves off."

"You're right about that!" she agreed, pointing at the line of customers standing at the front door now.

"Oh… yes, I can see it's going to be another long day," she laughed, heading over to let them in.

Chapter Two

By the end of the day, the two closed up and went out to dinner.

"Boy, what a day," Karen groaned.

"Yes, well you can certainly say that gain," Jodi sighed tiredly, while getting them a table at a local diner.

After putting in their order, Karen commented, "Well, now, why don't you tell me about these dreams of yours. I was meaning to ask you earlier, but we had gotten too busy. Just when did they start anyway?"

"Shortly after the girls left. At first the dreams were just your average dreams! But then they changed!"

"Changed? In what way?"

"At first, there was what I thought to be an old abandoned house, surrounded by trees, just like in Jessi's dreams. By then, it was getting dark, and I was standing next to my car, looking at the house. When out of nowhere, came this blue Chevy pick-up, followed by an old black, beat up looking Ford. The guy in the Ford looked pretty angry, while the guy in the Chevy, after having just pulled in, jumped out of his truck and ran up to the house!"

"Yes…! And what happened then?"

"The man in the other truck got out and followed him in, after kicking down the door," she explained, when the waitress delivered their coffee.

Meanwhile, looking astonished, Karen asked, "Well… don't leave me hanging! What did he look like?"

"The guy in the Chevy?"

"Well, yes…!"

"Angry. He looked angry! And at the same time, for some reason,' she sighed, "he looked familiar, as if I should have known him!"

"From where?"

"I'm not sure!" she shrugged. "He was tall, maybe six foot three, and looked to be in his early forties, with medium brown… hair…" she started, just as her voice began to drift off some.

"Jodi…?"

"Yes…" she hesitated, while thinking to herself.

"Jodi?"

"What…?"

"The man in the other truck…?"

"What about him? Oh! He was about five ten or so, and looked to be in his mid to late forties, with short black hair, as well as a rough looking face."

"And…" she asked hurriedly, "what happened next?"

"The…" she began, when her face went pale, and the hand, which held her coffee cup, began to tremble. At that moment, looking down at the cup, the words just froze in her throat.

"What…?" Karen asked, reaching over to touch her hand.

"The guy in the Chevy. He was trying to talk to the man, who by then had a gun pointed at him. When… all of a sudden…"

"What?"

"I heard the most horrible sound ever coming from the house!" she cried, looking up with tears in her eyes.

"Jodi…" Karen prompted. "What…?"

"Oh, Lord, Karen… h…his voice_____! He was crying out, no_____!"

"Oh… my… gosh_____! That must have been horrible."

"It was!" she exclaimed, playing back the reaction to her dream.

"Wow, this is awful. Just like what had happened to your cousin! But why, and what does it mean?"

"Yes, you're right, and I don't have the foggiest," she shivered, while sitting back when their food arrived.

Meanwhile, on the other side of the Diner, Alex, while huddled in a corner booth with his nephew, was asking if he had everything he needed out at his place.

"Yes," he grumbled, while adjusting his Chicago Cubs cap on his head to hide his identity, "I just wish things would hurry and get over with."

"It will. Just give it time."

"Yeah, time. I keep hearing that," he returned, but for some reason it wasn't because of his own life having been threatened, but his uncle's, as well. "You know, Alex, we're taking an awful big chance even being out here?"

"Yeah, but you needed some fresh air. Besides, we have plenty of guys outside watching. Not to mention, in here as well to keep a close eye on things. If Delgado is out there, he won't get close enough to hurt us."

Having said that, their waitress arrived with their meal, while on the other side of the restaurant, Karen went on.

"Jodi?"

"Yes?"

"What are you going to do if this dream was to come true, like…"

"Jessi's…? I hope not!" she shivered again, remembering what she had told her. *'A troubled spirit? No…way…!'*

"What…?"

"Oh nothing. Just remembering how she met Craig, is all."

"Well, come on now, he's after all, a real hunk."

"Yes, but still, I just wished I could have been there when they got married."

"Jodi, we've been over this already. You couldn't help being out of town when it came up. Your mom needed you."

"Yes, but I should have done something. Jessi is my closest cousin, and I should have been there for her."

"Well, you're helping her out now with the plans on those cabins she's wanting built."

"Oh, and yes, they are sure coming along nicely."

"Great!" she smiled, as the two went on to finish their meal.

After getting through, they got up to pay their bill. However, not seeing the two men huddled off in the corner, as if in a hushed conversation, Karen called out to her friend, while heading off to the ladies room, "Hey, Jodi, I'll be right out. I just need to make a pit stop first."

Hearing her name being called out, Jarred's head shot up like a bullet.

"What is it?" Alex asked, seeing his nephew's reaction.

"That name!" he returned, not giving Vince Delgado a thought, while looking around the diner, hoping to find the person the name belonged to.

"What about it?"

"Didn't you hear it?"

"No!"

Still looking hard, Jodi, at that time, was just getting their change back from the cashier, before turning to head out the door, when Karen returned to join her.

"Ready?" Jodi asked, closing up her purse.

"Yes, let's go," she agreed, while taking the lead.

Suddenly catching sight of them, he groaned, seeing the back of Jodi's long hair and shapely figure, while going out the door, "Oh, God, it can't be…"

Getting to his feet to go after her, Alex reached out, grabbing his arm. "Hold up there, you can't just go running off like that!"

"But, Alex!"

"But what?"

"That girl…!"

"What about her?"

"Didn't you see her, just now?"

"Yeah, and she looked an awful lot like Jessi, but that can't be, she and Craig are still on their honeymoon!"

"Yes, but…"

Seeing how he wasn't going to just let it go, Alex got up to check it out for himself. "Just stay put, while I go and see this person for myself."

"Sure. Fine. But do you even know what she looks like?"

"This, Jodi? Well, no, but…"

"Then let me go!"

"No, it isn't safe for you out there. Just stay put," he ordered, not wasting any more time, when he reached the door.

Spotting the woman right away, before she could reach her car, he growled quietly, finding her indeed looking a lot like Jessi, "What? This is crazy!" he groaned, standing back in the shadows, while quietly watching the two women walk out to their cars.

"Hey, I'll see ya in the morning, all right?" Karen called out, getting into her little red sports car, while leaving Jodi alone in the parking lot next to her own car, a small, red, Pontiac Lemans.

"Yeah, tomorrow," she grumbled, tiredly, while out of the corner of her eye, Jarred had just come out after paying their bill.

"Alex?" he spoke up quietly.

Shaking his head in disbelief, "I can't believe it. The resemblance is uncanny!"

"With Jessi?" he asked, peering out across the parking lot at the woman who had just gotten into her car.

"Yes, but that isn't Jessi," he continued, while shaking his head. "Damn…!"

"What?" Jarred asked, when Alex looked off across the street, where a couple of his men were parked, in case there was trouble.

"I've got to get you back out to your place, before you're spotted."

As for Jodi, her drive home didn't take long, as the house stood just on the east side of Ripley, not far from the antique store.

Pulling into the driveway, she thought back on all the happy times she had had there, whenever her parents went off to Florida, knowing how she didn't like long trips.

It wasn't until a few years ago that her grandmother had passed away, leaving her the house and business. "Oh, Granny," she cried softly, while sitting out in her car, looking up at the old two-story structure that looked so large and barren at that moment with all its lights off, "I wish you were still here!" she continued, before seeing how sitting there was doing her no good.

Getting out, she walked up to unlock the front door. Once inside, a smile came to her, while closing the door behind her. As it was then she realized the place still held the woman's familiar scent, which made it easier for her to handle her absence.

However, that night was no different than any other. When after getting herself ready for bed, the dream still played out in her mind, with the man's face looking familiar to her. *'But why,'* she wondered, as she continued to toss and turn in her sleep.

CHAPTER THREE

THE NEXT FEW DAYS, JODI dug into the mountain of paperwork, until she pretty much had it all caught up, before leaving for Charlottesville.

"Finished?" Karen asked, walking into the office with the Friday morning's mail.

"Yep! And I even called the girls to let them know I'll be out of town for a few days."

"Well, at least the weather looks good for it."

"Yes, and I'm sure everything will be all right. Besides, I'll be back with the furniture in no time," she announced, while getting up to smooth out her blue v-neck sweater, when a long strand of hair fell out of its ponytail.

"Good. Now, do you have everything packed?"

"Yes. And Hank has already brought Jessi's truck over," she replied, thinking fondly of her cousin's old stable hand, that had worked for Jessi ever since she had bought the one hundred and ten year old Victorian Inn, outside of Langley.

"So then, I guess this means you're on your way out?" she asked, following Jodi out to the front door.

"Just as soon as I give you the keys to my house! You won't forget to get the mail for me, will you?"

"No. But you are just going to be gone a few days, aren't you?"

"Yes!"

"Okay."

After giving her friend the keys, the two exchanged a few more pleasantries, before she got into her cousin's blue pick-up, and pulled away, waving goodbye.

The trip over, all but took a few hours to get there, with the town being ninety-five miles west of Ripley. While there, Mr. Murphy, the local antiques dealer, had a room set up at his place, on the north edge of town, in case she needed it.

"Well, I see you made it in all right!" the elderly man in his light gray suit and wire rimmed glasses greeted cheerfully, when she pulled up to the front of his old run down shop in the middle of Charlottesville. "You didn't have any trouble, or run into any bad weather, did you?" he asked, handing her a tall glass of iced tea, seeing how she could use one about then.

"No, and not a drop of rain, either," she smiled, while accepting the glass graciously.

"Good, because it's heading our way."

"What?" she complained, following the man back inside his shop. "But it said nothing about rain, when I checked out the weather report, before heading out. I don't like the sound of that one bit!"

Once inside, she got her mind off the pending weather, when she spotted, off in one corner, the most beautiful antique storage chest she had ever seen. Going over to take a closer look at it, she knelt down to open its lid.

"Do you remember that?" he asked, coming up behind her, before she could get it open.

Turning back, she saw the grin on his weather-beaten face. "Is this what I think it is?" she asked, afraid to believe her eyes.

"Open it and find out!"

Turning back, just when his wife, a short, stocky, silvered hair woman, walked in, she slowly lifted the lid, and sure enough, it was the same old cedar chest that used to sit in the far corner of her grandmother's bedroom. Even all her old blankets and quilts were still folded up neatly in it.

At that time, her eyes welled up with tears, when she thought back to those cold nights her granny used to tell her to go in and get one of her quilts out and cover up with it. "I can't believe it," she cried. "It's the same one that sat in granny's old room! And the blankets. I wondered what happened to all her old blankets."

"She must have forgotten they were there," Beatrice replied, kindly. "So knowing someday you would be back to claim them, we held onto them for you."

"Oh, thank you…" she cried, hugging to her favorite one.

"Well now, how about the two of you stop with what you're doing, and come on up to the house for lunch, before loading up these old things?"

Looking back at Jodi, Tom asked, "Are you hungry?"

"Starving!" she exclaimed, closing the lid.

"Good. I can get the boys to load up everything, while we're sitting down to eat."

"Sure, but first, if you don't mind, I would like to check out a few other things while I'm here."

"Sure, just take your time! We can wait!" he offered, going over to the front door with his wife.

Looking around the somewhat large single room, she found a few other items she wanted to get while there.

"Oh, that reminds me," Tom spoke up. "Those few items which belonged to your cousin's, husband?"

"Yes! How are they doing?"

"They're done!"

"Really? But you hadn't had them all that long."

"I got help! Would you like to see them?" he offered, leading the way to the storeroom.

Upon opening the door, she spotted them right away. "Wow…!" she cried, going over to run her hand across the top of the dresser.

"Looks like new, doesn't it?"

"Sure does! And I know they will be happy to see these."

"Well good! And now, if you're ready to go and grab a bite to eat, we can take care of the bill later."

"Sure, besides, I've seen enough," she replied, on the way out to the Murphy's car.

Heading up to their house, she told them what all she wanted, while leaving the truck behind to be loaded by his hired hands.

"You made a good selection. And better yet, I'll be getting in even more later."

"Great! I'll be back when you do!"

After dinner, they had all gone out to the front porch to get some fresh air. While there, they noticed how the air smelled of rain.

"It's coming!" Beatrice announced.

"Yep, it sure is!" he agreed, walking out to the edge to see some dark clouds coming their way. "And I sure don't like the looks of those clouds there either, Ms. Tate," he commented, turning back. "With those pieces of antiques on the back of your truck, they might get damaged if you were to get caught in a downpour."

"Not if I leave right now!" she announced, seeing his hired hands bringing her cousin's truck up to them.

"Oh, Tom…!" Beatrice spoke up, looking worried.

"Well, we do have that plastic out in the shed she could use!"

"Yes!" she agreed, while he headed out back to get it. "Oh, sweetie," she turned back to Jodi, "would you rather stay the night? We do have that garage in town that we can put your truck in until the weather passes!"

"No, but thanks. I have a feeling of déjà vu about this. So I'll chance getting home in hopes before I do get caught up in this," she smiled nervously, while turning back to watch the clouds. *'At least this way I'll be driving away from it. Just maybe I'll be able to out run it too.'*

Once they had gotten everything tied down, Jodi climbed in behind the wheel.

"Ms. Tate…" Beatrice called out, carrying out a wicker basket of food, "I don't want you to go off without this."

"Oh, but it's only a couple of hours to Ripley! I should be all right in getting there!"

"Yes, but just in case you run into trouble along the way, you'll have something to tie you over," Tom interceded, while taking the basket from his wife, to give to Jodi. "Now be careful, and drive just under the speed limit."

"All right," she replied, thoughtfully, while anxious to be on her way. *'So much for out running it,'* she thought, when feeling the wind pick up.

Pulling onto the main street of town, she looked back to see the

15

Murphy's waving good-bye. Doing the same, she waved, just before turning to head out of town.

Halfway home, she got caught in one of the worst downpours ever. If that weren't bad enough, the bridge up ahead was under water. "Darn…" she slammed her hand a little too hard on the steering wheel, "what now…?"

Looking around, she remembered seeing a road a short distance back, when turning around to head for it.

"I have got to get this stuff out of the weather, and soon!"

Taking the road that she had passed up, she soon found an old barn, and pulled the truck up to it.

"Well, it isn't in the best of conditions, but it'll have to do," she commented, while getting out to see how it looked inside.

To her relief, it was nearly empty. Turning around she ran back out to get the truck. Once inside, she shut it off and got out to stretch her legs, while walking over to the large set of double doors to have a look out at the growing storm.

"Well, girl, at least you have a roof over your head. Now let's just hope this doesn't turn into a really bad storm," she prayed, while turning to go over and have a seat on a bale of straw.

Nearly an hour had gone by, when what she had been praying for not to happen, did. Hearing the first sound of thunder rumbling overhead, she got up and went back over to look out at the storm, as it was gaining strength. "Oh great…! Now what?" she groaned, wrapping her arms around herself.

Soon she had her answer, when seeing a streak of lightning cross overhead. At that, she shrieked, backing away from the door.

Going over to the truck to get out a flashlight and jacket, it was beginning to get a little too dark, and chilly for her. Slipping it on, she headed back to the doors, when realizing what kind of mess she had gotten herself into. "Well, I can't stay out here!" she muttered, not knowing that just a hundred yards away was an old two-story house.

Having decided then to find more suitable shelter, after a few more minutes of loud crashing thunder, and eye blinding lightning, she spotted a house off in a distance.

"Great!" she cried, pulling the jacket up over her head, before making a run for it.

Not taking long to reach the front porch, she went up to knock on the door. To her dismay, there was no answer.

"This can't be good...!" she cried, looking around, when finding the place to look fairly empty. "Hmmm... well it at least it looks deserted!" she thought, while going on to try the door.

Finding it locked, she went around to the side of the house to try a few windows, before coming to one that opened for her.

"Yes!" she shivered, while crawling in out of the rain.

Once inside, brushing herself off, she waited until her eyes had time to get adjusted to her new surroundings, where off in one corner of what seemed to be the living room, she saw it. "Well, what do we have here?" she asked, stopping short of the doorway, where she saw an old sofa, and not far from it a fireplace with wood stacked up near it. "Okay, now, this is going to have to work. Now to find some matches."

Unaware that her presence was being monitored, she ran back over to the truck to grab her suitcase and a blanket. While there, she dug around in the glove box and found some matches. "Thanks, Jessi," she smiled. "Now to get my butt back to the house to get a fire going and just maybe a bed made up on that old sofa."

Afterwards, getting out of her wet things, she said a short prayer and got in under her blanket, before attempting to drift off to sleep. On the other hand, sleep wasn't going to come easy for her. When it did come, all she could do was toss and turn all night, dreaming the same thing, until she had awakened to find that she was thirsty. Not to mention, the fire in the fireplace was still going strong.

"Mmmm..." she reflect to herself, not giving any thought to the fire.

Getting up, she went into the kitchen and found an old fashion pump with a tin cup next to it. Filling it, she went back to the living room to lie back down. While there, she had found the fire somewhat soothing to her nerves, after all the tossing and turning she had done.

Staring off into it, she started to drift off to sleep again. "Good," she grumbled, sitting the cup on the floor to do just that. "Just maybe this time, the dreams will leave me alone so I can get some sleep."

CHAPTER FOUR

By morning, waking up, there he stood, a tall masculine man, smiling down on her. "Good morning! Didn't you sleep well last night?" he asked, looking amused to find a stray sleeping on his sofa. But not just any ordinary stray, when he couldn't help but wonder if this beautiful woman, lying in front of him, was the woman from the Dinner, and the one he had fallen in love with years ago. Like Jessi, they did look a lot like, yet there was something different about her eyes.

Meanwhile, finding she wasn't alone anymore, as she stared up at the tall, brown hair, blue-eyed man, with his nicely trimmed beard and mustache, still smiling down on her, she swallowed hard. Then it hit her, she wasn't dreaming anymore. This man standing over her was real. And yet unable to find her voice at first, she went to sit up. As she did, it was then she found that not only did she have one blanket on her, but one of his, as well, when she picked up right away on its scent. *'Masculine! Mmmm... very masculine.'*

Seeing her growing state of puzzlement, he offered, "You were cold last night, so I thought you could use an extra blanket, in case the fire went out."

"Oh?" Pulling the blankets up around her, she asked timidly, "W... who are you?"

"I think I should be the one asking you that question?" he chuckled, while continuing to smile.

Even though, she found nothing about the situation anything to smile about, she was in his house. Worse yet, beneath these blankets, the only thing she had on was an over sized t-shirt to cover her modestly shaped body.

"Are you all right?" he asked, not yet getting an answer from her.

"I uh…" She stopped to look around the sunlit room. Realizing then, she covered her mouth. "It was you I saw in my dreams. That man, he…he shot you!"

"Well, yes, I was shot a while back, but I'm alive and well now!" he went on, asking her how she happened to have been in his house in the first place.

Swallowing again rather nervously, she raked a hand over her ruffled hair, before answering. "Well, I uh… I had gotten caught in the storm on my way back from Charlottesville yesterday. And the bridge was flooded over. Seeing that, I had to turn back to get my load out of the rain!"

"Your load? What load would that be?"

"Some of my granny's antique furniture, that she had sold a while back to repair a plate glass window in her shop, when some kids had vandalized it."

Giving her a puzzled look at what she had just told him, the man turned to add a log on the fire, while at that same time, thinking back to a call he had gotten of a break-in, involving an old antique shop on the southeast side of town. At that moment, he began to wonder.' *Is it really possible?'* he asked, looking back over his shoulder.

"What?" she asked, wondering what that look was about. *'Why would the mere mention of my granny's shop cause him to react in such a way?'* Then a feeling came over her.

Getting up, she went over to her suitcase, not thinking how she must look in her over sized t-shirt, as she bent down to open it.

Catching a glimpse of her long shapely legs and bare feet, he turned away, feeling his blood begin to heat up. Getting up, he went into the kitchen and asked, "Are you hungry? I was just about to fix something to eat!"

"No," she replied, now holding a white cloth in her hand that bore the initials 'J. S.' in one corner, "I really should be getting out of your way!"

Hearing that, he returned just inside the kitchen doorway to protest, "No! Please, stay. It'll give us a chance to talk. Besides, the bridge is probably still flooded!" he stated, knowing how that bridge was when it rained.

"Oh, of course, you're right!" she agreed, forgetting about the bridge, when straightening back up, just as he went back into the kitchen.

Standing there for a moment longer, she wondered, *'Could this be…'* she asked herself. But then, when coming around to stand in the doorway to watch him going about getting things he would need to cook over the open fire in the fireplace, she thought, *'No, how could he be? He was younger then!'*

Turning, he saw the look on her face. "Are you all right?"

"What? Oh, yes, of course!"

"Good. I hated to think being out in the rain may have made you sick!" he grinned, realizing now that she just might be that girl. And with so many things adding up, while passing her in the doorway with an iron skillet in hand, he had one question that burnt at his mind. "Your husband, where's he?"

"I'm divorced!" she replied, driving herself crazy to find a way to ask him what his name was.

"Oh…?" He turned curiously and asked. "How are you getting by then?"

"I own my grandmother's antique shop on the southeast side of Ripley!"

Just then, the picture was becoming more and more clearer. But that left just one more question. "This shop," he asked, hoping with all his heart it was her, "what's the name of it?"

"Jodi's Antiques! Why?"

"I uh…" he began, when thinking back to her grandmother's objection to his wanting to ask her out. After that, it left him heartbroken.

"What?"

"It just sounded familiar, is all," he explained, while going back into the kitchen to get a few more things from the cabinet. While there, he sadly shook his head, *'God, if only she had known I wanted to ask her out. Damn…!'*

Still standing in the doorway, she studied him for a moment longer, before asking what she had wanted to for some time now. "Uh…" she began, while trying to get up the courage to do so.

"Yes?" he asked, not turning back to look at her.

"Do the initials J. S. mean anything to you?"

Hearing that, he stopped what he was doing to look back at her. "Only my name!" he exclaimed, hoping she had remembered who he was.

"Oh," she asked, holding out the handkerchief he had given her all those years ago, "then I suppose this must be yours?"

Seeing his old handkerchief in her hand, a warm smile came to his face, when reaching out to touch it. "Why, yes, it is!" he laughed. "I'm just surprised to see you still have it."

Smiling back, she looked up into those beautiful deep blue eyes of his. "You know, you never really told me your name!"

"I didn't! Well, come to think of it, I guess I didn't!" he continued to laugh. "It's Jarred Stanton. And yours, I recall, is Jodi! Named after the shop."

"Y...yes!" she shivered involuntarily.

Having seen that, he smiled. "Why don't you go on into the bathroom and get changed, while I fix us some breakfast. We can talk more when you get back."

"I should, shouldn't I?" she smiled, just as his gaze dropped down to her damp t-shirt, where the cool air had a rather interesting effect on her. Seeing this, as an eyebrow shot up at what he saw, she felt the warmth of his gaze go through her, when turning back slightly to head into the living room. Turning red, she cleared her throat, "Well, I think I'll do just that," she replied modestly, while going in to get out a change of clothes, before heading off into the bathroom. Before leaving, she looked back to see his grin at how her face had turned red. *'Come on Jodi, what are you thinking, you haven't known him all that long...?'*

After going off to change, Jarred laughed, and went back to doing what he was, when his cell phone sounded off, breaking into his thoughts. "Yeah?" he grumbled abruptly over his end.

Jarred," his uncle returned with a hint of concern, "are you okay?"

"Yeah! What's up?"

"I just got a call about a pick-up parked out in your barn."

"Oh?" he smiled. "Are you still at home, or on the road?"

"I'm still at home, and strapping on my shoulder holster. Though, I had already called one of the guys to see what's going on, before I come by to check it out myself. Why?"

"Are you sure you're ready for this?" he laughed heartedly.

"Jarred, don't play games with me. Just tell me what's going on there."

"It's…" he kept right on laughing. "It's Jodi! She's here!"

"What…?" he too, couldn't help but laugh. "But how…?"

Going on, he told him everything, right down to when one of the guys had called to tell him about a woman walking around in the rain. "Not feeling any danger, I had to laugh when she climbed in through one of the windows I had conveniently left unlocked to see what she would do."

"You what…?"

"Yes, but listen! Having seen her from the diner the other night, I had to know…!"

"If she was Jodi?" he asked, shaking his head.

"Yes. And after watching her from the top of the stairs, I was right, she is! God, Alex," he went on, "seeing her after all this time. Not to mention, sleeping on my sofa," he laughed, "was really wild!"

"Great…!" he roared, while the two went on talking a little while longer.

Upon her return, he was just getting off the phone, when she went over to sit on the sofa next to him.

"That was my uncle," he replied, laughing, when getting up to dish up their food. "It seems that one of my neighbors called to report a truck parked out in my barn!"

"Oh… that's your barn?" she grinned.

"Yes…!"

Seeing his rich smile, she blushed, yet, again. "Was he upset?"

"No. I told him what had happened. And I had also told him it was going to cost you," he added with a hint of mischief in his voice.

"Uh huh." Her face lit up in a warm smile, when unable to resist the temptation to come back with a comment that was sure to hit home. "Yes, well, if your cooking is all that bad, that would be payment enough!"

"Ouch…!" he roared out laughing. "She even bites!"

After breakfast was over, she went into the kitchen to help clean up after herself, when turning to thank him.

"You're welcome," he returned, giving the dishtowel a toss, before walking over to stop in the doorway. "Maybe we can get together again sometime?"

"Perhaps!" she smiled, while starting for the living room.

Though, out of pure orneriness, he blocked the doorway, just as she started to walk through.

Not realizing the effect in doing so was going to have on them, when their bodies brushed up against each other, the unexpected happened. From within them the heat rose several degrees, just as she looked up into his eyes. Seeing something that had almost frightened her, he was sad, and yet she didn't know why, but she did know she truly wanted to see him again.

'No...' she thought, changing her mind, while feeling the effects of what his nearness was doing to her. "No."

"No, what?"

"No," she laughed lightly, "I would really like that."

"I'm glad!" he smiled a sigh of relief, while they continued to look into each other's eyes for some time, before forcing themselves to look away.

"I...I should go. I...I really do need to get home," she stuttered nervously.

"Yeah, you're probably right," he swallowed hard. "The old bridge should be passable right about now." Not bothering to move, his breath warm against her cheek, his eyes taking in every curve of her face, he asked, while lightly touching her chin with his forefinger, "Can I call you later?"

Still seeing the saddened expression in his eyes, she replied, "Yes," and reached up, intending to kiss his cheek, when then, at the last minute, turning his head, he kissed her soft, warm lips instead. Feeling the warmth of his kiss, she began to respond in kind.

Sadly the kiss didn't last long, when he pulled back to look into her smoldering eyes. "Thank you," he murmured.

"Y...you're welcome!" she replied, pulling away, to go back into the living room, to get her things. "Well, I had better be going now. Karen's probably getting frantic, wondering where I'm at," she fibbed, knowing her plans included staying over for a few days in Charlottesville.

"Sure! I'll walk you out!"

"Oh, okay!"

With his help, as he went to hold open the front door for her, she walked out onto the sun drenched porch, where the air felt fresh and clean, after the previous night's rain. Meanwhile, seeing a few of Alex's men tucked away amongst the trees and a few bushes, he bowed his head to them silently and kept on walking.

As the two got closer to the barn, the silence was beginning to bother him, while he felt that he should say something, anything. *'But what?'* Clearing his throat, he spouted off the first thing that came to mind, "Jodi?"

"Yes?"

"I..." he stopped just inside the barn. "I don't have your number!"

"I suppose I should give it to you, shouldn't I?" she laughed, taking her things from him to give them a toss into the cab of her cousin's truck. Afterwhich, reaching in to get her purse, she got out a pad of paper and pen and wrote it down.

"Thanks!" he smiled, taking her number, before she turned to get into the truck.

"Well, I guess I'll be talking to you later?" she asked softly.

"Yeah, count on it!" he grinned, patting the door of the truck, as she started it up to leave.

Looking back, after pulling slowly out of the barn, she tried hard to smile, but seeing the sadness return, she just nodded her head and pulled on out.

"See ya!" he waved goodbye, as she pulled out onto the blacktop road with her precious cargo on board.

Slowly making her way down the road, she looked in the rearview mirror, just then, to see two men, one dark haired, looking to be in his mid forties, the other, lighter brown hair, somewhere in his twenties, strolling up to meet him. *'Must be the men keeping an eye on him,'* she thought, driving on.

On the way home, she called Hank to get a few of the boys together, to give her a hand, when she arrived.

"We'll be there!" he announced warmly.

"Thanks, Hank."

"Sure thing!"

By the time she pulled in, Hank, a fatherly-like stable hand, in his late fifties, with graying hair and blue eyes, was there to unload her furniture with Travis, a tall, brown haired man in his mid to late twenties, and Andy, young, sweet, tall, blond, but lazy at times, so Jessi had said.

"Did you have any trouble with that storm last night?" he asked.

"Yes," she smiled. "I had to stop and take refuge in an old barn!"

"Oh?" He quickly picked up on something hidden in her words.

"Hank...!"

"Well, it mustn't have been too bad! You look happy!"

"Well... you can say it was a storm I'll never forget."

"Good. Neither you nor Ms. Jessi cares much about storms. In fact, they rather terrify you both."

"That's for sure."

"Hey, Hank!" Travis called out. "Where do these things go?"

"In the dining room!" he hollered back. "Well," he turned back to Jodi, "I had better be giving them a hand."

"All right."

Going in as well, she instructed the guys as to where everything went, before going up to her room to call her girls.

Chapter Five

Later that night, Jarred called just as he said he would. "I hope this isn't a bad time?" he asked.

"No… I was just sitting out on my front porch with a glass of iced tea. How about you?"

"As good as to be expected!"

"Really?"

"Yes! That and I was just on the phone with my uncle," he was saying, while stretching out on his sofa. "Which reminds me, were you able to get your things unloaded okay?"

"Yes. Hank and the boys came by to give me a hand."

"Hank? Is he…"

"My boyfriend?" she laughed, picking up on his light humor.

"Well…?" he asked, not knowing Jessi's stable hand.

"Goodness, no…! He's…"

"No… no… no, you don't have to explain!" he teased.

"Jarred…!"

Laughing, he sat up, shaking his head, while the two went on talking.

After while, seeing how late it was getting, getting to her feet, she went back inside, while continuing with their talk.

"That sounds awful!" she exclaimed, while turning the deadbolt on her front door. "That explains the look on your face, when I was getting ready to leave!"

"Yeah, well, my uncle doesn't want the same thing to happen to me that had happened to my cousin two years ago."

"Your cousin?" she asked, thinking about Jessi's story.

"Yeah. Why?"

"No, it's nothing!" Stopping to lean back against her door, thinking of him out there with little to nothing to do, she was unaware that she was being watched from one of her side windows.

"Jodi?"

"Yes?"

"You got quiet there. Are you all right?"

"Yes. I was just locking up," she said with a pause. "Jarred?"

"Yes?" he asked, getting up to fix a pot of coffee.

"Do you ever get out much?"

"Yes, when my uncle comes by to take me up to his place for a weekend."

"Oh?" she asked, going on into her kitchen to check on the back door.

Never thinking, the whole time they had been talking, never once had he mentioned his uncle's name, nor his cousin's, for that matter. Not to mention, all the clues he was unaware he was giving her about his family, she never picked up on the connection between her cousin's new husband and Jarred. All she knew was he was a cop for the Crawfordsfield County Police Department. And with a name like Stanton, how was she to know? Let alone, her last name being different, she still looked amazingly like Jessi.

"I'm glad!" she went on. "Perhaps, if you'd like, I could come back out and see you sometime."

"That would be nice. But the place isn't anything like what you're used to!"

"Don't worry about that," she explained, reaching out to turn the lock on the back door, when the shadowy figure, after making his way around to the back of the house, ducked out of sight when he saw her coming.

Detecting the sound over the phone, Jarred asked, "What was that?"

"What was what?"

"That sound?"

"Oh, I was just locking the back door. Why?"

"You can't be too careful."

"Because of that man?"

"Yes. Right after you left, Marcose told me we had company."

"Jarred_____!" she nearly wanted to scream in fear, at hearing that.

"Hey, it's all right! He isn't here. And the guys we have watching me, are out keeping a close eye on things, as we speak!"

"Oh... good...!" she sounded out a sigh of relief, when walking back into the living room, after switching off the kitchen light along the way. "Mmmm... wha...t a day... for the bo...th of us...!"

Sensing her fatigue, he laughed, "Yeah, well for now you sound pretty tired. We'll talk soon."

"Mmmm... you're right! I am tired. I'll call you tomorrow...?"

"Fair enough."

After hanging up, she headed up to her room, while leaving on a nightlight. Once there, her mind went back to the previous night, when she climbed into his window, then waking up to those beautiful eyes of his. Not to mention, that smile. *'Oh... yes, that smile. Mmmm...'* she moaned, while slipping out of her things, before pulling on her pajamas.

Getting one of her grandma's quilts that she had brought up earlier, she went over to lie down, while continuing to think about him, just as she fell off to sleep.

By the next morning, it was much too early for Jodi's poor, tired body to have to get up, when all she wanted to do was sleep in. But that wasn't going to happen when her phone began to ring.

Picking it up on the second ring, she was greeted by her friend, "Good morning, girl...! I thought you were going to stay over."

"No, you can thank the weather for that. So I thought I would try and make it back before it hit, but I was greatly wrong about that."

"Oh? Hey, I was just getting ready to open up here. So why don't you save the story, and tell me about it when you come in!"

"Mmmm... I just woke up. Give me about twenty minutes and I'll be in."

"Good! I have some stuff here that I'm eager to show you."

"Oh? All right. I'll just grab a quick shower, and be right in."

"Okay! See ya soon," she said cheerfully, hanging up.

"Mmmm…, great," she grumbled, pulling back the quilt to get up, "so much for having a day to relax." In the meantime, going around gathering what she would need to get a shower out of the way, her mind drifted back to the day she received a letter from her grandmother's lawyer, telling her that she had inherited her grandmother's shop, along with her old two-story house. Having told her one day it would all be hers. Then that day came.

After having sat with the lawyer, she and her two girls moved into her grandmother's eighty year old house, and got started right away on fixing up the shop.

"Oh, great," her thoughts were cut short, when feeling the water turn cold, "just what I wanted to start off the day with."

Getting out, she quickly toweled off, and pulled back her hair in a braid, before getting dressed in a cream-colored three-piece suit.

"Well, girl," she groaned, giving herself one last look in a mirror, before heading out of the house, "not too bad!" she grinned, grabbing her keys and locking up the house.

On the way, she decided to make a pit stop and pick up some doughnuts, thinking they would give her some energy, since she hadn't taken the time to eat first. Meanwhile, pulling into the parking lot of their local bakery, she felt rumblings in her stomach, as she went to get out of her car. "Quiet now," she groaned, heading up to the door, "we don't have to make it quite so obvious that I haven't eaten, do we?"

After making her selection, she headed to work, and parked in front when getting there. "Hey there, is one of those for me?" she asked, seeing Karen pouring two cups of coffee, when carrying in the box of doughnuts and a stack of papers.

"Yes. It just so happens I saw you coming up the street. So I thought you could use some when you got here. Now, watchya got there?" she asked, turning back to give her, her a cup.

"That all depends!" she teased, knowing how her friend loved doughnuts too.

"On what?"

"On which one you want first?" she asked, going over to sit the box of doughnuts on their table.

"Well," she pondered the thought, but then, curiosity got the better of her, when she chose the stack of paperwork she saw in the other hand. "Those!" she pointed.

"Oh, these…! They're just some of granny's old paperwork I had decided to bring back in with me!" she smiled, while sitting them down next to the doughnuts, before taking her cup. "So now, enough about the paperwork! What do you say we dig into these doughnuts, while having our coffee?"

"Sure, besides, I haven't had much to eat this morning, and boy am I starved," Karen laughed.

"Good," she smiled, sitting her cup down, to open the box. "In that case, take your pick, I got plenty."

"No kidding!" she cried, as her eyes widened at what all she saw.

Getting themselves a couple of napkins, the two started eating, while Karen told her all about the auction she went to in her place. "It just came up all of a sudden. Heck, no one even knew anything about it, until one of our regular customers walked in right after you left!"

"Oh?"

"Yes. And just wait until you see all the things I got from it," she laughed, while getting up with her doughnut to show her. "The girls will even have fun going through it all."

"What sort of things are we talking here?" she asked, sitting her cup down to follow her over to the backroom door, having seen some boxes sitting there, when she first arrived.

"All sorts of things! Including some more old dolls and toys!"

"Great! I'm looking for just the right doll to set on my bed. Maybe I'll see one in here."

"Speaking of which, didn't you get any sleep last night?"

"No…!" she replied, but then seeing her friend's expression, she smiled at the thought of who they were talking about, before leaving for Charlottesville.

"Okay! What's going on?"

"You will never believe it," she laughed.

"Well, it couldn't be because of that same dream, you're too happy!"

"No, it wasn't the dream this time. And you're right. I am happy" she continued, while sitting aside the dolls, to walk back over to their table, to add a few teaspoons of sugar to her coffee.

"Well then, what was it?"

"Well, seeing how it isn't busy," she turned back to her friend, using that same line her cousin would use on her two friends.

"Jo…, come on, out with it."

"Well… you know I was just thinking how nice it would be to set up a few tables and chairs out front for the customers, while enjoying the fresh morning air. What do you think?" she asked, seeing Karen's twisted expression, and laughed.

Waiting patiently, Karen just shook her head and laughed right along with her.

"All right, I'll tell you," she thought for a moment. "Do you remember what we were talking about just before I left for Charlottesville?"

"Well, yes! I was saying you should find out who that police officer was that came to take your granny's statement."

"Well…" she smiled brightly, "I don't have to go looking for him now."

"What do you mean? Did you find him?"

"You might say that!" she frowned at her friend's surprised look.

"What…? Where…?"

"The other day, while in Charlottesville, loading up, we noticed how the weather was about to take a turn for the worse. So…, like I was saying this morning, I tried get back before it hit. Only I didn't make it."

"So… what happened?"

"The bridge on State Road Nine flooded out. So I turned around and went back to where I saw another road. After turning down it, I saw a barn off on the right and pulled the truck inside to wait out the rain. But the rain turned into a bad storm!"

"And you're terrified of storms, like your cousin, Jessi."

"Very! That was when I went looking for a house on foot."

"And…?" she asked, getting even more anxious.

"Well… I found one, and at the time, I thought it was empty. So I went back to the truck to get some of my things to hold up out of the storm!"

"And this house, it wasn't…"

"No! The owner was up in his room sleeping!"

"Oh… my… Lord…! You must have felt really bad!"

"Bad…?" she cried, shaking her head. "I thought I was dreaming at first. But when I woke up the next morning, he was smiling down at me."

"And...? And...? Who was he?" she asked, laughing at her friend's predicament.

"Who do you think? The cop who took granny's statement!"

"What...?" she cried, covering her mouth. "No...!"

"Oh, yes!" she laughed even harder, while fanning her face. "And his name..."

"Go on...!"

"His name is Jarred Stanton. He's a Detective now on the Crawfordsfield County Police Department."

"Oh, my, gosh, what luck to have wound up in his house of all places."

"No, kidding!" she agreed, getting up, when Karen noticed a change in her friends' expression just then.

"What is it, Jo? You looked a little lost there."

"Oh, Karen," she cried, turning back, "he looked so sad just before I left."

"Have any idea why?"

"No, not unless it's because he has to stay out of sight, until they catch the guy who shot him!"

"That can't be fun!"

"No, but I told him I would be back out to see him sometime."

"Good. And now, what do you say we go through all that wonderful stuff I got from the auction? It just might even cheer you up some."

"Yes, you're probably right."

Doing that, she was amazed at what all she saw, when right away she found the perfect doll. Not to mention, an old tin milk can, perfect for her front porch.

Chapter Six

By the time they were finished, after getting things cleaned up, a customer walked in, followed by a few more.

"Karen?" Jodi called out from her office doorway.

"Yes?"

"Can you handle things out here, while I'm in working on these papers?"

"Sure!"

"Thanks," she smiled, going on into her office, while leaving the door open. Sitting there for a moment, she heard voices filtering in from the showroom, as the crowd continued to pour in. "Boy, this is going to be a crazy day," she grumbled, while looking over her work.

Meanwhile, out in the other room, her mysterious figure from the previous night had walked in, eyeing the place, while Karen was busy with other customers. Seeing the office door open, he stared at it, sensing the woman he was looking for was in there. *'Huh... so you are here,'* he grinned, seeing her moving about to get a ledger off the shelf.

Hearing Karen about to end her conversation with a redheaded lady in her thirties, he made a beeline for the door, before he could be seen

"Karen!" Jodi called out, walking in just after the man got into his truck to leave. But then, stopping abruptly, just short of the door, the hair on the back of her neck began to prickle.

"Jo…" Karen stopped within a few feet of her, "what is it?"

Cocking her head to one side, she slowly looked over to the front door, just as the truck pulled away.

"Jo?"

"Karen…?"

"Yes!"

"Was there just a man in here a short while ago?"

"Well, come to think of it, yes! I was just about to see what he wanted, when he simply disappeared! Why?"

"That smell…! I feel as though I smelled it somewhere before!"

"Smell…? I don't smell anything! Are you sure you know what you're talking about? Maybe it was something that lady was wearing, before she left!"

"Yes. Maybe."

"Well, anyway, what were you about to say, before the smell thing came up?"

"Oh, I was about to go out to get some lunch. Did you want anything?"

"Yeah, sure!"

Giving her, her order, Jodi was just about to head out to their neighborhood deli, when one of Alex's men spotted her. Remembering her from the Dinner the other night, and again at Jarred's, where he and another man were watching over Alex's nephew, looking up just then, he saw the black truck, and its driver paying particular attention to her, when walking out to get into her car. "Well, what do we have here?" he wondered, while taking out his hand radio. Before he could make the call, the truck pulled away. "Damn, Alex isn't going to like that!" Marcose grumbled, while looking over at Jodi, as she too was about to pull away.

After making her run, getting back, the two ate, before Jodi vanished back into her office.

"Back to the grindstone again?" Karen teased.

"Yes," she replied, while looking around the shop at all the customers they had. "Looks like you're going to have your hands full for awhile. Call me if you get too busy!" she offered, getting to her feet.

"Sure!"

Tossing her trash away, Jodi was off once again, while Karen saw a customer coming her way.

After a few hours had gone by, the crowd started to thin out. "Hey," Karen called out from across the room, when Jodi walked out to give her a hand with the cleaning, "what do you have planned for this weekend?"

"With the girls gone, I thought I'd go over to Jarred's. However, I can't even think about that until I've finished up on those papers. And before I forget, I'm supposed to call him sometime today."

"Well... you had better be doing that!" she smiled, as Jodi went back into her office.

After dialing his number, she went over to have a seat at her desk to wait. However, the wait was soon cut short, when she heard his voice on the other end.

"Hi! Can you talk?"

"Sure! How was your morning?" he asked, knowing she hadn't had much sleep.

"Fine! How about yours?"

"I was up with the birds, having my coffee and thinking about getting out of here for a while," he replied, looking out the back door with one hand propped up on the door frame, the other, holding his cell phone.

"Are you sure that's a good idea?" she asked, thinking about the man who had shot him.

"Yeah, my uncle will be here soon. We're just going out back to cut some wood."

"Hmmm... I wish I could..." she broke off suddenly, feeling silly.

"Be here?" he finished warmly. "I wish you could too!" he went on, in a quieter voice, just when he heard a vehicle pull in around back. "Oh, great!"

"What?"

"That's my uncle pulling in now. I have to let you go."

"Oh, okay! I'll talk to you later?"

"Sure!"

After hanging up, a thought came to her, as she went to sit back. Remembering something he had said to her grandmother, while taking her statement, she wondered what had brought that on. *'Were they arguing about something? And if so, what? What would've caused him to call her an old biddy the way he did? And why an old biddy?'*

Meanwhile, sitting there a little while longer, she hadn't noticed how the hours had passed by, when Karen walked in. "Well, it's closing time, lady! What do you say to a late supper?"

Not saying a word, she got up and walked out of her office, taking her purse and keys with her.

"Still thinking about him?" she asked, following her out.

"Sort of!"

"What is it?"

Turning to look at her friend, she shook her head puzzledly, "Something he had said all those years ago to granny!"

"Which was?"

"He called her an old biddy!"

"What the heck would make him do that?"

"I don't know! For some reason I can't help but feel that they must have been arguing over something. But what?"

"You, maybe?" she teased.

"Me…? But why?"

"Jo, I was only kidding! But if you think about it, your grandmother had always been very protective of you. Perhaps he wanted to ask you out, and she said…"

"No…?"

"Yes! I mean no! I mean she said no! You know what I mean!"

Shaking her head, she headed for the door to leave.

"Jo…!"

"Listen, it's getting late," she spoke up tiredly, "and tomorrow is going to be another busy day. Oh," she was just about to walk out, when turning back, "as for dinner. Would you mind if we do it another time?"

"Yeah, sure! Are you going to be all right?"

"I'll be fine. I'm just tired. I'll see you in the morning, all right?"

"Sure! All right!"

Just before leaving, the black pick-up pulled up across the street again.

Not noticing it, Jodi got into her car and pulled out to go home.

Doing the same, the guy in the truck followed her, staying at a safe distance behind, until she reached her house.

All that night he sat watching her place.

Waking the next morning, after giving Jarred some thought, she came to a conclusion she had to know what the argument between him and her grandmother was about.

Getting up, she got herself ready and headed in early, even before Karen had gotten there. "Good," she thought, walking up to unlock the shop door. "I'll have enough time to get some work done, before she gets here, and then…" The thought of seeing him bothered her, but she knew she had to talk to him. Meanwhile, walking in, she shut and locked the door behind her, before going into her office to start on what was left of her paperwork.

After an hour and a half of sorting through what was to be kept and what wasn't, it was then she heard a key being slipped into the front door and turned. After that, she heard Karen walking in. Not getting up to greet her, more thoughts of Jarred crept into her mind.

"Hey! What's going on in that head of yours?" Karen asked, walking into Jodi's office.

"You don't want to know. But still yet, I'm glad you're here now."

"Oh?"

"Yes. I've got to talk Jarred and find out what the argument was about that day."

"Perhaps it was as I had mentioned, your grandmother didn't want the two of you going out after what you had already gone through with Stephen!"

"If that's the case, she's right! With Jarred's line of work, I can't go through that kind of pain again. Having already lost one man in my life, it was bad enough to see Jarred get shot in a dream. How do you think I would handle it if he were to get killed?"

"You have a point, but surely you aren't going to end it with him now! The two of you haven't really had a chance to get to know each other. Just keep it low keyed and see what happens!"

"That won't be all that easy to do," she replied, thinking of their kiss. "Besides, I've already called to tell him I'm on my way out."

"Yeah, but you didn't tell him why, did you?"

"No!" she replied, grabbing her keys on the way out. Calling back over her shoulder, she asked, "Could you keep an eye on the store while I'm out?"

"Sure. Don't I always?" she smiled.

"Great. I'll see ya later."

On the short drive out to Jarred's, her mind was in such a deep thought that she hadn't noticed the black pick-up behind her.

And now, having arrived, he met her at the front door. "Hello!" he greeted, when she got out of her car.

"Hi," she returned quietly, while not once looking up at him, when walking up onto the porch.

It wasn't until then, that the gleam in his eyes slowly disappeared, while seeing the expression on her face. Wondering what it was about, he asked, "Jodi, what is it? You look like you have lost your best friend!"

"Yes, well, we need to talk."

"Sure! Let's go inside!"

Nodding her head quietly, he held the door open for her.

Going in after her, he closed the door behind him, as the man in the pick-up drove by slowly. "So, you're not dead," he growled, glaring at the house, as he went on by.

Seeing this, Marcose, one of Alex's toughest men, gave him a call.

"Yeah?" Alex answered, recognizing his voice, while getting himself ready to head out.

"Hey, we've got trouble."

"What is it?"

"Delgado. He just drove by."

"Where is he now?"

"Gone," he returned from where he and a younger officer were hiding.

"Good. I'm on my way out now."

"Alex, that's not all."

"What now?"

"Jarred. He's got company."

"A young lady with long brown hair?"

"Yeah. She kind of reminds me of... "

"Jessi? Yeah, so I've noticed," he smiled. "She's all right. Oh, and Marcose?"

"Yeah?"

"Alert the others in case Delgado was to circle back and come up through the woods."

"Like our other unfortunate man did a few months ago?"

"I wasn't going to say that, knowing how mad you were, when you and Baker had gotten clobbered over the head, and then tied up. But yes." He thought back to that God forsaken day, being the Fourth of July, out at Craig's old place, while Marcose went on talking.

Having to stop David, Craig's best friend, from going after Tony, the man who killed Alex's nephew, Alex knew he couldn't let the same thing happen to his friend. So having tackled David to the floor, just inside the front door of Craig's old place, somehow, the gun, which David had taken earlier, got knocked out of his hand in the struggle.

'Alex…' he yelled. *'He's going to get away! We have to stop him!'*

'Not this way. And not without me,' he yelled back, unaware that while outside, Tony had doubled back and was now coming in through the front door.

'Well, well, well, what do we have here?' Tony snarled, kicking the gun off to the side. *'I've been waiting for this day, Storm!'* he laughed. *'Now I have the both of you right where I want you.'*

'Tony Belaro!' Alex growled, glaring up at him. *'You're not going to get away with it this time. You're going to pay dearly for killing my nephew.'*

'And just how do you plan on carrying that threat out? From where I'm standing, you don't seem to have a rat's chance of getting yourself out of this mess,' he laughed again. *'Your gun, toss it over here. Now!'*

Begrudgingly, Alex did just that. Pulling it slowly out of his shoulder holster, he slid it off to one side, opposite of where the other gun had landed.

'Good! And now for the driver of that other truck out there? Get him down here. Now…!'

'Leave her out of it, Belaro!' David yelled. *'She doesn't deserve to get hurt.'*

'So we have a girl here, do we?' he sneered, looking up at the stairs, grinning, while at that moment, both, Alex and David wondered where Craig was.

Though again, at the present time, he could only imagine, while smiling at the thought of his nephew, Craig and Jessi, now.

In the meantime, still locked away in his thoughts, upstairs, Craig was helping Jessi with Harry's wound, while trying to make him comfortable.

'*You're going to be okay, Harry,*' Craig was saying, after the man, who had been helping Tony do his dirty work against his will, had been shot by none other than Tony, himself.

'*I can see him!*' Harry whispered with a softened expression on his face. '*I can really see him!*'

'*Yes,*' Jessi turned to smile up at Craig, '*I know.*'

'*Matthews, it was Tony who did this to you. I didn't really want any part of it, I swear!*'

'*I know that, Harry. And Tony won't get away this time. He will pay for what he did to me.*'

'*Harry,*' Jessi started in puzzledly, '*if you and David were so close…*'

'*Why didn't I know that this wasn't David?*'

'*Yes!*'

'*At first, seeing the truck pull away, we both thought it was!*'

'*When did you first realize that it wasn't?*'

'*Here, when we came face to face with…*'

'*Me?*' Craig asked cynically.

'*Yes,*' he returned nervously, seeing the look on Craig's face go grimmer. '*I…I'm sorry Matthews. Really I am. But it all happened so quickly from then on out.*'

'*Go on…*' he instructed, folding his arms across his chest.

'*Well, Tony had his gun out and I…I was scared…! P…Please, you gotta believe me! I didn't want to do this!*'

'*Craig…!*' Jessi spoke up.

But instead, he turned away to look off in the direction of the stairway, the expression on his face went even more grim, as he thought back to when his nightmare had first started.

Just then, interrupting his thought, Alex called out sounding a little different, as if to warn them that Tony had caught them. At that, he recalled the sound in his own voice, when Tony sneered, hearing her name being mentioned.

'*Well, well, well, if it isn't Ms. Jess!*'

'*God, Jessi!*' Alex had also recalled, groaning inwardly, while looking up at Tony, and hoping she was smart enough to pick up on his warning, and tell Craig.

It had worked too, he smiled, while taking a seat on the sofa to listen in on more of what Marcose had to say, while the thoughts continued on in his mind.

'*Tony!*' Craig said, warning Jessi not to go. '*He's got them!*'

'*Alex...!*' she cried silently. '*No...! He can't...!*' she started, when Craig held up a comforting hand.

'*It will be all right. I won't let anything happen to him, but we have to get them back up here! I have to deal with Tony alone!*'

'*I know,*' she replied sadly, when thinking of a way to do just that. Just then a thought came to her.

'*Jessi, no...*' he groaned, picking up on what she was thinking.

'*It'll work, Craig! Trust me!*' she exclaimed, looking down at her blood-covered hands.

CHAPTER SEVEN

STUDYING HER FOR A MOMENT, he gave in, seeing the determination on her face. *"Okay, but just be careful."*

"I will. Besides, what could go wrong?" she asked nervously. *"I have you guys here to protect me!"*

"We will do our best," he grinned, while not liking what was about to take place.

"Okay, Harry," she began, *"you're going to have to go along with this if you want to get out of here alive."*

"Sure! What is it?" he asked eagerly, while Craig, too, listened intently to what she had to say.

After all was said and done, she took the bloodied rag and held it to her own shoulder to make it look as though she had been shot.

"Jess…" Craig looked at her with deep concern, *"are you sure you really want to do this? It's pretty dangerous, and Tony is not one to mess with."*

"I'm sure I don't want to lose you or Alex, but knowing how much you want for this nightmare to end, for your sake, I'll do it," she cried, as a tear found its way down her cheek, not wanting to see Craig go at all.

"Jessi…" he smiled sadly, while wiping the tear away,*" it's time to call them up."*

Nodding her head, she looked to Harry. *"Are you ready?"*

"Let's do it!" he replied, closing his eyes.

"Okay…" she replied, while taking in a deep, cleansing breath, as

she went to look for another rag to apply to his shoulder, though the bleeding seemed to have stopped.

Meanwhile, positioning herself for what she was about to do, Alex called up to her again, while watching Tony out of the corner of his eye, yet at the same time he wondered what was going on upstairs, and why his nephew hadn't shown himself yet. At that, he recalled his gun was not too far away, but knew that wasn't the time to go for it, while Tony's gun was still trained on them.

Just then, he heard Jessi's voice, yet there was something strangely odd about it.

"Alex…" she cried out, staging her voice to sound as though she were in great pain, *"I…I c…can't! It hurts too much!"*

Meanwhile, downstairs, he looked to David, while his own expression turned from being full of anger, to concern, as he silently shook his head, thinking, *"Damn it, Jessi… you weren't hurt when I left you! What the hell are you up to now?"*

Hearing her as well, Tony turned to look back at the two of them. *"How do I know she isn't lying?"*

"Jessi doesn't like to lie." David stated heatedly, sensing what Alex had.

"Well, we'll just see, won't we? Let's go!" he ordered, waving his gun at them.

"Where?" Alex asked, trying to stall for time, as he and David slowly got to their feet.

"Upstairs!" he pointed, going over to pick up Harry's gun.

At that time, Alex saw his chance to retrieve his own, while Tony's back was turned, and quietly, he swept it up and returned it to his shoulder holster, while David stood in between the two them in case Tony had turned back too soon.

Not realizing what he had done, Tony gave the two a shove toward the stairs. *"Let's go,"* he growled.

Presently, grinning to himself, while the thoughts went on, he gave David a knowing nod, when the two exchanged silent grins to one another, while tripping up the steps, ahead of Tony.

Upon arriving up in Craig's old room, Tony shoved them both over to where Jessi was slumpt over.

"Jessi…!" they both called out, stumbling over to sit next to her.

"Are you okay?" Alex asked, remembering how he had pulled her

43

over into his arms, as she turned to look up at him, where Tony couldn't see her expression.

Smiling quietly even now, he recalled how he growled his disapproval when David moved around to look her over for himself.

"How does it feel?" David asked, checking out her supposed wound, while glancing down into her eyes. When she turned then to look up at him, understanding the message he saw in them, he tried hard not to smile.

"Mmmm…I feel l…like I'm going to faint!" she replied weakly, turning back to look up at Alex, *"He's dead, Alex. H…Harry is dead!"*

"Oh…" Reading, the expression on her face, he knew then Harry was still alive. *"I'm sorry to hear that, Jess,"* he returned, going right along with her scheme. *"He should have never gotten killed."*

"No, he shouldn't h…have." At that, she turned to look over at Tony, when seeing Craig standing in the doorway behind him. *"Mr. Belaro,"* she began coyly, *"have you seen your prosecutor lately?"*

"What? What are you talking about?" he asked smugly.

Just then, both, Alex and David looked up to see Craig standing there grinning, when both their faces lit up in a big sheepish grin, as well.

"Why, I do believe," Alex went on, nodding behind him, *"that you're about to be prosecuted, Tony Belaro!"*

Turning just then, the look on Tony's face was one of utter horror, when seeing the ghost of Craig Matthews standing there. *"No…!"* he cried out. *"This isn't real!"*

"Oh, but I am real. And now it's your turn!" Craig thundered, throwing Tony one powerful backhand, sending him flying across the room, where he landed up against the far wall, while leaving several cracks in the old plaster, as he slowly slid down to the floor.

Remembering when he had finally straightened up, Tony stood, looking over at Craig, and then Alex. At that time, taking a moment, he aimed his gun directly at Alex. *"Not before I kill you…"* he yelled.

Just then, as if in slow motion, they all cried out, before Alex had time to get to his own gun out, when Tony pulled the trigger, spewing one very hot piece of lead out of its short, black barrel, propelling Alex back away from Jessi, and onto the floor, as the bullet penetrated his right shoulder, sending blood pouring out through the hole it had made along the way.

"Oh, God, no..." he remembered Jessi crying out, while reaching over to pull him into her arms, when Tony took off running out of the room. Meanwhile though, looking down into his pain stricken eyes, she continued to cry, remembering how she had last seen Craig in her nightmares. *"No... Alex...! Please... don't you die on me, too..."* she continued, while placing her hand over the area inwhich the warm, thick liquid oozed out of.

"Jess," he slowly reached up to touch her tear-dampened cheek, *"I...I'll be okay. R...really!"*

"Alex..." Craig too, he recalled, spoke up to see if he was okay, as did, David, *"are you sure you're okay?"*

"Yeah! I...I'm fine!" he replied, feeling the heat of the bullet, as he looked up at his nephew reassuringly. *"Now, stop him, Craig,"* he continued. *"Do whatever you have to, to get him for what he had done to you."*

Hearing that, Craig looked to Jessi.

"Do it, Craig. Whatever is necessary," she said, choking back the tears.

"I love you, lady!" he groaned, looking deep within her eyes.

"S...Same here..." she returned unhappily, when at that moment, he looked to the Heavens just as the sky turned dark and stormy, and the thunder roared out all around them. Though, just as the lightning lit across the sky, his spirit vanished, leaving David and Jessi to tend to the two wounded men, while downstairs, Tony was making a run for it.

"This is crazy..." he yelled, just as Craig reappeared at the front door, before he could get away.

"Crazy...!" Craig yelled back eerily. *"You took my life away from me and now I want it back_____!"* he thundered, throwing another powerful backhand, sending Tony back into the living room, before going on to do it again, only this time, up against the fireplace, where the blood now trickled down from his nose and mouth.

"Yeah, well," he asked sarcastically, while wiping the blood away with the back of his hand, *"what are you going to do about it now, you're dead?"*

Walking up, Craig glared down at him. *"You've heard a life for a life? Well now, meet your maker,"* he growled, shortly before disappearing.

"Is he out of his mind?" Tony yelled, while looking around the living room, wondering what was next.

Meanwhile upstairs, David looked as though he should go after him.

"No, David_____!" Alex spoke up, sensing his mood, while he attempted to get up.

"Alex, no_____!" Jessi protested. *"You shouldn't try to move. You'll start bleeding again."*

"I'll be fine. Besides, you're going to be needing some help with Harry!" he explained, turning to David, *"As for Tony, he won't be going far. Craig has to finish this war for himself now!"*

"I know," he replied sadly, when Harry began to move.

"Is Tony gone?" he asked.

"Yes," she replied. *"He's downstairs."*

With their help, leaning against the wall, near the window, Harry told Alex everything. *"Detective Storm, David didn't do anything to break the law,"* he added, looking up at David's empty expression. *"He really wanted out, and so did I, but…"*

"Thanks, Harry," David put in sadly, while walking over to the window to look out, *"but because of what I'd done, it doesn't matter much to me anymore."*

"David! What are you saying?" Alex thought back, asking, as David just stood, looking so lost.

"Just that," he said, looking back at Alex. Then with a heavy sigh, he turned back to the window to continue looking out.

Meanwhile, back downstairs, Tony was making a run for the front door once again, when Craig reappeared, cutting off his path.

"No_____, this can't be happening! You're dead! I killed you_____!" he yelled, shaking his head, as he turned to head for the back door. *"I'm out of here!"*

"Like hell you are!"

Before Tony could reach the door, Craig summoned all the power he could gather to bring down that corner of the house to stop Tony dead in his tracks.

Not realizing though, in bringing it down, it would also weaken the structure for the rest of the house. As it had, looking up at the same time, the ceiling in the kitchen, with all its plaster and beams, came crashing down on top of Tony.

"*No____!*" he yelled, covering his head, as the rubble began pelting him, until one beam struck the final blow, silencing him forever.

With that, the rest of the house suddenly began to shake.

"*Alex____!*" Jessi cried, just as a beam broke loose from the ceiling, as it came crashing down toward her.

Seeing this, as he turned away from the window, David threw himself in the path of the beam to knock Jessi out of its way. "*Ahhh_____*" he groaned, when stricken across the back of the head and shoulder by the heavy two by eight, knocking him to the floor, while rendering him unconscious.

"*Oh, my God, David_____*" she cried.

At that, the sound of her voice kept playing back in Alex's head, while still hearing Marcose's voice on the other end of the line, as the thought continued.

CHAPTER EIGHT

GETTING TO THEIR FEET, JESSI and Alex rushed over to move the beam off his back.

"D...David..." The thought just sent pains of sadness shooting through his heart, while thinking back on what he did to save Jessi from the falling beam, by taking the hit himself. *"David...!"* he called out again, while rolling him over. *"Come on, David, talk to me_____!"* he cried.

At that moment, seeing how much blood he had lost while holding him, she must have called out to Craig. And call, she did, by sending him a telepathic message, while Alex did all he could under the circumstances to keep his own shoulder from bleeding profusely.

By then, Craig had appeared in the doorway at the same precise moment the room had lit up overhead.

Looking up, they saw an Angel appear, hovering over them with her wings expanded out to its fullest extent. While at that same moment, raising her hands, she had temporarily slowed time to a near stop, causing the shaking of the house to stop, as well.

"Craig," she spoke softly, *"God has chosen to grant you, David, and even your prayers, Jessi,"* she smiled angelically down into her tear-filled eyes.

"I don't understand," she replied, looking up at the Angel.

"It's simple! Craig, you have been praying for a second chance, so that you can be with the one you love. And you, Jessi, you have already lost one

love in your life. You too, have been praying for the same thing, to be with Craig."

"But what about David," Craig asked about his best friend.

"David has been praying that God would take his life..."

"What..." they all gasped in horror.

"Yes, she went on, *so that you, Craig, could go on living, as you should have! And now, because of the guilt he has had to carry these past few years, his spirit has no will to live. Craig, God wants you to continue on with your life in David's place. You must hurry now, as time is running out. This house will be collapsing very soon!"*

Standing near his best friends' unconscious body, stunned by what he had just learned, he didn't know what to do.

"Craig..." Jessi cried, *"please come back to me...! I need you...! I need you..."* The words played over in Alex's mind.

"Do it, Craig," he remembered telling him, while looking into his nephew's confused eyes. *"Come back to us, for Jessi's sake, as well as the rest of us."*

"Oh, yes, Alex," the Angel then added, *"God has plans for you, as well."*

"Me? Why? What have I done?"

"Because of your willingness to give up your love for Jessi so that your nephew could be with her, God feels that you have sacrificed a lot for the love of your nephew, not to mention the love you recently had to forfeit. Thus, you too, shall be rewarded," she finished, turning back to Craig. *"Craig, you must decide, now. I can't hold back time for much longer."*

Looking into Jessi's tear-filled eyes, and then his uncle's, he shook his head. *"You could have had each other!*

"Yeah, right, nephew," he grinned just then at thinking of their love, *"no one could come close to what the two of you share with each other."*

But then again, going on with his thoughts, while it seemed at that moment Marcose had a lot to say, he was telling his nephew no. *"Do it for Jessi. It's you she loves, not me!"*

"Not me," he repeated to himself, while looking out the front window of his living room, inwhich he didn't live much farther from Jarred.

"What do I have to do?" Craig asked, turning to the Angel, while kneeling down next to his friend.

"The same thing you have done to your uncle!" she smiled sweetly, as

her hands went up to open the gates for David's spirit to be released, and as she did, her wings had risen once again to their fullest width.

Before long, David's spirit had arisen. And while looking to Craig, he sadly said, *"I'm sorry for not telling you the truth. And when the time is right, tell mom and dad that I just couldn't go on like this anymore. Tell 'em,"* he stopped to look at the others. *"Tell 'em I love them."*

"Damn, you, David, why...?" Alex cried, while feeling the pain striking at his own heart once again, as he fought back the tears, while the memories of the event went on, while even adding a few yes's and uh huh's into his conversation with Marcose.

Thinking back then again, with a smile, the two exchanged their farewells, with Craig entering into David's body, as David's spirit left with the Angel. Not long afterward, the joy of seeing Craig starting to come to, as the house, once again began to shake. That in itself was one of the most exciting things he had experienced, seeing his nephew Craig come back to them.

"Craig_____," he recalled calling out, *"can you hear me?"* he asked, bending down to help him up.

"Y...yeah," he replied lightly at first, until he was able to think more clearly.

With their help, he was soon able to stand on his own. However, while looking into Jessi's tear-filled eyes, he tried to smile. But then, as he carefully pulled her into his arms, he cringed at the pain he felt at the back of his head and shoulder. The pain of knowing what it's like to be alive again.

"Are you all right?" both, Alex and Jessi asked.

"Yeah!" he laughed. *"But man... I sure know that I'm alive now!"*

"How's that?" Alex smiled at recalling their laughter.

"Because it hurts like hell...!" he continued laughing, while carefully rubbing his head.

"Well, I'm glad to see that you are okay!"

And glad he was, to have his nephew back, while thinking about what took place next.

While going over to get Harry, the real excitement was about to take place, as they went rushing out of the bedroom, missing all the falling debris and crackling floorboards, while racing down the stairs to reach the front door.

At that point, recalling the sound of approaching ambulances, as they pulled in, he recalled the feeling pouring through him, as he yanked open the front door.

But then it hit him, the thought of the house no longer standing, when they all took one last look at the place. At that, all three of them were going to miss it when it was gone.

"Come on," he recalled giving the order, while holding Harry up with his good arm, *"let's get out of here!"*

Remembering too as they cleared the front porch, they heard Ted's voice in the crowd, as he, Beth and Jarred ran up with a few ambulance attendants to take him and the others to where they would be safe. When just then, they all heard the most horrifying noise ever. Coming from the house was the sound of wood groaning and glass crackling, as it echoed throughout the air.

Looking back on it now, he remembered Ted crying out, when seeing the roof come crashing down. *"Clear the way_____!"* he yelled. *"It's coming down_____!"*

And so it did. Just as they jumped in behind the vehicles parked out front, the house, itself, came crashing down around them with the wood and glass scattering out all over the place.

Meanwhile, still crouched down behind his truck, Ted, Alex's now, old partner, turned back to the others, once all the dust and debris had settled. *"Is everyone okay?"* he asked, looking at Jessi first, then Alex. Seeing what had happened to his right shoulder. *"Alex...?"* he became alarmed at seeing the blood oozing from its wound.

"No. I'm fine, but we need to get Harry and Cra..." he stopped, recollecting what he was about to say, when remembering the look on both, Ted and Jarred's faces when he had nearly slipped up, by saying Craig's name. And then remembering the concern Beth showed, when coming around to check on him for herself.

"And what about you?" she asked.

"I'll be fine!" he recalled smiling at her. *"I just want to get them taken care of first."*

"Oh, I think we can fit you into the ambulance, as well," Ted ordered, while flagging down an attendant.

Recalling too, just how much he wanted to tell them the news, he had more important concerns on his mind, and that was to see to his nephew's injuries. But then, with Jessi and Craig standing at the back of the ambulance, while he was being looked over, he recalled, how he looked sadly into Jessi's eyes, when obviously Craig must have exchanged thoughts with her.

"*Go to him, he needs you!*" Craig prompted, nudging her toward his uncle once they were through with him.

Doing so, she went up to give him a hug, before thanking him once again for everything he had done.

"*You're welcome! However, it's I, who should be thanking you,*" he recalled the grin, while looking down into her smiling, yet blood smudged, dust covered, and tear-dampened face.

"*Oh, Alex...I...*"

"*No,*" he remembered putting up a protesting finger to her lips.

"*God, those lips...*" he groaned inwardly, before going on. "*Jess,*" he spoke softly, not wanting to draw any more attention to what had taken place in the house, "*it's because of your belief in Craig that had brought him back to us. You're the one who deserves the thanks.*"

And then the kiss that was to follow, to say; thank you anyway.

"*Damn...*" he continued to think about that kiss, until his thoughts were called back to the present.

"Alex...? Alex...?" Marcose was calling out over and over.

"Y...yeah? What?"

"Thinking about what had happened with Craig's situation?"

"Yes."

"Me, too."

At that point, the two went on a little while longer, while inside, both, Jarred and Jodi were in the middle of their own conversation.

Meanwhile, concerned about what was bothering her, he began to get worried. "What's going on, Jodi?" he asked once again, when she stopped and turned around.

Lifting her chin to look down into her eyes, he saw the hurt look in them that could only mean one thing.

"Jarred," she tried to look away, but he wouldn't let her, "I remember now, the conversation between you and my grandmother. You called her an 'old biddy'! What I don't understand is why?"

"Oh, God... we had an argument that day I saw you in her shop. I had just asked her if I could ask you out, but she said no. She wouldn't say why. But then she was just about to, when you walked in." Looking puzzled, he wondered what her grandmother was about to tell him. "What was it, Jodi?" he asked. "You know, don't you?"

"Yes, I think I do!" she replied, tearfully, while pulling away to avoid his inquiring eyes.

"What...? What was she about to tell me?" he asked, turning her back to face him.

"Jarred, no...! I can't tell you...!" she cried, while attempting to pull away again.

"Why?" he asked, seeing the tears forming in those beautiful eyes of hers. "Jodi, I have the right to know!" he went on, while his voice sounded both angry and hurt, while at the same time, trying to understand what was taking place in front of him.

"Oh, Jarred, I can't. I just can't allow myself to get involved again. Especially now, with a man whose life is in so much danger, now! Lord, it was hard enough seeing you get shot in my dreams. How can I go through that sort of pain again if he were to succeed?"

"What do you mean, again? Come on, girl, you're not making any sense here! What do you mean, again...?"

Looking up into his confused expression, the tears kept coming. "I..." she began, while thinking back to when she had lost Stephen.

"Jo, what...? What were you about to say...? Please, tell me!"

"I...I had already lost one man in my life. And seeing the pain in your eyes when..." she broke off into sobs. "God, please____!" she cried out, attempting to leave, when he reached out to take her into his arms, just to hold her.

But then the urge to claim her trembling lips took over, and as it did, the heat began to grow between them once again.

"Mmmm... No...! No____!" she moaned, shaking her head, as she felt herself about to give into it. At that moment, knowing if she didn't pull away then, she would never be able to.

Doing so, Jarred pleaded with her, "Jodi, no____! Please, give me a chance____! Give this a chance____!"

"Jarred, I can't____!" she cried, hating what she was doing to him. "I...I just can't...! Not now! Maybe not ever____!"

Just then, hearing the familiar sound of his uncle's black Chevy Blazer, with its tinted windows all around, pulling in, he had let up on her, not realizing in doing so, she would take that moment to make her break.

Looking up at him one last time, she turned to leave, brushing right past his uncle in the doorway, without even looking where she was going.

While watching the distraught woman fly out the door, he turned to his nephew. "What was that about?"

"That was Jodi."

"The one you were telling me about over the phone?"

"Yeah. She came out to tell me she didn't want to see me anymore. I just wish I had more time to understand why!" he exclaimed, with a look of puzzlement on his face.

"What exactly did she tell you?" he asked, while casually walking over to the front window to see her drive off down the road.

"Something to do with already losing someone in her life, and that she couldn't go through it again."

Turning back, Alex looked surprised, thinking about what Jessi had gone through. And too, she and her cousin had so much in common. "You say she had already lost someone?"

"Yes, but I don't know how it happened, or even who it happened to!"

"What were you telling me the other day about this dream she had?"

"She saw me get shot here in the house. Why?"

Laughing briefly, he thought once again about Jessi having had a similar experience. "It's just odd that she just happen to wind up on your sofa, and on a stormy night just like someone else I know."

"Are we referring to Craig and Jessi's situation?" he asked, jokingly.

"Yeah, it happened the same way for them, too! With one major exception," he said, looking back out the window, thinking about just how much he had loved Jessi, then, only to have to give her up for the sake of his other nephew.

"You still love her, don't you?"

"I probably always will, but she and Craig belong together," he stated, when turning back to his nephew. "But enough of that, I really didn't come over here to talk about them."

"Oh? What's going on? Has our friend chose to come out of hiding?" he asked in a more serious tone, when seeing the look on his uncle's face pretty much told him what he already suspected. "He has, hasn't he?"

"Yes, and he's been seen hanging around outside your friend's store."

"Jodi's Antiques?" he asked, as his eyes widened with surprise. "Why Jodi? What does he want with her?"

"He must have been watching your place, when she was out here the first time! Just how well do you know her anyways?"

"You know the answer to that, ever since her grandmother's shop was broken into. And then how I wanted to ask her out, but her grandmother was against it," he explained, just as his expression saddened once again at the thought of losing so much valuable time with her. "Damn it, Alex, I wish I would have known that she had gone through a divorce. I would have pursued her then after her grandmother had died." Stopping, he saw the look on his uncle's face. "Christ, I know that must have really sounded lame. But the woman was so dead set against her going out with me."

"Did Jodi know that you were interested in her then?"

"No, not at the time, but then if that wasn't bad enough, she had to overhear me call her grandmother an old biddy."

"Damn, you sure screwed that up!" he roared out laughing.

"Yeah, I know," he shook his head sadly. "Damn him, Alex, I have to protect her from Delgado."

"Not without me you aren't," he glared. "I'm not about to let something happen to you now! Just hang tight. I'll work on getting someone over there to keep an eye on her."

"Thanks."

CHAPTER NINE

MEANWHILE, THE NEXT FEW WEEKS were the hardest for Jodi, while she avoided his calls and kept herself busy working late at the store. At the same time, the man in the black pick-up continued to lurk around out in the shadows, while watching and waiting for her to be alone.

And then one night it happened, as she was working late in her office, Karen walked in. "Jodi?"

Without looking up, she answered, "Yes?"

"How long are you going to keep ignoring his calls? He has called at least three times today. Not to mention, all the times he had in the last few weeks!"

"You know why I have to do this."

"Yes, I know, but you're not being fair to him. He isn't Stephen, for cryin' out loud."

"I know he isn't! It's just that I…"

"Can't bear to see him get killed…?" she cut her off, adding bluntly, while going over to shove the phone into her hand. "Call him!"

Looking at the phone after her friend left, she wondered if Karen was right. *Have I been so unreasonable?*

Putting the phone back into its cradle, she got up to walk out to the front door and lock it. While standing there for a moment, she found herself thinking about her reaction to Karen's comment.

Unaware of the ultimate danger that lurked about in the darkness of the showroom, without so much as a sound, suddenly a strong pair of hands came out of nowhere and covered her mouth and shoulders.

"Mmmm_____!" she attempted to scream, while trying to fight off her attacker.

However, to her misgivings, all attempts were muffled out by his overpowering hands, when he sneered deep into her ear, "That's it, lady," he laughed, tearing at her sweater, "fight all you want. You aren't going anywhere," he continued, while dragging her back into her office.

Fortunately, a man was just passing the shop, when he saw what was going on inside, and ran off to call the police.

Meanwhile, back at Jarred's, he and his uncle were talking over what they were planning to do with the news of Delgado's recent actions, when the call came over his radio. "We have a code 211 in progress at Jodi's Antiques. Address, 777 North Haven Road. I repeat," the dispatcher said, "we have a code 211 in progress at Jodi's Antiques. Address, 777 North Haven Road."

"Alex_____" Jarred turned in horror at hearing the name and address.

"I know," he returned, heading for the door. "Just stay here and I'll take care of it."

"Like hell I will!" he yelled, grabbing for his motorcycle helmet, as he ran out past him, heading for his garage, where his bike was parked.

Attempting to stop him, Alex went out the door after him. "Jarred…" he yelled.

"I can't, Alex!"

Catching up to him at the garage, he grabbed his nephew's arm to pull him away from his bike. "Just what do you think you're going to do by putting yourself out there in the open? You know Delgado will just try to shoot you again. Only this time he just might not fail."

"I know that, Alex, but I have to go to her!" he informed him, while pulling away sharply to put on his helmet.

"No you're not, damn it! We'll take care of her. Just stay here!"

"You'll take care of her? Alex, you were to have a man on her at all times. Just what the hell happened to that?"

"I don't know, but I will find out. Just stay put!"

"Alex, normally I would listen to you, but not this time, and not when it concerns Jodi. Now, you can either go with me, or get the hell out of my way, 'cause I'm out of here."

Hopping onto his motorcycle, he started it up and looked one last time at his uncle, before peeling out of his driveway, sending rocks flying out behind him.

"Damn you, Jarred____!" Alex growled, running for his Blazer to go after him.

"Should we follow?" Baker asked, while he and Marcose stood back to see the rocks fly.

"Possibly," he replied, pulling out his radio to call Alex.

Getting the word, the two Detectives ran for their vehicles to follow.

Meanwhile, back at the antique shop, Jodi was still putting up a struggle with her attacker. "What do you want with me____?" she cried, feeling his icy cold hands through her thin sweater, as his fingertips bit into her flesh.

"It isn't you I want. It's your boyfriend, and his partner that I want."

"But why____?"

"Oh, let's just say that they owe me."

"But what do I have to do with it?"

"Oh, come now, you aren't that stupid!" he scowled, while dragging her over to her sofa that sat up against the far corner of her office, near the cabinet that held the coffee maker. "Let's just say after I get through with you, your Detective Stanton won't want to stay in hiding much longer."

"No____" she screamed out in horror at what was about to take place, when feeling his cold hand slid up beneath her sweater. While trying to push him off her, she continued to scream, but just as she did, he pinned her hands together behind her back, as she tried to get off the sofa.

"Oh, no you don't," he growled, coming down on her even more with his weight, while finding the bottom of her sweater once again. "Let's just see what you have here, huh!"

"Oh… God, please help me_____!" she cried, feeling his hand coming up even closer to capturing one of her breasts.

Just then, her prayer was answered, when hearing sirens off in the distance, as they vastly approached her shop.

Hearing this, her attacker looked back toward the door. "Damn..." he swore, less than thrilled that his time there was soon to be cut short, as he went to bring his hand back up to cover her mouth. "Don't think that this is the last you'll see of me, lady. I'll be back. Tell your boyfriend that, too!"

Before he could do anything else, they both heard the back door being kicked in.

"Jodi_____!" a man's' familiar voice called out, making his way through the dark back room. "Jodi____!"

"Mmmm____!" she muffled out a cry from beneath her attacker's clinched hand. Just then, biting down on it, while trying even harder than before to get free, it caused him to rear back in pain. "Jarred___!" she screamed even harder. "In here___! I'm in here..." she cried, while jumping up, as he and his uncle rushed into her office to attempt to apprehend her attacker.

Unfortunately, he had slipped away in the confusion, while pushing Jodi into Jarred's arms, as he rushed passed Alex in the doorway.

"Go after him, Alex____!" Jarred yelled, turning back to look Jodi over. "Are you all right?"

"Oh, Jarred___!" she cried frightfully. "How..." she started, when he pulled her up into his arms to hold her.

"Alex was at the house, when the call came through. I couldn't just stand by, knowing you were in trouble."

Feeling his warmth radiating through her, she buried her face into his shoulder, while continuing to cry.

"Jodi," he whispered softly, while pulling back a little to look down into her face, "you know this goes both ways."

"What do you mean...?" she asked, studying his angered expression.

"He could have killed you, and then how the hell do you think I would have felt, knowing that you were dead?" he asked, with his expression coming across so cold and so very hard, when he suddenly went to claim her lips, as they parted to answer him.

As the time passed, his lips became even more gentler, when he felt her arms coming up around his neck.

"Oh, Jarred, I'm so sorry!" she whispered, just as they heard Alex clearing his throat from the doorway.

"Sorry for the interruption, folks," he couldn't help but grin, "but we have a much more pressing matter here than we could have imagined."

Looking up at his uncle, he saw the concerned look coming back over his face. "What is it?" he asked worriedly, while turning to drop one arm from around her waist.

"That wasn't just any ordinary attacker, but I think you already know that," he stated, while looking deeper into Jodi's eyes, now that he had gotten a better look at her.

"Then who was it?" he asked, looking from his uncle to Jodi puzzledly.

"It isn't good," he shook his head. "After seeing his truck, I ran his plates through the B.M.V. It turns out that Vince Delgado has decided to go after your friend here after all!"

"Why her though? Why not just come after me if he knows that I'm still alive?" he asked, looking down into her frightened eyes.

"Are you saying that, that was…"

"Yes, the guy who tried to kill me a month ago."

"But why…?"

"We put him away for drug smuggling two years ago."

"And again just recently," Alex added.

"He said he was going after your partner next!" she exclaimed, looking back at Alex, who had a look of deep anger in his icy blue eyes.

"Did he tell you that?" Alex asked, looking hard into her eyes.

"Yes!"

Taking in a breath, Jarred looked down at her, then back to his uncle. "It was also something she had heard in a dream she had."

"Oh, no, the dream you were telling me about? I could have sworn I've already been down that road before," he grinned, shaking his head.

"I don't understand!" she replied, seeing the amused look coming over Jarred's face, as well.

"Ms. Tate," Alex was just about to ask with a hint of laughter in his voice, when he had noticed even more of a likeness between the two women, "you aren't by any chance the Jodi Tate that is related to Jessi Rae, are you?"

"Yes, I am. She's my cousin! Why?"

"No particular reason," he replied, looking back at his nephew, while still shaking his head. "I'm just glad that you weren't killed back then too," he laughed at Jarred.

Walking out into the other part of the shop, he went on thinking. *"Damn you, Jessi, I thought you were the only one who had those types of dreams."*

In the meantime, still standing in the office, she turned to see even more of a gleam in Jarred's eyes. "What was that all about?" she asked.

"Oh... I'm sure he will tell you when he is ready," he laughed, remembering back on something Jessi had said to him about her having a cousin who was a spitting image of her. And now he knew beyond a shadow of a doubt just who she was referring to, while the two walked out into the other room.

"Oh, but there's something else about him I just remembered," she announced.

"What's that?"

"The smell, he was here a few weeks ago, before I went out to... Well."

"It's okay. Alex," Jarred turned.

"Yes?" he returned, when coming over to join them.

"Vince was here a few weeks ago," Jodi explained.

"Did he talk to you then?" he asked.

"No. I was in my office, when he came by. Karen remembers seeing him, but when she was about to wait on him, he took off!"

"He won't be doing that again," Alex returned.

"What do we do now?" Jarred asked.

"Well, after I get through checking out Ms. Tate's place, I'll have an officer stay with her, until we can catch him!"

"Yes, but you had already had one on her. Did you happen to find out what happen with that?"

"He got pulled off her when the department didn't think she was in any more trouble. They were wrong."

"But he's gone now. Is it really necessary to go through this again?" she asked, looking from Alex to Jarred, just before Alex went out back to where he left his Blazer.

"Yes, it is," Jarred explained, taking her by the elbow to turn her back around. "I don't want to see anything happen to you now. Can you understand that?"

Feeling the warmth of his hand on her elbow had coursed right through her, she tried to smile. "But..."

"But nothing!" he placed a finger up to her lips to hush her. "I have waited a long time to finally be able to see you, not to have something like this come between us now."

"I wish I had known."

"If you had, what would you have done?"

"Fainted!" she laughed.

"What...?"

"I... would have fainted!"

"Why?"

"Oh, Jarred..." she looked away, not wanting him to see her blush again.

Turning her back to face him, he saw with the help of her office light, the soft crimson blush on her cheeks. "Really?" he smiled, while leaning down to kiss her lips once again.

"Oh, yes, really..." she smile fondly, while losing herself in his kiss, when she reclaimed his lips with so much warmth in her own, this time, while tasting the day old coffee that still lingered in his mouth. Though, that didn't bother her one bit, she loved what the feeling of his lips were doing to her.

After calling the station, Alex walked back in to let her know her new roommate would be at her place after they arrive to check it out. "And now that that has been taken care of, are we all ready to go?" he grinned, seeing the look on their faces.

"Sure," Jarred replied, while taking her out through the back room.

But then, once outside, coming to a sudden stop, she turned to look at the door leaning up against the building. By then, she turned to look over at Alex, "What about that?" she pointed.

"It'll be taken care of first thing in the morning. For now, I'll just temporarily patch it up, and have a guard placed here until we get it fixed," he offered smiling. "I can't allow for my new niece's cousin to go without being taken care of now, can I?"

"Your new niece's cou..." she began, when it all started to come together. "Oh, my, gosh...! You're Craig's uncle...?" she asked, watching him go to get some tools out of his Blazer. "You're Alex Storm...?"

"Yes, I am," he replied, bowing sheepishly with a hammer in one hand and a few boards that he had in the back end of his Blazer in the other.

"Oh, my, Jessi has told me so much about the hot headed, arrogant cop, who has mellowed out with age."

Seeing his expression, she had to laugh at the mention of his age.

"Oh, great, first Jessi, and now you," he laughed boldly. "I just hope that you aren't as temperamental as she is."

"No, I'm not," she smiled. "Jessi has the lead on temperament in our family."

"Good, I'm glad to hear that," he replied, as he went on to fix the back door, when she turned to see what Jarred was riding.

Pulling away from him with a look of fear returning to her face, he reached out to stop her, "No, Jodi," he shook his head, "not this time. I'm not letting you go, and I'm not going to get killed like he did, either."

"What do you know about how he died?"

"It was in the way you just looked at my bike! That is how he died, isn't it?"

"Uh huh!" she cried sadly, turning away.

"Oh, Jo… you're going to have to start trusting someone again. And that someone might as well be me."

"B…but i…it isn't that easy!" she choked back on the words, while fighting from looking back at his bike.

"Jodi, look at me!" he ordered, while turning her back to face him. "I'm not going anywhere. You hear me?" he groaned, pulling her back into his arms. "I'm not going anywhere."

"I want so much to believe that, but…" she cried softly into his shoulder.

"But nothing, Jo. You can again if you'll let yourself," he returned, while running his fingers in through her long, silky-like hair.

"But I'm so… scared…! Jarred, this man isn't going to just stop, until he has gotten you both. He said so himself, before he left."

"That's just what he thinks, Ms. Tate." Alex turned back at what he just heard. "I'll be damned if he gets anywhere near my nephew again."

"And you?" she asked. "What about you? He wants you just as bad!"

"He'll just have to wait in a very long line of enemies who have been wanting me out of the way," he announced, while gathering up his tools. "So, if the two of you are ready."

"What about her car?" Jarred asked, assuming she would be riding with him.

"What about my car?" she asked.

"Jo, I'm not about to let you drive anywhere alone. Not with Delgado out there."

"He's right," Alex agreed, looking at his nephew's bike. "Ms. Tate, do you have a garage back at your place?"

"Yes, I do! Why?"

"Jarred, why don't you ride back with her in case we run into trouble? We'll come back and get your bike later. For now, Chase can keep an eye on it, along with the shop, until we get it over to her garage."

"All right," he agreed, turning back to Jodi. "May I?" he asked, taking her keys to drive.

Chapter Ten

Arriving at Jodi's place, Alex went around checking it over, while she and Jarred spent some quiet time together in the living room, before he had to leave.

Meanwhile, standing next to her fireplace, he turned back to look at her. "These next few days are going to be rough for the two of us. Alex isn't going to want me out in the open, and it won't be safe for you either."

"I know….," she sighed heavily, walking over to her sofa.

"Jo, talk to me, please?" he pleaded, seeing her begin to close up again, while going over to join her. "Tell me what you're thinking!"

Pulling her knees up to her chest, she lowered her head to think, before going on. "My cousin went through something like this. Now I feel just like she did. Like everything is closing in on me."

"We're just wanting you to be safe!" he exclaimed, while turning her around to face him. "Besides, I've kind of gotten used to looking into those beautiful blue-green eyes of yours."

"I feel the same way, but…" She stopped, when feeling his thumb gently caress her cheek. "Oh, Jarred…!" she whispered his name, as he went to take her lips to his.

As he did, their kiss began to grow, as he felt himself wanting her, but knew better than to try at that time. Groaning, he pulled away, looking down into her eyes. "Oh, Jodi, I've got to stop this before I…"

he continued to groan, while running his fingers through her hair, and his lips lightly over hers.

Feeling it too, she stopped to slip out from under his embrace. "I know, it's all so sudden! We need time to get to know each other all over again, before we can even think about anything else."

"Yes, your right," he laughed nervously. "I'm sorry, it…it is too soon."

Just then they heard the front door bell ring.

"Alex?" Jarred called out, hearing his uncle coming down the stairs.

"It's okay. It's probably Beth, now!"

Going up to answer it, Jarred helped Jodi to her feet, with a thoughtful smile, as he ran his fingers through his hair.

With a blush, she smiled back, just when hearing faint voices coming from the foyer.

"Yes. She's in here," Alex was saying, when walking into the living room to introduce Jodi to her new roommate. "Jodi," he spoke up, seeing the blush on her face, as he went on to grin at the two, "this is Beth Lamb, your new roommate. She will be staying with you for a short time," he explained, looking from Jodi to the short, slender, strawberry blonde, with baby blue eyes, in her late twenties. "I think the two of you will get along just fine, since you have something in common with each other."

"Oh?" Jodi returned, when he went over to take Jarred by the arm to leave.

"Let's leave these two to get to know each other."

Reaching the front door, Jarred turned to see the look of saddened come over Jodi's face, just then. "Wait, Alex," he said, going back over to hold her one last time. "I'll call you. I promise."

"Oh, I hope so…!"

After kissing her goodnight, he looked one last time into her eyes, while gently running his thumb over her parted lips.

Closing her eyes against the oncoming tears, she lingered at the warmth of his touch, until she heard the sound of his voice break the moment.

"Goodnight, Jo," he whispered softly, touching his lips to hers, before she had opened her eyes to see his warm, smiling face looking down on her.

Reaching up to hug him tightly, she whispered, "Watch yourself out there. I've kind of gotten used to seeing those beautiful eyes of yours too."

He laughed. "I will," he replied, pulling away. "Besides, I've got a great watch dog, here," he roared out laughing even more, when pointing to his uncle.

Returning with his own hearty laugh, Alex growled, smacking Jarred on the shoulder. "Come on, before I have to get rough. Besides, Marcose and Baker are waiting on us."

"Oh? Then who's out at the house?"

"Kevin, as you already know and a few other guys went out after I put the call into the station."

Turning back, he smiled. "Well, I'll call ya!"

"All right!" she smiled back, while hiding her tears, until they left.

Outside, Marcose and Baker were right there to escort them over to Alex's Blazer.

"Any news?" Alex asked, getting in.

"No. It's as if he's dropped out of sight again," Marcose returned, while keeping a close eye on their surroundings.

"Good. Let's get back out to Jarred's so I can call Ted. It's time to get him more involved, as well."

"Might as well," he laughed, "since you have the rest of us here!"

"Yeah, I do, don't I?" he grinned, looking back at the house, before pulling away.

After seeing them off, Beth turned to see Jodi's tears flowing freely now. Giving her a gentle hug, she told her, reassuringly, "He will be fine, you'll see."

"He has too! We've lost so much time already!"

"What do you mean?"

"A long time ago," she began, while going back into the living room to get comfortable, "my grandmother's antique store was robbed, and Jarred was the officer that took her report."

"I think I remember hearing about that!" she laughed. "There was talk that he had called her an old..."

"It's okay. I know why. It was one of those times I overheard her one day talking to my mother."

"What about? If you don't mind me asking."

"He asked her if he could take me out!" she smiled, thinking back to that day, one late August morning. "I had forgotten all about that, until earlier this week!"

"Yes, but what did she say to get him to do that?"

"She said *no*!" she laughed.

"Why…? He's such a nice guy…!"

"Because he's a cop, and his life could come to an end like…" Her voice broke off, as she turned away to avoid having Beth see her cry.

"Hey…" she said softly, "it's not easy loosing the one you love."

"How did you know that I…" She turned back, looking surprised.

"Alex told me. I take it Stephen was your first real love?"

"Yes," she returned, looking down into her open hands. "When granny told him that he wasn't going to see me, she never told him the reason why."

"Why didn't the two of you get together after she had passed then?"

"The timing was all wrong."

"What a shame, the two of you look so good together."

"It feels so right too, but…"

"But you're afraid he'll get killed, too?"

"Yes," she replied, getting up to head for the stairs.

"But, Jodi," Beth stopped at the steps, when following after her, "your life is in danger now, too! How do you think he feels? And I for one know the answer to that. I think the two of you care more about each other than you both are letting on!"

"Oh, Beth, but how could I be feeling this way about him so soon? I'm not ready to handle this if he were to get killed right now."

"Then you are just going to have to start praying that he doesn't."

"I have been, ever since I realized who he was!"

"Then don't stop," she explained, taking her by the shoulders to study her for a moment. "Jodi, Jarred, from what I've heard, has been burying himself in his work to avoid his heartache over some girl he had fallen in love with years ago. I have a feeling you're that girl from what Alex had told me, while on our last case."

"Jarred? Fallen in love with me?"

"Yes. Having something to do with seeing your tears, when you were just seventeen, which brought him to his knees. And since then, well!"

"But that was so long ago! Surely he had been with other women!"

"Not anything serious, and not like what he had felt that day at your grandmother's shop."

"Oh, my, gosh…" she sat herself down on the steps, "I didn't know!"

"He loves you, Jodi."

"I…I don't know what to say!"

"Then don't say anything. But don't give up on him either."

Seeing how late it was getting, she got back up. "It's getting late."

"Yes, if it's all right with you, I'll just stay down here for the night, in case our visitor decides to show himself."

"All right, I'll just get you some blankets and a pillow."

After doing so, she thanked Beth, before going on up to her room.

Glad the subject had been dropped, Jodi cried herself to sleep in the confines of her room, after calling her girls to say goodnight. Just before getting off the phone with them, she talked to her mother about needing for them to stay a little while longer.

"Is everything all right? You don't sound like yourself," she asked.

"It's been a rough couple of weeks, and we had some trouble at the shop tonight."

"What happened?"

"I…" she started, when the words got caught in her throat. "I was attacked. But I'm all right, now. A passer-byer saw it happen and called the police right away."

"And this is why you want the girls to stay on a little while longer?"

"Yes, while they are looking for him. Will you keep them, then?"

"Well of course! But I have to ask, do they have someone watching over you, while they are looking for this man?"

"Yes. Her name is Beth. She's here now, staying downstairs in case he shows up here."

"Jo, do you have any idea who he was?" she asked, knowing her daughter had been keeping to herself, while staying busy with the shop and her girls.

69

"No, Mom." She fibbed, not wanting to tell her everything.

"Well, get some sleep. We'll talk later."

"Goodnight, Mom. And tell dad not to work the girls too hard," she laughed, thinking of all the cattle he had to feed.

Getting off the phone, she changed and slipped into bed, after saying a prayer.

The next morning, awakened by her phone, Beth went to answer it.

A few minutes later, hearing a knock at her door, Jodi called out from beneath her blankets, "Yes...?" she mumbled.

"It's Alex!" Beth called back in from outside her door.

Suddenly, feeling her heart heavy at hearing he was calling so early, not thinking, she jumped out of bed and threw open the door. "Has something happened to Jarred?"

"He's fine!" she replied, warmly. "Alex just wants to know what your plans are for today, is all."

"Oh, I just have to go out to feed Max and Maggie!" she exclaimed, feeling as if a great weight had been lifted off her shoulders.

"Who?" she asked, not thinking of Jessi's two dogs.

"They're my cousin's dogs," she smiled, while going back in to get her bathrobe on, before heading downstairs to put on some coffee.

"Oh? Okay!" she returned, while going back downstairs to finish talking to Alex, while Jodi headed for the kitchen, by way of the back staircase that the old house had to offer.

After getting the coffee started, she went over to stand at the back door to look out over the yard where the grapevines growing along the back fence ever since she was a little girl.

Not hearing Beth when she walked into the ample sized kitchen, she had quietly called out, interrupting Jodi's thoughts, "Jodi?"

"Yes?" she replied, not turning around.

"How about after we go out to feed the dogs, we go and get us some breakfast?"

"Sure!" she returned, while going over to pour herself some coffee.

"Mmmm... something sure smells good."

"Oh, I'm sorry!" She looked back at her company. "Where are my manners? Would you like a cup?"

"Sure! That sounds good!" she smiled, while going over to take a seat at the table.

Just as she had, the phone on the kitchen wall started ringing, which caused Jodi to jump, when answering it, "H...Hello..." her voice sounded a little different at first.

"Jo Jo... is that you?"

Hearing her cousin's voice, she cried out, "Jessi... where are you?"

"Still on our honeymoon...! Are you all right?" she asked, detecting trouble in her voice. "You don't sound good, and are the dogs all right?"

"Yeah, I'm all right! And the dogs are fine too. We were just getting ready to head out to feed them soon!"

"You and the girls?"

"No! Jarred's uncle has a female officer assigned to..." She stopped abruptly.

"What_____?" Jessi cried out, before Jodi could retract her statement.

"I'm fine_____! Really! As it turns out the man who tried to kill Jarred has been following me around, too!" she explained, leaving out the fact that he had attacked her the other night at her shop, when she went on, "Her name is Beth!"

"Beth...? By any chance, is her last name Lamb?"

"Yes! Why?" she asked, turning back to see the puzzled look on Beth's face, while drinking her coffee. And then it came to her. Not seeing Beth at the Inn the day she was there, the look on her face had given it away. "Isn't she the one who worked with Annie?"

At the mere mention of Annie, Beth sat her cup down, and came over to the phone.

"Yes...! Is she there now?"

"Yes, she's standing here in front of me, now!" she smiled.

"Oh, my, gosh...! Put her on! Put her on!"

"All right!" Handing Beth the phone, she continued to smile. "She wants to talk to you." Still yet puzzled, Jodi quickly explained, "Jessi Rae is my cousin."

"Really...?" Turning back to the phone, Beth's hands began to shake. "Jessi...?"

"Hello, Beth! Surprised?" she laughed.

Meanwhile, hearing the two chatting on, Jodi went over to collect their cups, while thinking to herself about the story her cousin told her about Craig and his uncle.

It wasn't too long after, that Beth had hung the phone up and walked over to the sink to thank her. "I can't believe it. Alex told me I was in for a surprise, and he was right!"

"Well, guess what!" she turned and smiled. "It just so happens that we're going out to the Inn to feed her dogs!"

"Great, it'll be so nice to see Annie and the others again."

"Yes, well, not until after I get dressed," she laughed, leaving the coffee cups for Beth to wash, while heading upstairs to do just that.

After locking up the house, the two headed for Jessi's Inn, a white, one hundred and ten year old, two storied, Victorian, with its black shutters, and wraparound porch, located outside of Langley. The drive itself had only taken twenty minutes from Jodi's, while making it easy for her to go out and check on the dogs from time to time. Even though Annie and the others were there to do it for her, she still loved going out, while taking her girls with her to see their cousins.

Upon their arrival, they were greeted warmly by Ashley, one of Jessi's closest friends, who along with Renee, Jessi's other friend, ran the Boutique, just inside the Inn, across from the front desk, then Annie, Jessi's beloved cook and confidante, who was now bringing out a breakfast cart for the guests and employees.

"Annie...!" Beth cried out, getting out of her small, blue, Pontiac Sunbird.

"Beth...?" the middle aged, matronly woman called back, when looking up to see them coming up. Recognizing the petite red head, Annie stopped with what she was doing to welcome her with open arms. "Well, it sure has been quiet around here without you!"

"Yes, and I've missed being here to help you, too!"

Smiling at the two, while they went on talking, Jodi went on into her cousin's office to call Jarred.

Once again, her wait was kept short, when she heard his handsome voice come over the other end. "Hello!"

"Hi!" she smiled, while leaning back in her cousin's office chair to get comfortable.

"Hey, how are you doing? Are you all right?" he asked.

"Yes, I just wish we could live a normal life."

"You're not the only one. I hate being stuck out here all the time."

"That can't be any fun."

"No, but don't get me wrong, I love the country, but due to circumstances and all."

"Yeah, exactly!" she replied, but then got quiet.

"Jodi?" he spoke up, getting worried.

"Yes?"

"Are you sure you're all right?"

"Sure! I'm just..."

"Unhappy?" he asked, detecting sadness in her voice.

"You know me too well, you know that?"

"Yes!" he smiled on his end, while sitting on the edge of his couch, wishing she were there. "Hey?"

"Yes?"

"Where are you, anyway?"

"Why?" she asked mischievously.

"Because I called over at the shop and your friend said you probably won't be in today."

"No. Beth and I are out here at the Inn."

"Serenity Inn? Your cousin's place?"

"Yes! While she's out, I come by once in awhile to feed the dogs and give them a little extra runtime."

"Sounds nice!"

"I'm sorry."

"Why?"

"I suppose, because of all the freedom I have."

"Yes, but still..."

"I know. I'm not safe either," she grumbled over the phone. But then hearing his laughter, she perked up right away. "You think that was funny?" she laughed.

"Have you heard yourself?"

"I suppose you're going to say that I sound like a spoiled brat?"

"No... I wouldn't think of it!"

"Jarred, you're a brat...!"

CHAPTER ELEVEN

AFTER LAUGHING OVER SEVERAL THINGS that had taken place to each of them in the past, and other things, Jodi went to get up and stretch her legs. "Mmmm... I had better be getting off here, I need to go and check on the dogs, and see how the others are doing."

"All right. And Jo...?"

"Yes?"

"I'm sorry you had to get involved in this mess."

"Why? You didn't cause the dreams to happen! They just came on their own!"

"So I'm finding out," he nearly laughed, which made her feel a little better about having to hang up.

"It's good to hear you laughing."

"It's nice to be able to laugh again."

"Jarred," she began, while going over to look out the front window, "I can understand now why my grandmother did what she felt was necessary, but I just wished she would have talked to me about it."

"She was only acting out in your best interest. I just wish I hadn't stayed away so long."

"Yes. Who knows where things could have been today. But then, I wouldn't have had my two girls!"

"Oh... I don't know about that!" he laughed.

"Jarred...!" she blushed, wondering, *'What if...,'* while laughing to herself.

Not realizing he heard her little laugh just then, he asked, "What were you just thinking?"

"Jarred...!" she cried, feeling as though she had been caught red handed. "And just how would you know that I was thinking anything?"

"It was in the way you laughed, just then."

"Oh...? And now you're an expert in reading a persons' laughter?"

"Sure! In my line of work you have to be able to read a person's body language."

"Have you been reading mine?" she asked, halfway teasingly.

"It's hard not to," he laughed. "You have a lot of good qualities!"

"Mmmm... granny told me the same thing, just before she died."

"I can only imagine how much you must be missing her right about now."

"Not as much as I'm missing Jessi! We could always tell when things were bothering us."

"Just like my uncle and I."

"He's just like Jessi had described. He goes the length to protect his family."

"Yeah, but he suffered when Craig got..." he stopped, not sure what all she knew.

"I know. Jessi told me," she returned, thinking back to the nights she and her cousin sat up late after their kids had fallen off to sleep. *"The whole thing was so... horrible!"* she thought quietly.

Not hearing anything over the line, he became worried once again. "Jo, are you worried that it's going to happen to me, too?" Not getting an answering at first, he went on, "Jo, Alex is doing his best not to let things go that far."

"But..."

"But, nothing. He has the best men on the job looking for this guy."

"I'm sure he does, but..."

"What is it, Jo?" he asked, unable to help but wonder what else she had on her mind.

"It's nothing," she fibbed.

"Jo, please don't shut me out. Let me help you. Tell me what's bothering you."

"I can't. Not now. I...it hurts too much j...just thinking about it," she cried, while turning back to go over to the desk to ponder over the memories of her far past. And now that things are just beginning to blossom between the two of them, she couldn't bear to see anything happen to him now.

"Jo...! Please...!"

"I really should be going! Beth is waiting on me, and I still need to tend to the dogs."

Giving up for the time being, he let things lie, as they were, but not for long. He cared for her too much to just let her go now. Not to mention, there had been too much time lost since he first laid eyes on her all those years ago. Now, he was bound to get her to open up and let him in. "Okay, but we will talk about this later, when you have had some time to think about it."

"No...! I don't want to talk about it. Not now or later!" she cried, tightening her grip on the phone.

"Jo, you have got to let it out. This is too much for you to hold in on your own."

"Just how do you know how much is too much? You've never lost someone you loved in your life."

Coming back at her a little harder than he had wanted, he said, "No, maybe not the way you have, but I have seen what it did to my uncle!"

"Oh, Lord, yes, you're right. You did!" She felt bad for being quite so harsh. And with that, she nearly gave into the tears that burned at the backs of her eyelids.

"Jo, I just want to help. Is that so wrong of me to care?"

"No, I suppose not," she returned quietly, just before saying goodbye.

"We will talk later."

"Okay. Call me tonight?"

"Count on it."

After ending their call, she went down to let the dogs out to run. "Ready you two?" she called out, walking in.

Both excited to see her, they ran up to the door with tails a wagging.

"All right," she smiled, while opening the doors.

Out in the backyard, she watched Max, Jessi's German Shepherd and Maggie, the Rottweiler, run while she walked about, thinking to herself, until Beth came up.

"Jodi?"

"Yes?"

"Alex just called. He wants me to take you back to get some of your things to stay out here for awhile."

"Why...?"

"He feels Delgado may try to come after you, back at your place. But if you're here, he won't know where to find you."

"Can we take Max with us?"

"Sure!" she replied, when Max came running up to jump on them.

"Well, Max, what do you say? Do you want to go for a ride?" she laughed, while he continued to jump excitedly, when turning to head back up to the Inn. "Hey, what do you say we grab a quick bite, before we head out though? That and I still haven't gotten the dogs fed yet."

"Sure. Annie was just wondering if we had breakfast yet!"

"Good." Going back into her cousin's quarters, Jodi dished up her dogs food and set it out on the private patio, before hooking them up on their leashes. "I'll be back to get you, boy," she smiled, while ruffling his fur, before heading upstairs to join the others, as they ate on the front porch.

Once they were done, Jodi hurried off to get Jessi's dog, before saying their goodbyes.

"Don't worry about Maggie," Hank spoke up, while walking up to give her a hug, "I'll take care of her, after she and I do some work out in the stable," he grinned. "I saw some little four legged critters that need chasing off."

"Thanks, Hank," she smiled, on her way out to Beth's car.

After pulling away, the drive back to her place was quiet, while she went on thinking about how hard it would be leaving her grandmother's house to stay out at the Inn. Even if only for a short time, this was something she really didn't want to do.

When she did say something, her voice came out wavered, "Beth, I...I can't do this. I...I can't go back out there just yet. I have so many things at home that I need to do, and I don't like the feeling of having to leave it right now. Lord... this was my granny's place, and now it's mine and my girls' home. How can he expect me to just up and leave it like that?"

"But, Jodi, Alex is expecting me to get you back out there!"

"I'm sorry… but you're just going to have to tell him that I won't do it! This is my home, and I am not some poor little girl that can be scared out of it quite so easily."

"Jodi, I know how you must be feeling, but…"

"But, nothing!" she cried, resenting what was going on, when they reached her house.

Just as Beth was shutting off the car, Jodi began to get out. But then, without warning, Max jumped over the front seat and made a beeline for her door.

Seeing this, Beth became alarmed and cried out, while rushing around to her side of the car to grab her arm.

"What is it?" Jodi asked, looking just as alarmed, when Max tore out across the driveway for the front porch of the house, growling.

"Someone has been here!" she noted, while pulling Jodi back around to the other side of the car.

"Oh, God…" she cried, as Beth kept watch on the house, while pulling out her phone to call Alex.

After putting in the call, Jodi called Max back to the car.

"Great. We'll be waiting for you," Beth returned, hanging up her phone.

"Was that Alex?"

"Yes. He'll be here soon," she explained, while placing her phone back into her pocket. "He's overseeing the repairs on your shop, as we speak."

"Wait. If Alex is there, who's out at Jarred's, watching him?"

"Jodi, he's all right. Alex sent Ted Jones out to stay with him."

"But of course! He's the other one who helped you guys out at the Inn?"

"Yes," she smiled. "Alex brought us both back to help him on this case."

It wasn't long when Alex and another cop showed up.

Coming around to join them, he asked, watching the house, while pulling out his service revolver, "Anything?"

"No. Nothing. It's been quiet so far," she explained, when he absentmindedly put his arm around her waist.

"All right," he replied. Turning to the other officer, "Mike!" he instructed the twenty-seven year old rookie to take the back. "I'll go through the front."

"Yes, sir," the rookie replied, heading out first.

"Beth..." Alex turned back to her.

"We'll be right here."

"All right then. Stay close to her."

"Okay," she returned, watching, as he headed for the front door.

It wasn't long after, Alex returned, placing his service revolver back into his shoulder holster, after sending the other officer away.

"Did you see anything?" Beth asked quickly.

"No, but I can't be too sure," he replied, coming up short of her driver side door, when he saw something moving around in the backseat. Getting a closer look, he broke out into a large grin at seeing Jessi's dog, who was looking eager to get out to him. "Max____?" he laughed, opening the door to let him out.

Getting out, the dog started in right away on jumping up on him, like a long lost friend.

"Well, it's good to see you too, boy!" he roared, while giving him a big hug.

Seeing their display of affection, Jodi just shook her head and smiled. "So is everything all right inside?"

"Yes, but still I plan on calling in another officer to keep an eye on this place, while you're out at your cousin's. Which brings me to my next question," he asked, while still fondling Max's fur, "when will your kids be getting back?"

"In another week or so. I had called my mother last night to see if they could stay longer."

"Good. And now..."

"Mr. Storm?" she interrupted.

"Yes?"

"I talked to Jessi earlier..."

"Oh? And how are they doing?"

"They're fine. Though, she did say they would be heading back pretty soon."

"That's great! I'll be glad to see them. However, as I was about to say, we need to be getting your things together and get you back out to her place, where Hank and the others can help keep an eye on you. And that goes for you too, Max," he added with a laugh, as the dog let out a gracious bark.

"No, Alex," she spoke firmly, while interrupting his moment with Jessi's dog, to tell him she won't be going just yet. As she did, she stood back to watch his expression change.

"You what…?" he nearly yelled, glaring down at her. "What the hell do you mean; you're not going just yet? Have you forgotten about that man who had attacked you is still out there?"

"No, I haven't," she glared back, with her hands propped on her hips. "And for your information, Storm, in some ways, I am a lot like my cousin. As in, this is my home and I won't let some jerk, Detective, or otherwise scare me out of it. Do I make myself clear?"

Taken aback by what she said, he looked at her in a whole other light. "Yes," he returned, "and yes, you're right about that," he half laughed, "you sounded a lot like her, just now."

"Good!" She stood proud.

"Okay," he grinned, "just for the sake of argument, what do you think you're going to do then, stay here by yourself?"

"No, and I won't be alone! Max will be here with me."

"Jodi, Max is a great watch dog and all, but the man does have a gun, you know?"

"Alex," Beth spoke up, "I'll stay with her."

"What? Are you sure you want to do that?" he asked, turning to see the expression in those baby blue eyes of hers. And just like it was with Jessi, he was lost in them.

"Yes, Alex, I'm very sure. Besides, knowing how I had felt when I lost everything after my parents' death, it was really h…hard…" She broke off suddenly at the thought of losing them at such a young age.

Feeling her pain at what he saw through her eyes, he understood. "Okay, but keep your cell phone handy in case he was to show up. And Max," he turned to kneel down in front of him, "take care of them for me. Or Jessi will have my hide if her cousin were to get hurt. Not to mention, someone else," he said, raising an eyebrow up at Jodi, knowing full well he was referring to Jarred. "He told me, you had been feeling like Jessi did. So, I'll try not to make this any harder for you, than it was for her."

"Thanks, Alex. It seems Jessi and I have a lot more in common than you bargained for."

"Does this mean that you're just as bullheaded as she was?" he asked, grinning.

"What do you mean, was? We still are!" she stated, smiling, when he went to stand back up.

"Damn, my nephews!" he swore, when they all began laughing, as he shook his head.

"Oh, Alex, are you afraid you'll just get more gray hair from all of this?" she laughed, as he turned to look back at her.

"I don't need any more gray hair, lady. Your cousin caused enough of this," he continued to laugh, while running his fingers through his hair.

"Oh, but it looks so becoming on you!"

"No," he glared back playfully, and then shook his head, while heading back to his Blazer to leave. "Beth," he called back in a low-keyed voice, "be careful, and call me if you run into trouble."

"I will," she replied, as the two turned then to go up to the porch.

"You know," he started, but then looked around in case they were being watched, "I would have preferred that the two of you were out at the Inn!"

At that moment, Beth turned and gave him one of her reassuring smiles.

"All right." And with a sound of defeat in his voice, he got in behind the wheel and pulled away.

Chapter Twelve

That night, after going to bed, their mystery truck returned and right away Max's ears perked up at the sound of the kitchen doorknob being jiggled. From the foot of Jodi's bed, he got up and made his was down to check it out, while leaving her asleep, as well as Beth, who was down, sleeping on the sofa, in the living room.

Reaching the door, while their attacker was attempting to get in, Max began growing in such a low tone that it had brought Beth out to the kitchen to see what was going on.

"Max, I want you to go and get Jodi up. Okay, boy? And while you're doing that, I'm just going to call Alex," she whispered.

Turning, he bounded up the stairs, and headed right for Jodi's room, where he leaped up onto her bed. "Err...uff! He barked, waking her.

"Max..., what is it, boy?" she grumbled tiredly.

Barking again, she laid there for a moment longer, when hearing it for herself. "Oh, Christ...," she threw back the blankets to get up, "we have to get Beth up."

Jumping down off the bed, Max took off for the back stairway again. Turning back, as she hurried out of her room, he barked again to get her attention.

"What is it, boy?"

"Arr...!" he wined, wagging his tail. "Arr...!"

"Beth..., is that it? Is she down there now?"

"Err…uff."

"Okay, let's go, boy!"

Getting down to the kitchen, where Beth was keeping guard in the shadows, she turned back to Max, "Did you get her up, boy?" she asked, reaching down to pat him on the back.

"Yes," Jodi whispered, just as Max began growling again. Only this time, he's growls had gotten a little more angrier, while Beth, having held off on putting the call into Alex at the time, did so then.

Upon hearing him over the other end, while staying out at Jarred's, she began quietly, while keeping an eye on the back door, "Alex, it's me. We have trouble at the back door."

"Delgado?" he asked, getting to his feet, along with Jarred, when hearing the name.

"Yes, he's here now, trying to get in…!" she explained, with a hint of fear in her voice.

Detecting Max in the background, he asked, "Is that Max growling?"

"Uh, huh! And Alex, it *was* Max who warned us of the intruder."

"I'm glad," he admitted, while strapping on his service revolver.

"Alex?" Jarred sensed trouble, as he went to strap on his own gear.

Seeing his concern, he went on, "What about Jodi? Is she all right?"

"She seems to be! But I have to admit, we're both feeling a bit shaken right about now."

"Hang in there, we're on our way," he replied, hanging up, while turning back to Jarred.

"I'm going with you," he told him pointedly, while heading for the back of the door to get his black, leather motorcycle jacket.

"Who am I to stop you," he grinned, while grabbing his helmet to hand to him. "At lease this way I can keep an eye on you!"

Grinning, Jarred thanked him, while the two hurried out the door together.

"You're welcome. Now let's hit it…" he hollered out, running to their vehicles.

Meanwhile, taking the lead on his bike, with Alex hot on his trail, the two were off heading down the dark and wooded country road toward Jodi's place.

Back at the house, the intruder suddenly paused, when hearing Max growling inside. "Damn… what next?" he groaned, while standing quietly off to one side of the door.

Hoping the dog would simply go away, inside, Jodi looked to Beth worriedly. "He's still out there, isn't he?"

"Oh, yes," she whispered, while listening closely for signs of Alex's Blazer or Jarred's motorcycle.

Soon, after waiting a little while longer, they heard a motorcycle coming up from the alley.

Hearing it, Jodi cried, covering her mouth. But was it too much to hope for? When just then, they heard Delgado's voice growing over Jarred's coming out into the open.

"No…" Beth cried, hearing bits and pieces of his threats, when he went to move further off to the side of the back porch to hide, when the sound of Jarred's bike got closer.

"Beth…" Jodi cried, going to the back door, "he'll be gunned down if he isn't warned!"

"No_____!" Beth stopped her, when they heard yet another vehicle up front, slammed on his breaks, before jumping out to come to their rescue. "It's Alex! He's here, as well!"

Just then, hearing Delgado's voice outside the house, growling at his dismay, they heard the sound of footsteps running around from the side of the house to capture him, before he could make his getaway, again.

"Damn, him…" Delgado repeated. "Doesn't Stanton ever go anywhere alone anymore?" he growled, as the footsteps got even closer.

Seeing how his attempt there was futile, he made good on his escape, just as Jarred appeared, pulling in alongside the garage, out back.

"Jarred…" Jodi cried out, while Beth went to unlock the door, just as he came running up.

Finding her in the darkened kitchen, he called out pulling her into his arms, "Jo_____!"

"Jarred_____!"

"Are you all right?" He pulled back to look at her.

"I am now_____! Thanks to these two…!"

Turning to Max, he knelt down to pet the dog, knowing him from being out at Jessi's place. "Hi, Max, it's nice to see you again!" he smiled gratefully. "Man, Alex was right, he is a great dog," he commented, while standing back up to look Jodi over again. "And now, you, are you sure you're all right?"

"Yes," she cried nervously, while going back into his arms, shaking.

By then, Alex came running into the darkened kitchen. "Beth?" he called out, flipping on the light, after closing the door behind him.

"Right here," she replied, while still feeling a little nervous herself.

"Good! I'm glad to see that you're both all right," he returned, looking back at Jodi with a slight glare. "And now, Ms. Tate," he said in a more authortive-like voice, "will you please put some things together, and come with us back to the Inn, so we can watch over you there?"

"Alex," Jarred interrupted, before letting her go, "I know I've asked this before, but damn it, why is he still going after her? Why not just come after me now that he knows that I'm not dead? Damn it, he knows where to find me!"

"Because there are too many men watching over you there. This way he knows if he can get you out in the open by going after her… Well, just think about it. Why not go after your friend? Tonight and the other night at her shop just proved it."

"That's not all," Jodi added. "There's something else, too!"

"What's that?" Jarred asked, looking down at her.

"He was upset when he heard Alex pulling up out front!"

"Why? What did you hear?" Alex asked.

"He said…" Beth began, "'doesn't Stanton ever go anywhere alone anymore?' I think he wants to deal solely with one of you at a time. As a team…"

"We're too much for him," Alex grinned proudly. "Damn… that has to be it! Together, we are too much for him," he laughed.

"Perhaps," Jarred returned. "But he's not going to give up until he does get each of us alone. Yet you've been alone plenty of times, Alex!" he stated, looking to his uncle.

"Unless he feels that Alex is a much harder target?" Jodi spoke up just then.

"What do you mean?" they asked, studying her.

"From the impression I got from Jessi, Alex, you have made a name for yourself. Taking you down last would mean a much better trophy for him. For now, he wants you, Jarred!" she turned back to look up into his eyes, sadly.

"No, that's just not going to happen," he returned. "So, for now, please do as my uncle asked. Go out to the Inn with them, until they can catch Delgado? I couldn't bear it if I were to find you hurt or worse yet..."

"Dead?" she groaned, seeing his pleading eyes. "All right, I'll go," she agreed, turning to head up to her room to pack her things.

Just before leaving to go to her cousin's, she stopped short of her bed, where she saw the old quilt that had belonged to her grandmother hanging there. Grabbing it up, she didn't hear Jarred walking in just then.

"Are you ready?" he asked, seeing what she was holding.

"No, I'll never really be ready," she cried, holding tight to the quilt. "This used to belong to granny!" she added, when turning to face him.

"Then by all means, take it with you!"

"Thanks!"

Meeting her halfway, he brought her back up into his arms to hold her. "I wish it didn't have to be this way."

"Oh, Jarred..." she continued to cry, "I really don't want to leave here! This is mine and my girls' home!"

"And it always will be!" He pulled back to look down at her. "Just not right now, because it isn't safe for any of you. Neither you, or your girls."

"I know...!" she sadly whispered, as they turned to head back down the front stairs to find Alex and Beth waiting at the front door.

"Are we ready?" he asked, sensing Jodi's reluctancy to leave what she had always felt so safe in. "The guys are here to follow us out to the Inn. And Jarred, I had already brought your bike up front for you."

"Meaning?"

"You're going to ride it out there," he groaned, reluctantly.

"Thanks," he replied, smiling.

"Yeah, thanks," Alex growled, not liking him to be on it, out in the open, and especially now, not knowing where Delgado might be. "In any case, Ms. Tate, do you have everything?"

Thinking for a moment, she looked to her kitchen. "I have some things in the refrigerator that I had just gotten."

"Go get them. Beth, give her a hand."

"It's quite a bit, since the girls were supposed to be coming home," she was saying, after leaving the foyer.

"We can get it," Beth smiled sweetly.

Soon they were back with four bags, looking to be weighing down their arms.

Taking a few, Jarred grinned.

"Okay, is that it?" Alex asked, picking up her other things, for when he went out to toss into the back of his Blazer.

"Yes," Jodi returned.

"Good, just give me a minute first, to check things out with the guys, before we go."

"Okay," they agreed, while going back into the living room to get comfortable.

Getting out to his Blazer, Marcose and Baker walked up to join him. "Any word?" he asked, while quietly loading her things.

"As far as I can tell, he's not in the area," Marcose informed him, while keeping himself ready, in case he was wrong.

"Damn it to hell!" Alex growled, heatedly.

"Alex, what is it?" Marcose asked.

"Why won't he just go after me for awhile? I could handle it better if he did!"

"Because you would know what his next move would be."

"Exactly! But going after Jarred, I can't always be certain."

"What now?" Baker asked.

"Jarred is going to want to take his bike back home with him. For now we're heading out to the Inn."

"Serenity Inn?" the two asked, mostly surprised, but happy too.

"Yes," he practically grinned, knowing what they were probably thinking.

"And Ms. Tate?" Baker added.

Shaking his head, "I'm certain he will want her to ride with him."

"On the bike? Out in the open?" Marcose growled. "Isn't that a little dangerous even for her?"

"Yes."

"Fine, and don't worry, we'll stay close by," Marcose assured him.

"They should be all right as long as Delgado doesn't return," Alex glared, closing the hatch. "For now, let's get the show on the road, before he does come back."

"You got it," the two said, heading to their vehicles, while Alex went in to get the others.

"All right," Alex called out, walking in, "got your things loaded, all but the groceries. So let's get out of here, while we can."

"Jodi?" Jarred asked, warmly.

Seeing she was still feeling a little hesitant, Alex offered reassuringly, "Ms. Tate..."

"Alex, it's Jodi, please! I mean after all if we're family now, we might as well be on first name base," she smiled briefly.

"You're right, we are family, now, aren't we?" he grinned. "Well in that case, Jodi, Marcose says that Delgado isn't in the area now. So if we're careful, we can get you out to the Inn without detection."

"Alex," Jarred interrupted, "my bike?"

"Well, Ms... Jodi," Alex teased to lighten the mood, "it's up to you! You can either ride with me, Beth, or..." he laughed, looking to his nephew, knowing already what he would want.

Looking to Jarred, as well, she smiled nervously. "I'll... I'll go with Jarred."

"Well then, shall we?" Jarred grinned, heading for the door.

"Go head, I'll see to the locking up of the house, myself," Alex offered.

"All right!"

Going out to their vehicles, Alex went around with Max to check out the house.

Meanwhile, having gone out to get on his bike, with a brief hesitation, Jodi smiled even more nervously.

"Well..." Jarred turned smiling, while handing her his helmet, "climbing on?"

"Yeah, sure!" she nodded, while taking the helmet. Afterwards, she got on, wrapping her arms around his waist.

"Comfortable?" he asked, smiling, as he went to brush a hand over her upper thigh.

"Uh, yes!" she replied, while his touch caused a sudden rush of heat to flow though her loins. *"Not now…"* she cried. *"Not until all this is over…!"*

Walking back out to his Blazer, just then, Alex gave out last minute instructions, while opening the door to let Max in, "Marcose, I want you right behind them, and Baker…"

"Behind Lamb?"

"Yes." Looking to his nephew, Jarred smiled brightly. "Just watch yourself out there," he growled, when getting in behind the wheel. "Ready?" he called out on his radio to each one of them.

"Ready," Jarred came back first, followed by Marcose, then Beth, and then Baker.

"Let's go."

"You heard him. Shall we?" Jarred turned back to giving her leg a gentle squeeze.

"Yep!"

With that, they were off after making sure it was safe.

CHAPTER THIRTEEN

ARRIVING AT THE INN, JODI went down to her cousin's quarters to unpack, before attempting to get some sleep, when Jarred knocked on the door, at the top of the stairs.

"Hi!" she greeted, when seeing him come down see her.

"Are you up for some company, before you call it a night?"

"Sure!" she replied, going into the kitchen to get a hot cup of tea to help her relax.

Just then, hearing the radio playing in the other room, she listened closely to hear a slow tune playing on it.

Coming out of the kitchen, he took her into his arms and began to dance with her, when once again the mixture of emotions began to stir, as he went to claim her lips.

As he did, her tears began to fall, while the heat between them built to such dangerous heights that she had to break it off. "Jarred…"

"Jo," he placed a finger to her lips, "Alex says I have to go back first thing in the morning."

"Oh…," she cried, feeling his heart beat against her breasts, "then that doesn't give us much time, does it?"

"No, but at least we have this moment!" he exclaimed, holding her near the fireplace.

"So we do!" she agreed, looking up slowly into his eyes, as her tears fell one by one now.

Seeing them, he frowned. "You know," he went on trying to think of something more upbeat to talk about, "I was down here not all that long ago."

"What…? When…?" she asked, not thinking how Max had taken to him so easily, back home, in her kitchen.

"During the Fourth of July shindig!"

"No…! That couldn't be! I was here then."

"Oh! Which day?"

"Wednesday! And you?"

"Thursday!" he laughed, shaking his head.

"Oh, my gosh… that's what you meant, when petting Max. You met him here!"

"Yep!"

At that moment, they both started laughing.

"Damn…"

"What?"

"I could have been seeing you then."

"Oh, really?" she smiled, when suddenly thinking of something. Looking up at the mantle, where her picture sat in next to her cousin's, she wondered.

"What?" he asked, following her gaze.

"Well then," she began, while reaching up to get it, "if you were here…" she turned back to look at him.

"Yes… down here in fact, where I stayed the night, talking to Alex."

"Well then," She stopped to hand him the eight by ten frame, "how is it, as a Detective, did you miss this?"

Taking it, he turned it over to look at the picture. "Oh, no…" he shook his head. "How long has this been here?"

"At least a year!" she smiled, taking it back.

"Oh, God, how could I have missed seeing that?"

"Don't know!"

"No way…!" he groaned, looking up to see Jessi's picture, as well. "God, she said she has a cousin who was the spitting image of her."

"And she was right!" Alex put in, joining them for a short while.

Turning to look up at his uncle, she smiled.

"Well," Alex smiled, as well, "you do look a lot like her. I saw that at your shop the other night, and before then at the diner, when you were on your way out with your friend. I thought at first, how could that be, but look at you."

"Yes," she continued to smile, "and as for that day I was here, I remember it well! Jessi said you were out watching some guy named Tony!"

"Yeah, I remember that day. That explains how I happened to miss meeting you!" he grinned, while going on into the kitchen to put on a pot of coffee.

"The hardest thing for me, though, was missing her wedding. I was away seeing a dear old friend of my mother's, who passed away," she explained, while turning to hide the new tears, while acting as though she were straightening the pictures.

After both coffee and tea were ready, the trio sat around the living room talking.

It wasn't long after, they called it a night. Alex went up to the room he had first started out in, back when he first came to the Inn in June, while leaving Jarred to stay downstairs.

Taking their cups back into the kitchen, Jarred announced that he, too, should be getting some sleep. "It's late and you need to get some rest, as well," he put in, while coming back out to see a blanket and pillow on the floor next to the couch, where Alex used to sleep.

"Yes, you're right," she yawned, while getting to her feet. "You'll be all right out here, won't you?"

"Yes."

"Okay. I'll see you in the morning?" she asked, before heading to her cousin's room.

"Sure!" he returned, as she got started down the hallway. At that moment, he had to think hard as she got further and further away. "Jo, wait!" he called out, going up to her.

"Yes?"

"I uh…" he fumbled for the word to say, before just giving her a kiss goodnight. And like all their other kisses, it had taken off, sending them spinning out of control.

"Oh, Jarred," she groaned, filled with desire, "what's happening here?"

"Don't you know?" he asked, while running his hand down to the small of her back, to bring her up even more into his arms.

Feeling what was about to happen, as he went to reclaim her lips, she moaned, wanting to escape into the world he was paving for her. But once again she broke it off, while looking up into his smoldering eyes. "Goodnight, Jarred," she smiled timidly, as she pulled away, knowing he was as flustered as she was.

"Jo...!"

"Goodnight," she repeated, leaving him to go into her cousin's room.

Going back into the living room, he smiled, while looking back down the hallway at the door, which had just closed. "Goodnight, pretty lady," he whispered, while going on to get himself ready for bed.

Meanwhile, doing the same, she pulled her kid's pictures out of her suitcase to set out on the nightstand next to the bed, as she continued to smile, while turning to look over at the closed door. "Sweet dreams, Jarred," she grinned, sliding down under the blanket. "Sweet dreams."

When morning came, getting up early, Jodi went into the bathroom to get washed up and ready to head upstairs to offer a hand at the front desk. Once she had finished, walking out into the living room in her stocking feet, while wearing a pair of jeans and a light weight top, she heard a faint groan coming from the couch. "Well, what do we have here?" she smiled, as Jarred rolled over to see her standing there.

"Good morning," he smiled up at her.

"Good morning to you too! Did you sleep okay?"

"Mmmm... ask me after I get some coffee in me," he teased, coming up off the couch in one fell swoop, as he headed for the bathroom, but then stopped long enough to give her a small kiss on the forehead.

Laughing, she went on into the kitchen to put on some coffee for him. "Jarred?"

"Yes?" he answered, while splashing some water on his face.

"What time do you think Alex will want to leave?"

"Don't really know. But soon, I would think," he replied, walking into the kitchen to give her a hand. "What are you going to be doing in the meantime?"

"Go up and offer a hand at the front desk, since Lisa, the regular clerk, is out!"

"Hmmm... from the looks of things, it looks as though the Inn is going to be buzzing with people all day long! If anything, that will be the perfect time to go. Just as soon as he gets done talking to the guys he has covering the place."

"Oh, okay!"

After the two shared a simple breakfast together, they headed upstairs after getting their shoes on, and straightening up their beds.

As for the rest of the morning, and into the noon hour, it had stayed busy, when Alex and Jarred came walking down the stairs to say their goodbyes, feeling it was safe to go.

"Hey there," he called out, stopping by the desk.

"Getting ready to head out?" she asked, turning to see him and his uncle looking like they were ready to go, while she and Beth were standing next to each other.

"Yeah."

"Beth," Alex turned, "do as I told you, and if you have any, and I mean any trouble, call me immediately."

"All right."

"As for you," Jarred smiled at his lady, "I'll call you this evening!"

"I sure hope so!" she returned his smile, while he leaned down to give her a kiss.

"See ya," he grinned, walking out the door to hop on his motorcycle, which had been hidden away in Jessi's garage overnight.

Watching them leave, she soon turned to walk off into the kitchen.

"Jodi," Beth called out, following after her.

"Beth, I know what you're going to say…, but please, don't…!"

"Jodi, I can't help it. I know you're worried, but you have to believe everything will be all right!"

"Will they?" she asked, not meaning to sound quite so sharp, when she went over to look out the back window, where Annie was busying herself doing up the breakfast dishes.

"Yes."

"How do you know that?" She turned back to see the young policewoman's expression.

"Because, back when Tony was here, Alex had to go undercover to keep his identity a secret."

"I don't understand. What does this have to do with…" She

stopped, when remembering more of the story Jessi had told her. "Ah...
yes, it was because he wanted him dead, too!"

"Yes, and because of it, I was scared, too!"

"You...?" she shook her head, not being told of Beth's relationship
with Alex in the past, when turning to look back out the window to
try and sort out her own feelings.

CHAPTER FOURTEEN

SOMETIME LATER, AFTER LEAVING BETH with Annie, Jodi went back up to the front desk. Lost in thought, she never saw Ashley and Renee walk over from the Boutique to take the registration book out of her hand.

"Hey, how about a break?" Ashley suggested, when seeing how tired she looked.

"Yeah, sure!" she agreed, sitting her pen down. "What about Beth?"

"Right here..." she called out, walking up to join them.

"Would you like to join us out on the porch like old times?" Ashley asked.

"Sure!"

"Good! Let's go then!" the forty-two year old, brunette smiled, while leading the way out to their favorite table, at the far end of the porch, where Annie brought out a cart of food for everyone.

Getting there, everyone looked over the food Annie had prepared with Beth's help.

"Boy, this sure looks good!" Renee, a pleasant forty-five year old, Hispanic, smiled.

"Sure does!" Alex grinned, while taking them all by surprise, when walking up.

"Alex," Beth spoke up, blocking the sunlight from her eyes, when seeing his brilliant smile, "when did you get back?"

"Just a few minutes ago," he replied, looking down to see Jodi's growing concern. "It's okay, I left someone with him."

"Thanks, Alex. That really takes a load off my mind. Would you like to join us?" she asked, noticing how the sunlight brought out his graying hair, and that beautiful tan of his. Not to mention, his icy blue eyes, which, at that moment, were looking off toward Beth. *"Hmmm... am I imagining things?"* she asked herself, when noticing Beth's own shy expression.

Just then, Alex cleared his throat. "No thanks, I'm waiting on a call."

"Oh?" she asked, getting herself something to eat, when his cell phone started ringing.

Taking the call inside, where he was able to talk more privately, Ashley looked over at Jodi curiously, "Hey girl, what was that about?"

"Yesterday, after leaving here, we had found the front door of my house ajar, when we got home. So he's checking it out."

"Oh? What has he found so far?" Renee asked, taking her plate of food over to the table.

"Nothing yet," she was saying, when Alex returned, not looking all that happy.

"Ladies," he interrupted, taking Jodi's arm, "I'm sorry, but I need to borrow her a minute. May I?" he asked politely.

"Sure!" she returned, looking over at Beth, before going with him.

Once inside, she turned back, looking concerned, as usual, "Okay, Alex, you got my full attention. Now what's wrong?"

When he didn't answer at first, she began to get even more concerned.

"Alex, please... you're beginning to scare me. What is it?"

"From what I've learned so far, Delgado has been hanging around outside your place ever since we left. I..." He stopped, not wanting to divulge too much information. Though, when he didn't go on, the look on his face said it all.

"Oh, Lord, just what were the two of you involved in?"

"Jodi," he began, when turning to see Beth walk in, "I'm sorry," he said, turning back to face her, "but I can't tell you anything more without causing you more trouble."

"You can't, or you won't?"

"Oh, Jodi, please… not you too…!" he grumbled, shaking his head.

"Alex, if things start to get out of hand…"

"I know. I hear you," he interrupted, remembering that very same speech that was made not all that long ago. "But damn, if you don't sound just like your cousin," he half laughed, while looking up at the ceiling, amusingly.

"Then, I'm sure you also know…"

"Yes, damn it, I know! I know! And yes, of course I wouldn't do anything to endanger the guests here or your cousin's friends or the help. Now," he turned to take Beth's arm, "if you will excuse us for a moment, I need to talk to Beth."

Nodding her head, Jodi excused herself to rejoin the others.

"Alex…" Beth started in, as he took her aside to fill her in on what had been going on.

"Beth, I have my reasons."

"Oh?" she asked, seeing his expression go even more grave. "Alex, what is it then?"

"Delgado. He's been hanging around Jodi's place, and the neighbors are really starting to get worried."

"Great! What are we going to do now?"

"Just pray her girls don't decide to come back home early."

"Oh, my, God!" Her face paled at the thought.

"Yeah."

Later that evening, having called Ted to come by the Inn, he arrived as Beth went out to greet him. "Where's Alex?" the tall, black, distinguished looking, gentleman asked, while walking up onto the porch.

"Down in Jessi's quarters, talking to Jodi!"

"Is she really a lot like Jessi?" he asked, walking on inside.

Laughing at his question, she nodded her head, "Oh, yes. She sure is."

"Oh, boy, just when he thought he got through handling one hot tempered woman," he started laughing, when Alex walked into the foyer. "Just like old times, huh?"

"Your right about that!" he grinned. "Do you have anything new for me, since we talked earlier?"

"Yeah."

"Great. Let's go on out on the porch and get us some coffee. We'll talk there."

Going back out, Alex walked over to pour himself a cup from the cart that was left there earlier.

Seeing it, Ted thought back to the first time the two came out to drink their coffee. "Man, some things just never change, do they?" he grinned, while going over to get himself a cup of that hot, black liquid.

"No, but let's just hope for another happy ending," he replied, while walking back over to sit down at the table. "Now, what do you have for me?"

"Nothing you would really want to hear!" he exclaimed, while going over to join him.

Knowing the look on his friends' face, Alex asked, "Damn it, Ted, where has he been staying?"

"Close, Alex, real close. It's that cheap motel, outside of Logan, to be exact. Which we both know isn't far from here, or her place."

"Damn!"

"Yeah, and he's been sticking close to Jarred's place, as well. But that isn't all."

"What now?"

"I have a feeling he's about to make his move, and soon!"

"Not if I can help it. For now let's just keep a tight watch on what he's going to do next."

"You want me to see about getting more men out there?"

"I've got a couple more already going out tomorrow. That should cover it in case he gets ready to move."

"And what about this place, do we have enough coverage here in case he gets wind of her being here?"

"Yes, we should."

"Good. Right now all I want to do is get my gear taken up to my old room. That's if it's still available!"

"Yeah, I've already taken care of it."

"Good, then, shall we?" Ted suggested, while downing his coffee.

Coming back inside, where Jodi, Beth, and Ashley were standing at the front desk, talking amongst each other, they looked up.

"Is everything okay?" Jodi asked, giving Alex a questioning look.

"Yeah, everything's just fine! I'll be up in Ted's room, helping him get settled back in."

"Okay..." she was just saying, when they all heard a commotion out front.

"What the heck?" Alex growled, going to the front door, where everyone looked out to see what was making such a racket.

Just then, recognizing the truck that had just gone by, Jodi backed away from the door, where she ran into Ted, crying quietly to herself.

"Damn! How the hell did he know to find us here?"

"Not a clue!" Ted replied, while pulling out his service revolver along, with Alex and Beth.

"Ashley..." Alex turned.

"Say no more," she turned to head back into the Boutique to stay with Renee, while Jodi went off into her cousin's office, closing the door behind her.

Taking out her cell phone, she called Jarred, while out in the foyer, Alex and Ted looked at each other, wondering what went wrong with their plan to keep her hidden away.

Just then, Jarred's deep voice came over the other end. "Hello?"

"J...Jarred...!" she cried out, going over to take a seat at the desk.

"Jodi, what's wrong?"

"It's Delgado! He just drove by the Inn!"

"Is Alex still there?"

"Yes!"

"Get him for me. I have to talk to him."

"A...all right!" she replied, getting up to go out to the door.

Meanwhile, still looking out at the roadway, the three continued to talk quietly amongst each other.

When just then they heard Jodi clearing her throat, while standing in the office doorway, "Gentlemen, will you please step in here? Now!" she asked, before turning to go back into her cousin's office.

Making sure his people knew what they were to do first, Alex and Ted went in to see what she wanted, when she closed the door behind them.

"Jodi, what is this all about?" Alex asked, sounding a little heated, when then she handed him her cell phone.

"He wants to talk to you," she returned, looking into his, now, steely blue eyes.

"Who?" Alex asked, taking her phone to put up to his ear.

"Me," Jarred replied, with a hint of humor in his voice.

"Jarred?"

"I heard that Delgado drove by."

"Yeah."

"Alex, there's something you should know about Jodi that I haven't told you."

"What?" he asked, looking back into her tear-filled eyes.

"I think you might want to bring her out so that we can both tell you."

"Jarred, I don't want her getting any more involved in this case than she already is. It's just too dangerous."

"It's too late, Alex," she spoke up, "I'm already involved. The moment he attacked me at my shop, I became involved."

Not able to argue that point out, he gave in. "We'll be right out," he said coldly, while handing her back the phone. "He wants to talk to you now."

Taking the phone, she stood solemnly for a moment, before putting it to her ear. "Jarred!" she tried hard not to cry, when her voice began to tremble.

"Are you all right?"

"I... don't know! Seeing his truck... Well, it really got intense!"

"You think that's intense," Alex spoke up, heatedly. "It may get worse yet!"

"Jo," Hearing his uncle, Jarred spoke up in his behalf, "Alex is a good guy. He's just pretty upset over the whole situation, surrounding this case. Please, understand, he's just trying to catch the guy."

"I know!"

After hanging up, she turned to look up at Alex.

"Stay out of it, Jodi, please, before you really do get hurt," he told her, feeling the same pain and sadness that Jessi had expressed to him before.

"I know what he did to Jarred, Alex. So I can't stay out of it. It's too late," she announced calmly, going over to the door.

"I really wish I didn't have to ask, but what do you mean, 'you know what he did?' You weren't there when he got shot, were you?" he asked even more puzzledly, while not wanting to think of her connection to Jessi, at that time.

"No, of course not. Well at least…"

"No. Don't say it."

"I'm sorry, Alex, but I promised that I wouldn't run away again. So, please, I want to be with him." With that, she turned and walked out of the office, while closing the door behind her.

"Damn it!" he thundered, looking back at Ted. "Why do I suddenly feel I'm about to repeat what had happened with her cousin?"

"It sure is looking that way!" he mused over the look on Alex's face. "What are we going to do now? Delgado won't hesitate to go after her again!"

"I know," he replied, running his fingers through his hair. "How would you like to play desk clerk again?" he smiled, dropping his hand to his hip.

"Why not! I kind of liked playing the part before!" he laughed, going back out to the front desk with his old partner. "Oh, yeah, this ought to be fun!" he laughed quietly, when seeing Jodi and the others standing around talking.

Stopping to look into her eyes, remembering how Jessi looked up at him the same way, he turned to make an announcement, "Ladies, due to the surrounding circumstances, I want you to meet your returning desk clerk."

"Oh…" Jodi asked puzzledly.

"Yes, I'm sorry, but I need the freedom to move around. And until all of this is over, Ted will be keeping an eye on things, here, mostly at night, though."

"Detective Jones, I presume?" she extended out a hand to him.

"Yes, and you, I understand to be Ms. Jessi's cousin, Jodi," he smiled politely.

"Yes, I am!"

"Jodi," Ashley interrupted, "what on earth is going on? Does it have anything to do with that truck that went by?"

"Yes," she returned, while turning to start for the backstairs, to her cousin's quarters, to get a few things together.

"Jodi…" Alex called out.

"Alex," Beth spoke up, "I'll just go and see if she's all right."

"Hold up," Ashley spoke up, going after her, "I'll come with you!"

"Alex?" Ted took his turn then, while the two walked over to stand in the open doorway.

"Yeah?"

"When will you be getting back?"

"I don't know. I'll have to give you a call, when we get out there."

"You know, things have a way of working themselves out."

"Yeah, let's just hope that this will too."

Meanwhile, down in Jessi's quarters, the two went into Jessi's room to check on Jodi.

"Hey," Ashley spoke up first, "are you going to be all right?"

"All right...?" she broke off with a sarcastic laugh, while turning to look back at them. "How...? Just how did she do it?"

"I don't really know! But I can tell you this, what went down then was definitely scary," Ashley replied, while taking a seat on the edge of her friends' bed.

"Perhaps," Beth added, "going out to Jarred's will give the two of you time to sort things out, even if only for a day or so, while Alex is trying to figure out how Delgado knew where you were going to be!"

"You don't think he talked to Karen, do you?" Ashley asked, puzzledly.

"No, but if he did, she would have called me first to see if she should say anything. Besides, she knows about the attack at the shop, and not knowing who had done it, she isn't going to just open up to anyone."

"The what...?" Ashley cried out.

"Jodi?" Beth asked, seeing her reaction.

"It," she began, "h...happened a couple of nights ago."

"Oh, my... gosh_____! How? And are you all right?"

"Yes, I'm..." She stopped to take a breath, while trying to put the thought out of her mind on what he had nearly done to her. *His cold, clammy hands...* she though horridly.

"Jo..." the two spoke up almost at the same time.

"I had just gone out to lock up after Karen left. He was already there, hiding in the shadows."

"Alex said some guy went by and saw what was happening," Beth offered comfortingly.

"Yes, while he went and called the police!" she added, while going around to gather up a few things to take with her, while having every intention of spending some time with him.

"What about this, Jarred, guy, Alex's other nephew...?" Ashley asked. "Where does he come into all this?"

"He was shot by Delgado," Beth explained. "And now Delgado is back to…"

"Let me guess, finish the job?" she laughed.

"Yes."

"Alex, too?" Ashley asked.

Telling the rest of the story, Jodi then took her small overnight bag up, along with her two companions, to meet with one, not too happy, Detective at the front desk.

"Wait…!" Ashley called out, stopping the two, just inside the back hallway. "Are you saying that Jarred has been in love with you since…"

"I was seventeen," she smiled, as she turned red-faced at how he made her feel, whenever he was around.

"Oh…?" she laughed quietly, as she went to read something into it.

"No…! Nothing has happened," she blushed even more.

"Yeah, but…"

"But, nothing," she grinned, while going on up toward the front desk.

"Are you ready?" Alex asked, turning back to see her.

"Yes."

"You know how much I don't like this."

"I'm sorry, Alex, but I won't go through what Jessi did. So, now, if you'll excuse me, I'll see you when you get out there," she announced, going on out the front door.

"Just hold up there!" he called out, taking off after her. Grabbing her arm, he went to spin her around to face him. "How exactly are you planning to get out there? Your car is back at your house, remember?"

"Yes, that's why I'm taking Jessi's truck. She won't mind!" she announced, showing him the keys.

"Fine, but you're still not taking off without me. I'll be following close by just in case we run into trouble."

"Fine! Then I suggest you keep up," she grinned, while pulling away to walk over to the garage to get out her cousin's truck.

"Damn you, woman…" he swore. "You lied to me!"

"What?" she spun around.

"You said you weren't the temperamental one in the family."

"I…" she started, but then smiled. "I guess I was…"

"Wrong?" he growled, musingly, while going on over to get into his Blazer. "But I have to give you credit," he got her attention once again, as she went to open the doors, when seeing Hank walk up to offer her a hand.

"And what's that?" she called back, handing Hank the keys to pull the truck out for her.

"Jessi's truck!" he smiled, thinking back to when he had driven it. "You're smart enough to know that your car can easily be spotted, had of you brought it with you."

"Yes, but I didn't. So that only leaves me with driving her truck!" With that, she bowed her head, and started to turn to Hank, when he was just getting out, to hold the door for her. "Wait a minute," she laughed, turning back. "What about your own vehicle. Don't you think he would know that one on sight?"

She had a point. It had been everywhere. Looking back at the others, standing in the doorway, Ted walked out to talk to him.

"Don't say it," Alex advised. "Just find me something to use by time I get back. Oh, and get another plate for it too."

"In the meantime?" Ted asked.

"Hide it," he ordered, handing him the keys. "I'm going to drive Jessi's truck out to Jarred's, but hide it in the barn, with a few guys to keep an eye on it."

"Sounds good. Call me when you get out there to let me know you made it okay."

"With a nod of his head, he turned to Hank. "Thanks, Hank, but I'll be driving," he announced, passing Jodi up in the doorway. "Oh, and Hank."

"Yeah?"

"Still got your gun?"

"Yep!"

"Keep it on you, and keep your eyes open out here. If you see or hear anything, get a hold of Ted, though I do have other guys out walking the grounds, just be careful."

"Gotchya."

Seeing the blue pick-up pulling out of the drive, with both them in it, the others shook their heads and kept watch for Vince's truck. Including the guy Alex had up the road now.

CHAPTER FIFTEEN

AFTER TWENTY MINUTES OF DRIVING, and making sure Delgado was nowhere around, Alex called Marcose to have him meet them at the barn, while filling him in on what was going on. Soon they pulled up to the partially opened doors, where Marcose stood, waiting on them.

"Alex!" the man nodded, while Alex and Jodi got out.

Tossing him the keys, Alex ordered, "Take it on inside, while we head over to the house."

"You might want to wait on that!"

"Oh? Why?"

Opening one of the doors the rest of the way, he gestured inside, off to the right.

"Jarred?"

"Yeah. He came out with me. But not to worry, we took the woods getting here."

Going in to see his nephew, he grumbled, "Okay, you got us out here, what the hell is going on?"

Looking to Jodi, then his uncle, he asked, "Do you want to talk out here, or up at the house?"

"Up at the house, both of you."

Taking her hand, they headed out the back door of the old wooden barn, and through the woods to shield their presence there, while Marcose kept an eye on their surroundings.

Getting to the back door of the house, they went in to tell Alex about the rest of her dreams.

"Now wait a minute," he growled, going over to a side window to look out, then back at them, "Jessi had told me the same thing when I was working on Craig's case. How can that be?"

"But it's true!" Jodi insisted. "I wouldn't make something like that up."

"I never said I doubted you," he stated, confoundly. "It's just that it's kind of strange to have all this happening again. First, Jessi... and now you...!"

"But... I..." She shook her head miserably, and ran out the back door, before either of them could say anything.

Hearing the back door close, Jarred turned to his uncle looking alarmed, "Alex!"

"Yes, I know, we've got to get her back in here, and now!"

Going after her, Jarred called out for her first, "Jodi_____! Jodi...!"

"Jarred...!" Alex called out, seeing one of his men running up to see what was wrong. "We got it," he said, waving him off, just when Jarred spotted her standing off in a grove of trees, while trying hard not to cry.

"Alex..." he called out, going to her, "she's over here! Jodi...!" he ran up, apologetically, when turning her to face him, "I'm sorry!"

"But I wasn't making it up____!" she broke down sobbing.

"I know that, Jodi," Alex replied, while walking up behind them. "I do believe you. It's just how you knew about all this in a dream, just like your cousin?" he laughed, shaking his head. "Way to go, Jarred!" he looked to his nephew. "You would have to find this one during a storm, sleeping in your living room, as well."

"Yeah, just like Craig," he laughed, smiling down at her. "Just like Craig."

Seeing they needed some time to be a lone, Alex backed away. "Hey, I'll just leave the two of you alone with the extra security here to watch over you. Just call me in the morning so I know you're all right."

"We will," he replied, walking him back over to the barn, with Jodi at his side.

"Alex, please be careful," he commented concernedly, when reaching the barn.

"I will. Oh, and Jodi, thanks for pointing it out to me about my Blazer. It does give away our location. So as for when you are ready, I'll be back to get you. As for what I'll be driving, I won't know that, until I talk to Ted. Again, thank you." Turning then to Marcose, he ordered, "Have Kevin keep a watch on things here, while you stay close to them. Kevin, I would prefer it if you would stay up in the loft, in case Vince were to come up on foot, so he doesn't see you, when you call it in."

"Sure thing," he returned.

Turning to leave, he looked back one last time and smiled. "Oh, and I like what you did with the vehicles!"

Jarred laughed, "That was Marcose's idea. It makes it to look like there aren't as many guys out here!"

"Yep!"Marcose added, grinning. "Pity the guy, when he tries to come after him again!"

"Yep! Well, seeing how late it's getting, while it's quiet out, I'll just be heading back to the Inn to see what's going on there."

"Yeah, since there hasn't been any signs of Vince since the other day. So you should be good to go," Marcose smiled.

With a nod of his head, he started up the truck and left the two of them with his man.

"Well," Jarred turned, holding her in his arms for a while longer, "would you like to go for a walk out back, away from the road? I know of a place you would really love to see!"

"Sure!"

"Marcose, would you mind?"

"I'll be watching close by," he grinned. "Kevin, if you need anything have Mike get it for you."

"We should be fine. We have plenty hidden away up top," he grinned, "and a pit for bathroom facilities hidden, as well."

"You did all that this afternoon?" Jarred asked, grinning.

"No, sir. We had all that done awhile back, right after your lady friend, here, had her cousin's truck parked out here during that storm!"

At that, they all laughed, and went on their way, with Jarred taking Jodi's hand, to head out back, and down a path toward a place he liked to go and think.

At the end of it, she saw what he was telling her along the way, while Marcose kept his distance.

And now with the sun going down behind some hills, she went up to see how they slopped down over the ridge, while overlooking a vast lake. "Oh, how amazing," she gasped, while taking in the fresh country air.

"Yes, it is. And if you look real hard, you can almost see the wild flowers all around here," he smiled, while taking her over to sit on a thick blanket of grass.

"Mmmm..."

"What?"

"The air," she sighed. "It's so fresh out here!"

"Uh, huh...," he murmured, when going back to lean on one elbow, while admiring her soft features, as the breeze blew back a few strands of her hair.

"Jarred," she laughed softly, feeling his hand slowly travel up her arm, as she turned to gaze into his eyes, "are you always like this?"

"Hush..." he whispered, smiling, while slowly lowering her back onto the grass. "And no, I'm not always like this. It's just seeing you looking so beautiful. If you only knew how many times I have seen you, and wanted to tell you how much I wanted to go out with you."

"I'm sorry my grandmother kept you from asking me, yourself. But then there were other times that you could have asked."

She was right, but he didn't want to tell her just yet.

"Jarred..." she turned to lean next to him, "what?"

"It's nothing!" he said, tracing her lower lip with his finger, before reaching over to kiss it. "I just find it hard to believe sometime that you are really here! Jo, if I were to... let's say, get too carried away, I want you to know that I'm not meaning you no disrespect. It's taking everything I have not to want to take you right here and now."

Knowing he meant every word, she just stayed, and gazed at his strong jaw line, as it flexed itself from time to time, and loving what she saw when it did.

Slowly reaching over, he started out first touching his lips softly to hers, until its sweet taste drew him in to want more. Soon the heat between them began to stir, until he was unable to help from wanting more. "Jo..." he whispered softly between kisses, when feeling so much pent up passion start to break loose. "I want you so... bad," he groaned, while going on to run his lips lightly over her neck.

"Mmmm..." she moaned in return, when feeling her own senses

coming to life, after so long of being ignored. Yet fighting to keep control of her emotions, when feeling his hand move down to gently run over her thigh, at that moment, the realization hit that what was about to take place, if she didn't stop it, she would wind up giving in to their passion, and she just wasn't ready for that. "Oh, Lord… Jarred… we have to stop!" she smiled up at him, when feeling her body about to betray her. "I know I'm going to hate myself for this, but I can't do this," she laughed. "It's still too soon…! And too, Alex's men are not that far away! It just wouldn't look right!" she said, pushing herself away to get to her feet.

"Jo…" he called out, reaching out to her.

Looking back into his eyes, she shook her head lovingly, "No, Jarred," she smiled, and then got up and started for the house.

"Jo, I'm sorry," he offered, when getting up to go after her.

Reaching the house, before he did, passing Baker along the way, Baker asked him if they were all right.

"Yes, we're fine. And things out here?"

"Quiet."

"Good."

Meanwhile, inside, stopping long enough to get out a change of clothes, she headed into the bathroom, before he could stop her.

Coming in shortly after her, when hearing the bathroom door close, he knew if he didn't slow down, he would risk pushing her away, and that was one thing he didn't want to happen. "No," he shook his head, and went on into the living room to fix up the sofa for her.

Coming back out shortly after that, in a light weight pair of pajamas, she still held a smile on her face to let him know she wasn't mad at him.

"Are we all right with each other?" he asked, turning back to see her in the doorway.

"Yes, and too, Mr. Stanton, if I were really bothered by it, I wouldn't have let things go on as long as they did."

"Really?"

She laughed softly at his childish grin. "Jarred, it's been a very long time since I've been with anyone. And out there, it took all that I had, not to want to give into to the passion your kiss was stirring up in me. Will you forgive me, and just be patient with me?"

"There's nothing to forgive!" he grinned with such relief. "As for patience, I will certainly try to be a gentleman. You have my word on that."

Coming over to sit with her on the sofa, the two snuggled together, while enjoying the fire he had built, when the evening air had turned chilly. Not long after, she felt herself begin to slip off to sleep in his arms.

Feeling this, he hated to leave her, but knew they both needed their sleep, and carefully slipped out from beside her to lay her down. "Goodnight, beautiful!" he said, covering her up, before heading up to his room.

Stopping though to check on the doors, he spotted Marcose out on the front porch with Kevin, when he opened it a crack to say goodnight.

"You turning in already?" Marcose asked.

"Yes. Alex will be here soon enough after I call him in the morning! Aside from that, any change since earlier?"

"No. It's still pretty quiet!"

"Good. Do you or the others need anything from in here?"

"No, we're set for the night. Just get some sleep. We'll keep our eyes open out here," he grinned.

"Yeah, sleep," he grinned in return, wondering if he or the others had seen anything between him and Jodi earlier. Closing the door, he looked back in at her, sleeping peacefully, and thought to himself, *'I have got to be more careful with her. She isn't like those other women I have been with, nor ever plan to be again,'* he grinned, going on up to his room. "Sweet dreams, pretty lady," he said on his way up the stairs.

Later that night, the dreams came back again and again, and there was certainly nothing sweet about them.

"No____! No____!" she screamed out, tossing and turning in her sleep. "Jarred…!"

At that moment, clear up in his room, having been awoken from his sleep, he thought he had heard something, and then it came again.

"No____! No____! Jarred, help me____! Please help me____!"

"Oh, Lord, Jodi____!" he cried, jumping out of bed to run down the stairs, and into the living room. Seeing then how she was having a bad dream, he rushed over to try to wake her.

Meanwhile, having heard this, Marcose came rushing in to see if she were in trouble. Getting there, he saw Jarred in the dimly lit living room, clad in only a pair of jeans. "Jarred," he spoke softly, "I heard screams. Is she all right?"

"She's been having bad dreams! I'll take care of her. Thanks."

"Certainly."

Leaving the two alone, he went back out to rejoin the others, who had come running to see if they were needed. "It's all right!" he called out, sending them back out to walk the area, all but Baker, who stayed behind, having partnered off with him, since their last case.

"What was it?" he asked.

"Bad dreams, he says. For now, why don't we stay near the house," he suggested, while they did just that for the remainder of the night.

Inside, Jarred continued to call out repeatedly, until she finally woke, while all shaken over what had just happened. "Jo, I'm here. It's going to be okay!" he continued, while soothing her long brown hair, back out of her face.

"Jarred?" she cried, throwing her arms around his neck. "Oh, Jarred...!"

"I'm here... I'm right here."

"I'm so... scared...! Oh, God...!"

"I know. It's going to be all right though! It was just a bad dream. That's all it was, just a bad dream!" he repeated, holding her tight, now, until she began to relax.

At that point, he went to lie down next to her, as she looked up wantingly.

"Jo," he whispered her name, "you know that if I stay, something just might happen."

"Jarred..." she returned, lowering her hand down to lightly trace over the thin line of hair, which disappeared just beneath the jeans, "I..."

"Oh, Jo..." he moaned quietly, while stopping her hand, just as her fingertips started to disappear beneath the waistband, "no, we can't," he continued to moan, when feeling his own arousal begin to return. "Oh... God, woman, I want you so... bad, but not like this. Not while you're feeling so vulnerable," he whispered roughly, while making himself get up to go build another fire.

"But..." She broke off in quiet sobs, just as he turned back to face her.

Seeing she had curled up on the sofa like a little lost kitten, shivering, from what had obviously been a really bad dream, it hit him hard. "Hey… no…! I'm sorry…!" he exclaimed, going back over to her. "It's not that I don't! Believe me, I do, but not like this!"

"Jarred…" she whimpered, "please… just hold me for awhile!" she cried, sounding so lost, while holding out a hand to him.

Lying back down next to her, he covered them both, while laying a light kiss on the top of her head. "Get some sleep now. I'll stay right by your side for as long as you need me too."

"Mmmm…" she softly replied, as she drifted back off to sleep, while feeling the heat of his body so close to hers. As for the dreams, they seemed to have stayed away, or so that part of them did, when she did dream again.

When morning arrived, he woke to find her still snuggled up in his arms, while looking down on her soft gentle features. *'Oh, Jo…'* he thought sadly to himself, *'if only we had gotten together back then, none of this would be happening with Delgado, now!'*

Just then, hearing her soft little moans, she began to awaken. "Mmmm… Jarred…?" she whispered at the same precise moment his cell phone started to ring. "Mmmm…"

"It's okay," he murmured softly, as he went to sit up and answer it. "Hello…!" his voice sounded deep.

"Jarred…?" Alex's voice thundered over the phone.

"What…?" he snapped back.

"Are you all right?"

"Ask me later when…" He stopped to look back at Jodi's soft smiling face, then grinned. "Never mind."

"Oh, did I interrupt something?" he teased, while going on, before giving him a chance to comment. "Anyway, I called to let you know that I'm coming out to talk over some things with you. So, tell that lady to take it easy on you in the meantime."

"I will," he laughed, seeing her getting up to go into the bathroom. After hearing the door close, he turned, lowering his voice, "Alex, we do need to talk."

"You sound serious. What's up?" he asked, going over to sit on his bed, back at the Inn.

"Late last night, she had a real bad dream. I haven't a clue what it was about, but she woke up screaming, which brought Marcose running in to see if she were in trouble!"

"Oh? And she hasn't said anything about it, yet?"

"No, but you can tell it was bad."

"How's that?"

"She was shaking pretty hard, and from what I could gather, someone was after her in this dream."

"Someone, like our Mr. Delgado?"

"Yes. And, God, Alex, she was crying out for me to help her! To help her, Alex!" he groaned, getting up to go into the kitchen.

"Yeah, and we both know why!" he growled, getting up to put his shoulder holster on. "She saw him shoot you, right? And now he's back to finish the job. Let alone, being attacked just made things worse. Now she has that plaguing her mind."

"Yes. So what are we going to do?"

"I'll work out something. For now, we're just going to have to play it by ear."

"Okay, I'll see ya later, then. Oh, but wait! What are you driving now?"

"A cream colored sedan, the Commander had setting aside, in case we needed a back up vehicle. And let me tell you, this thing has unbelievable power."

"And the plates?"

"Registered to a Lois Miller, from Toledo, Ohio. Oh, but she was checked out before the plates were made."

"Let me guess, she doesn't exist?"

"Or she had up and moved!"

"Good. In that case, are you still planning on stash it away in the barn, to keep it out of sight?"

"Yes, but have it out at the Inn, so he would think it belongs to a guest."

"And the Blazer?"

"In Jessi's garage. And if we're lucky, and he goes by a few more times, not seeing it, he may give up on the Inn!"

"Good. In that case, see you when you get here," he was saying, when she walked into the kitchen.

Hanging up, he turned back to see the questioning look on her face, while standing in the doorway.

"Alex?"

"Yes. He was wondering how you're doing?"

"A little scared," she said, turning to lean against the door frame, "but I'll make it."

"Sure you will. And now, are you hungry?" he asked, going over to the refrigerator to get out a few things.

"Starving!" she smiled, before going over to give him a hug. "Thanks for staying with me last night."

"Sure! Do you want to talk about this dream of yours, and what made you so scared?"

"No. I would rather not," she replied, feeling herself about to pull away, when he tightened his hold on her.

"Okay, we just won't talk about it if it bothers you that much," he surprised her by smiling down at her. "Hey, I have an idea!"

"What?"

"How about the two of us go for a walk after breakfast?"

Seeing that he was trying hard to ease her fears, she couldn't help but smile, while at the same time, drawing her arms up around him again. "That sounds wonderful. Can we take a blanket with us this time?"

"Sure!" he agreed, pulling away to get things ready for them to eat.

CHAPTER SIXTEEN

AFTER BREAKFAST, JARRED CALLED MARCOSE up, to the back of the house, to fill him in on what they were going to do. "Any sign of Delgado?" he asked.

"No, but the two of you should be all right. Word has it that he's still up at the motel getting something to eat."

"Good. And how about you? You have got to be dead on your feet. Do you have anyone to cover for you so you can get some rest?"

"Already did that. Once we made sure Delgado was tucked away for the night, Baker kept watch, while I grabbed a few winks!"

"Great!"

"So, what do you say," he grinned, "take that lady of yours and go for that walk, while it's safe."

Smiling, he turned to go back inside to get his service revolver strapped on, before getting Jodi. Soon the two were off on their walk to relax a little, before Alex got there.

"I have always loved coming out here to get my mind off things," he was saying, while walking hand in hand down a trail toward the same spot as the night before.

"Now that it's daylight, I can really see why!"

"About last night..."

"No, forget it, that was then, this is now. Let's just enjoy the peace and quiet while we can!" she laughed lightly.

Shaking his head, he let it alone, though, he was thinking about the dream, as well.

Not long after they arrived, going over to lay out the blanket near an old elm tree, he asked, "How's this?"

"Oh… it's perfect!" she sighed, seeing that rich smile of his, as she walked over, taking his hand when he reached out to her.

Joining him on the blanket, she sat in front of him, while listening to the sounds of nature all around them, along with the breeze blowing through the trees.

"Comfortable?"

"Mmmm… now if only it could be like this forever," she breathed in a sigh of bliss, while feeling his arms come up around her.

"Mmmm… me too."

Lying back in his arms, she closed her eyes for what seemed like an eternity, while feeling him running his fingers over and through her own. Liking the way it felt, she cried silently, *'Oh, Lord, please don't take this man from me. Not now that things are going so beautifully out here!'*

"Jo?"

"Hmmm…?"

"What are you thinking?"

"Mmmm… of Heaven!" she smiled. "This must be like Heaven. It feels so… beautiful."

'In comparison to you…' he thought, looking down on her, *'it sure… is!'*

Looking up into his eyes, she saw something, but didn't quite know what, when turning in his arms to ask, with a warm generous smile on her face, "Now, what are you thinking?"

Smiling back, he just shook his head. "Nothing!"

"Oh…?" she cooed, while taunting him with her lips, as she reached up to kiss him along his jaw line.

"That's not being fair!"

"Then tell me!"

"I'd rather show you instead!" he returned, when coming around to lift her chin to claim her lips hungeringly. Feeling the heat explode within, he brought himself around more to lay her back on the blanket, while continuing their kiss, until he couldn't handle it any longer. At that moment, feeling himself running his hand down along her waist, he pulled away to look down into her smoldering eyes, as a tear came streaming down her cheek. "Jo… I'm so sorry, I…"

Placing a finger to his lips to stop him, with an arm still up around his broad shoulders, she brought him back down to reclaim his lips. And as their kiss deepened, she brought herself up into it, while causing their passion to take off even farther than before.

"Oh, Jo…" he pulled back, as his breathing labored. "Are you sure this is what you want?"

"How much privacy do we have?"

Looking around, when seeing Kevin, the man bowed his head and turned to walk away to give them all the privacy they wanted, knowing they were safe for the time being. "We're fine for now," he replied, looking back down on her.

"Then, hush," she returned, using the same words he had the other night, "and kiss me."

And kiss her he did, over and over again, until they were lost in the moment with their legs intertwined with each other's.

But then, feeling his groin begin to throb, he found his hand sliding up under her top to where Heaven seemed to be waiting for his caress. But then, suddenly, remembering Alex was on his way out, he growled.

"What is it?" she asked, looking up to see his frustration.

"We're not going to be alone out here for long."

"What?" Her first thought was of Delgado, when forgetting about Alex.

Seeing her alarm, he smiled down on her. "No, it's not him. It's our watchdog and our guys!" he laughed.

But then, as he went to pull away, she stopped him. "No. Please!"

"Jodi, we can't!"

"I know, silly! But at least…"

Reading into her thoughts, he smiled taking her lips to his. "Oh… you know what this is doing to me?" he groaned, holding himself up on one elbow.

"And me…" she moaned, only with a smile playing at her lips.

"Oh. Right! Cute," he teased, nipping at her lower lip, until they heard a twig snap back along the pathway. After that, it wasn't long before hearing Alex walking up behind them.

"Well, here you are!" he laughed, when the two looked up to see him standing over them.

Bringing himself to a sitting position, Jarred grinned sheepishly, while looking back down at Jodi, who had her own little grin going on her face at seeing his tall, handsome, uncle standing over them.

"Are the two of you up for a cookout?" he asked, seeing the gleam in their eyes.

"It's up to you!" Jarred aimed the comment at Jodi.

"Sure!" she agreed, sitting up to face Alex better.

"When are you wanting to do this?" Jarred asked.

"Anytime the two of you can pull yourselves away from each other to come on up and join us!" he grinned, while turning to head back up the trail. "Oh, and by the way," he stopped, "Beth is up at the house, waiting on you guys. I'll just let her know you'll be up, soon!" he winked, before heading back that way.

"Yeah, we'll be right up!" Jarred called out, shaking his head at his uncle. "So much for our peaceful moment!" he grumbled, while the two got up, and gathered up the blanket.

"Well then again, it was probably for the best!" she smiled up at him. "Things could have gotten a little out of hand!" she teased.

"Mmmm... just a little?" he grinned, shaking his head.

"Jarred?" she asked along the way.

"Yeah?"

"Why isn't Alex involved with someone?"

"He was interested in someone once, but then it came a screeching halt, because of some departmental rules."

"So he moved on and fell in love with someone else?"

"Yes, but she was already in love with someone else."

"Jessi?" she recalled, something her cousin had told her.

"Yes."

"Surely he could find another well deserving woman now that she has married Craig!"

Stopping along the way, though, not far from the house, he looked down at her. "What are you thinking?"

"Oh..., maybe..." she was just about to say, when Beth walked out of the house, seeing the two of them standing along the pathway.

"Hello you two!" she called out, walking down the pathway to join them.

Seeing Jodi's smile, he turned back to look at Beth. "Jo...?"

"Uh huh...!" she smiled to herself, just as Beth reached them.

As for the rest of the day, Jodi thought if she could put her mind on fixing Alex up with someone it would keep it off the disturbing dreams, and for a while it worked, until Beth took her off to the side, while the men worked on cooking the steaks Alex brought with him.

"Hey," she began, while the two walked over to a group of lawn chairs that had been set up in the backyard for the cookout, "I know we don't really know each other very well, but after getting to know your cousin, I hope you and I can be friends too."

"I'm sure we can! Jessi speaks highly of you." she commented, while wondering just where this conversation was leading.

Then it came, just as Beth finished pouring them some iced tea.

Handing Jodi her glass, she asked, "Is there something bothering you that just maybe I can help with?"

"No!" she returned a little more sharply than planned. "I'm sorry, but no, no one can help me..." she cried, feeling the grip on her glass tighten. By then, the need to get up and run back into the house to avoid any more questions hit, as she did.

In doing so, Beth looked to Alex and Jarred, and shook her head.

"Did she say anything?" Alex asked, walking over to join her.

"No! But whatever is troubling her, I have a feeling she would only feel comfortable enough talking to Jessi about it."

"In that case, I sure hope she and Craig gets back soon!" Jarred commented, worriedly. "She can't keep all this bottled up for very much longer, it's killing her."

"Are you sure you have no idea what the dream was about?" Alex asked his nephew again.

"No, I don't!" he said, shaking his head, sadly. "But if you'll excuse me, I think I'll go in and see how she's doing."

Leaving them, Alex and Beth went for a short, casual, walk, but not too far, in case trouble was to show up.

"What do you think?" Beth asked, looking up into the trees, as a gentle breeze caught a strand of her hair, blowing it across her cheek.

"I don't know! It disturbs me, though, how much this has affected my nephew. And at the same time, I wish Jessi would high-tail it back here."

While brushing the strand of hair away, she turned to study his troubled expression.

"No, it's not what you think," he replied, quickly, seeing that look of hers. "I care a great deal for Jessi, but it's Craig she belongs to."

"Yes, and I wish I had that kind of..." She stopped and turned away to remember the feelings she had for Alex back in the academy, and still yet. *'God, if only...'*

"Beth," he sensed her own sad thoughts, "we couldn't continue down that path, and you know why?"

"Yes, of course, you're right!" She shook her head, while heading back up to the house to find Jarred and Jodi out getting things set up to eat.

Before she could get too far, he reached out a hand to turn her back to face him. The look in his eyes was so deep, and the pain of losing her was still so fresh on his mind. "Beth, I have never stopped caring for you. I want you to know that."

Smiling up at him, sadly, she took the hand that was holding her arm and put it up to her lips, "And I'll always care for you," she returned, as a tear found its way slowly down her cheek, when he went to wipe it away with his free hand.

'Oh, Beth... God how I still love you!' Wanting so much to take her into his arms, he couldn't, out of fear that one of his men, not including Marcose, or his nephew, would say something to their Commander about what they had seen. "We should be getting back," he groaned, breaking the spell between them.

"Yes, we probably should," she smiled, while still having a hold of his hand, before joining the others.

"How was the walk?" Jarred asked, looking up to see his uncle looking rather unhappy.

"It was all right," he replied, quietly, when walking over to get himself a plate.

Later, Alex and Beth took things back over to the barn, to pack up the car, to head back to the Inn.

"Jodi..." he called out, walking back up, "we need to be getting you back."

"All right," she replied, turning to look back at Jarred. "Wow, where has the time gone?" she asked, holding his hand. "I wish..."

"I know," he agreed, frowning down at her, "I wish we had more time, too!"

With a warm smile, she went into the house to get her things, while Alex walked over to talk to his nephew. "Keep your eyes open out here. If you see any signs of trouble, call me right away."

"I will. And Alex…" he hastily added, while shooting his uncle a warning look, "take care of her for me."

"You do know something, don't you?"

"I'm not sure, but there is one thing that keeps coming to mind."

"What is it?"

"How much do you know about her cousin?"

"Enough, why?"

"Jodi told me about this gift Jessi has. Just supposing she has a different kind of gift. One that warns her that she's in danger or that someone else is?"

"Wouldn't she know that?"

"Did Jessi know all along that she could perceive troubled spirits?"

"No, that came later when she met Craig," he explained, when turning back to see Jodi coming out of the house, while talking to Beth. "She and her cousin are very close! Just maybe I ought to give Jessi and Craig a call, to speed up their honeymoon a little. She sure does need her cousin back here."

"Yes, well she can't get back soon enough to suit me!" he was saying, when the expression on his face grew darker with concern. "And by the way, who takes up to a month or so for a honeymoon?"

"They do…?" Alex laughed.

CHAPTER SEVENTEEN

AFTER LOADING UP HER THINGS, Alex took that moment to talk to Beth alone, while the others were saying their goodbyes. "Well, it was nice out here, not having any problems with Vince showing up to ruin it."

"It sure was!" she replied, smiling up at him, before going around to get in on her side of the car.

"Hey…" he started, then changed his mind, when she turned to see what he wanted.

"Did you say something, boss?"

"No, it wasn't important!" he grinned, while opening his car door. As he did, he looked across the roof of it, and shook his head at the thought that entered his mind, while watching her get in.

"Well, it looks like Alex is wanting to go. So I guess I'll call you later?" Jarred was saying, when walking her over to the car.

"You had better!" she threatened, slyly, while reaching up to kiss him goodbye, before getting in.

Letting out a low guttural groan at the back of his throat, he growled, "You are so mean."

"And don't you ever forget it," she gleamed with joy, knowing she got his attention.

"Hey," Alex called out after she closed her door, "watch yourself!" he reminded, when Mike walked up.

"I will. I promise," he returned, when leaning down to tell Jodi goodbye one last time.

Pulling out of the barn, Alex looked back in his rearview mirror to see his nephew watching him leave, before turning to walk away.

On their way back to the Inn, Jodi commented on their relationship with Delgado. "He really hates you two, doesn't he?"

"Yes, but then it goes with the job, I hate to say!"

"So it seems!"

"Jodi, it isn't always this bad," he put in, seeing her expression change. "Jarred has been a cop for a long time now, and this is the worst it has ever been. We'll catch Delgado, you'll see."

"And if you..."

"No, Jodi," Beth spoke up from the front seat, "they will."

"And I won't rest until he has paid for shooting my nephew. I promise you that."

"Thanks, you two. I'm sure you will do your best."

Shaking their heads, Alex, then, just had to know what this dream of hers was about.

"Jodi," he treaded carefully, "this dream of yours. Won't you please, at least tell me if it was about Delgado? Was he chasing after you? And if so, did he..."

"No!" she cried abruptly. "No, h...he didn't!"

"Oh?" he asked, looking into the rearview mirror at her.

"After Jarred woke me up, I fell back off to sleep in his arms, and the dream came back. Only..." She stopped, when recalling something different about it now.

"What?" Beth asked, turning in her seat to look back at her.

"In the second dream..."

"What about it?" she asked again.

"Jarred came to my rescue on his motorcycle." Stopping once again, when thinking back to the face she had vaguely recalled seeing behind the tinted shield of his helmet. Somehow it wasn't quite Jarred's face in the darkness of an oncoming storm. As a flash of lightning lit up the sky, she saw something in his eyes. '*Was it...*' She stopped once again. Then suddenly, remembering those eyes, she cried softly, "Stephen...?"

"Jodi...?" Alex called out, seeing her face turn pale, as the tears began to form.

"Jodi, what is it?" Beth asked, concernedly. "Are you remembering something bad about the dream?"

"Jodi…" Alex was really getting worried. "Did something happen to Jarred?"

"No. No of course not. He…" She stopped, when recalling Stephen's smile. Then the person in front of her on the bike changed, and now it was Jarred smiling at her.

"Go on!" the two prompted.

"He was…"

"There to protect you?" Beth smiled, when seeing the glow come over her face.

"Y e s… P r o t e c t… m e…" she replied ever so slowly, when realizing, now, who had first appeared to her rescue.

Not asking what she meant by that, having arrived back at the Inn, Alex got out to give her a hand. "Are you going to be okay?" he asked, when she got out. "Jodi…?" He shook her shoulder slightly.

"Yes. What?" she asked, snapping out of her dream-state, once she realized they had gotten back to the Inn.

"Jarred? Your dream?"

"He was wonderful!" She looked up to see his worried expression, and smiled. "He came to my rescue. He and…"

"This first love of yours?" he asked, sensing something totally out there, when she hadn't returned his answer before.

"How did you…"

"It was in your eyes. The tears, they weren't, how do I put it? They weren't of this time! And I think I may have heard you call out his name. However, I don't think you were intending for us to hear it."

"No. I'm sorry."

"No, don't be," he returned, going on down to her cousin's quarters with her. "Now, what are you going to be doing for the rest of the day?"

"Get a shower and work on getting some more of my paperwork done that I've been falling behind on," she explained, while heading down the hallway to her cousin's room to gather up what she would need to go into the bathroom.

"All right, I'll check in on you later," he replied, going back up to his own room to make a few calls. One in which was to Craig and Jessi.

After getting her shower, she felt a lot better, and decided to go up to her cousin's office in hopes to get some work done.

When getting there, she saw just how much she had to do. Though, some of it was her cousin's that she had promised to help with. Going over to sit down, she groaned miserably, *'I have got to get some help with this.'*

Getting back up, she went over to the window to look out, thinking back to the last part of her dream, when recalling Stephen's smile, and how it warmed her heart.

"What are you thinking about?" Beth asked, interrupting her thoughts, when walking in, closing the door behind her. "Jarred?"

"How did you guess?" she fibbed, while coming away from the window to go back over to the desk.

"It shows!"

"Well, it was a pleasant thought! What about you? Is there someone in your life that you find yourself thinking about?"

"There was someone once, but…" She stopped, to look away, remembering what Alex told her.

"Beth…" Jodi spoke up, recalling how whenever Alex was around, her face would light up, "is it, Alex?" Seeing her reaction, she smiled. "It is, isn't it?"

"Yes! How did you know?"

"Well, as you said, it shows!" she laughed. "Why haven't you told him?"

"He knows, but…"

"But what?" she asked. Then suddenly remembering something she was told. "Oh, my, gosh, Jarred told me…"

"Yes," she returned abruptly, knowing Jarred would know the whole story, "it isn't allowed in the department. And now, enough about me, I came by to see if you wanted to go out on the front porch for some lemonade."

"Sure, but what if Delgado drives by again?"

"Not a chance. They say he's at a bar shooting pool."

"Great! But that brings me to one question. If he shot Jarred, why don't they go and arrest him?"

"Because the person who called it in wouldn't give us his name! So we have to wait until he slips up again."

"But what about the attack on me?"

"Jodi, that would only get him off the streets for a little while. When he gets out he'll be right back at it again."

"Yes, I see what you mean."

"Hey, it's no disrespect aimed at you. Alex… Well we all want him sent away for a very long time."

"You won't get an argument out of me. So now, what about this lemonade?" she smiled. "I'm ready for it. And besides," she added, looking at the stack of paperwork piling up on the desk, "this isn't going anywhere."

"Good."

Going out to the front porch, after getting settled in at their favorite table, Ashley and Renee came out to join them.

"Have you seen the groundskeeper, yet?" Renee asked with a hint of mischief on her smiling face.

"No. Why?" Jodi asked, looking puzzled at her quirky expression.

"Well, get ready," Ashley announce, grinning, "because here he comes now!"

Turning to see a tall man, with dark brown hair and wire rimmed glasses, walking up, Ashley spoke up first, "Jake, this is your new boss, Ms. Jodi Tate. She will be filling in for Ms. Jessi, until she returns. Jodi, meet Jake Green, the groundskeeper."

"Well, Jake," she fought hard to keep from cracking up, laughing, after having heard all about Alex's alias. "Jessi has told me so much about you. I sure hope you're ready for some real work, now, because I have a long… long… list of things that need to be done around here."

"I just bet you do!" he laughed quietly. "I just bet you do."

Later that evening, after having called Jarred, Jodi went out to greet her girls, when their grandparents came by to drop them off, after hearing how much she had been missing them.

"Mom…!" Kyleigh cried out, running up to her.

"Kyleigh…? Madison…?" she cried back, seeing her girls running up to the front porch.

Kyleigh, Jodi's oldest, at sixteen, was the toughest, after her mother went through a bad divorce from their father, when the time came to go into the hospital to have her younger sister.

"Alex told us that we are supposed to call him Jake," Kyleigh said, on their way to the dining room, with everyone, to eat.

Looking up to see Jodi walking in with her girls, he smiled, "I may have come up with another idea to make sure everyone is kept safe, until Delgado is caught."

"And what would that be?" she asked, curiously, while taking a seat next to her kids.

"I can't say for sure, now, but after I iron out a few bugs, I'll let you know in the morning, after talking it over with Ted, to make sure it will work."

"All right," she replied, as everyone sat down with a plate of food.

That night though, after talking over his new plans with his old partner, Alex stayed down in Jessi's quarters, while Jodi and her girls stayed up watching a movie.

"Mom?" Kyleigh spoke up.

"Yes?"

"Is he really Jarred's uncle, too?" she asked, seeing how Alex had fallen off to sleep on the couch, or so she had thought, when the movie was nearing the end.

"He sure is!" she answered with a warm smile, while going over to get a blanket out to cover him with. Then leaning over, she whisper, "Goodnight, Uncle Alex."

"Goodnight, meanness," he grumbled back, smiling, before rolling over onto his side.

With that, she and her girls went off to bed, making sure the patio doors were locked, and the dogs were inside, while leaving Max to go over and plop himself down next to the couch, to be near his favorite buddy.

Turning to see that, she had too smile, "Goodnight, Max. Take good care of him," she laughed quietly, while turning to head back down to her cousin's room.

Looking down at the side of the couch, Alex laughed too at seeing him lying there. "Goodnight, boy," he petted him on the back. And soon they were all snuggled down for the night, while upstairs, Ted and the other undercover officers were out doing their jobs.

Getting up the next morning, at the crack of dawn, to go out horseback riding, walking into the stable, Jodi ran into Alex, while brushing down one of Jessi's newest mares. "Well, if it isn't Jake Green!" she laughed. "How about joining me for a ride?"

"Sure! By the way," he lowered his voice, "your new accountant, and your assistant cook will be here this evening."

"My new... what? I knew I needed help in the office, but I didn't know I needed help in the kitchen, as well!"

"Yes, I asked Beth to work in the kitchen for awhile, while she stays with you. It seems she had taken a real shine to it when she was here before. Besides, she's really a sweet girl, and Annie loves her quite a bit."

"You're right, she is!" she agreed, when he stopped to bring out a couple of horses to saddle up. "Alex?"

"Yes?"

"About you and..." She stopped.

"What?" he asked, looking back to see the puzzlement on her face.

"It's nothing," she shrugged, while pulling up the collar of her denim jacket, which she had elected to wear, since it was so early in the morning, and the sun hadn't had time to warm things up a bit.

"Which horse do you prefer?" he asked, favoring the black stallion for himself.

"Maggi will be fine," she smiled, seeing the mare she normally rides, out grazing in the pasture.

"Maggi, huh?" he grinned.

"Yes, she's..."

"I know, Jessi's baby. Okay, Maggi it is!"

Once he had her saddled, she was ready to ride.

Once in her saddle, Jodi gave the girl a soft pat on the neck. "Good girl, Maggi!"

Shaking his head, he continued to grin, while going to climb up onto Joe.

"What?" she asked, reining Maggi around to head out for her favorite path that led down to the lake.

"You and your cousin. The two of you could easily pass for twins."

"Our mothers are sisters, and most generally girls favor their mothers."

"Is that why your daughters look as though they could pass as her girls, with the exception of the younger one?"

"Madison?"

"Yes. How old is she?"

"Fourteen."

Still, he couldn't help but grin.

After a short time of riding in silence, he suddenly reined up on his horse to bring him around to face her. "Do you love my nephew?" he asked, catching her off guard, as Joe took a few side steps, while at the same time Alex went to shift himself in the saddle.

Stopping her own horse, she looked surprised at his unexpected question. "Alex!"

"Do you?"

"Yes, I do! I just haven't told him, yet."

"Well, I know he is in love with you. And because of it, he is hell bent on putting his life on the line for you, as well as you have for him. You know, the two of you are making my job even harder for me than necessary? I hope you're aware of that."

"Ah… but Alex, isn't love grand?" she laughed, riding on ahead with him having to catch up. But then, feeling somewhat spirited, she suddenly gave her horse a slap on the rear with the reins to get her up to a full gallop.

"Jodi…" he laughed, doing the same.

"What's wrong, Alex?" she called back over her shoulder. "Can't handle it?"

Growling under his breath, "So it's a race you want. I'll give you a race, Ms. Tate."

Having ridden Joe quiet often in the past, he knew the layout well.

But then, just when the race was really getting good, she surprised him, when coming to a low area in the fence line, which she had used quite often to jump, when wanting to take a short cut.

Taking it, Alex, though, having brought his horse to a full stop, watched as her mare made the jump with such grace and precision, just like a pro at work. "Damn… she's good," he grinned, taking his own horse back a few yards or more to give him a good run for his money.

"Let's do it, Joe," he prodded, powerfully, with the use of the reins and his booted heels.

With a snort of his nostrils, Joe made the jump, as well, but not before getting back to the stables, where Jodi came riding in, feeling triumphant.

"Thanks, Hank!" she smiled, while pulling up on Maggi's reins.

"Sure thing, Missy!" he grinned, seeing Alex come riding back in winded.

Catching a glimpse of his reddened, yet handsome face, she smiled even more, while hurrying off her horse to rush off out of the stables, before he could rein his own to a full stop.

"Now that wasn't fair!" he laughed, handing the reins over to Hank, before catching up to her just outside the stables.

"Oh, but Alex, I would have thought that you, of all people, would've known that there are a lot of things in life that are not fair."

"Meaning?"

"For some of us, not to be able to have our lives back to normal," she said, heading back up to the Inn.

"Hey, hold up there a minute!" he called out, catching her by the arm.

"Alex…!" she cried, laughing, when turning to face him. "Hey," she changed the subject, "we're going to have breakfast out on the porch. Would you and Ted care to join us?"

"Sure, that sounds good! By the way, what are you planning on doing later today?"

"I'll be in the office, trying to get caught up on the rest of my work. Why?"

"No particular reason," he grinned, leaving her, to go on up to his room, to call Jarred, before joining her and the others out on the front porch.

Getting there, he had just closed the door, when pulling out his cell phone to make the call. "Jarred?" he spoke up, hearing his nephew's voice.

"Yeah?"

"How quick can you throw some things together?"

"Not long, why?"

"You win."

"What?"

"You heard me. You win. I want you up here."

"Really…? Are you sure about that?"

"You heard me. And Jarred."

"Yeah?"

"Stop off and get your Tux from Donna's. They're expecting you," he a smiled. "Oh, and yes, this is supposed to be a surprise. So don't tell Jodi that you're coming, if you happen to hear from her later."

"All right!" he replied, looking out the front window of his living room with a great sense of joy, knowing he could finally be with the woman he had loved all those years, and not having been able to tell her that. "Alex?"

"Yeah?"

"Thank you."

"You're welcome, nephew, you're welcome," he repeated, hanging up.

Turning to see Ted standing in the doorway, he hoped that he wasn't making a mistake, bringing him out into the open.

"You're doing the right thing," Ted stated, thoughtfully.

"I just hope it doesn't get him killed," he groaned, going over to look out the window.

"Maybe doing this will force Delgado's hand!"

"It just might," he stated, turning back to look at his old friend, before going downstairs. "By the way, we've been invited to join the others for breakfast."

"Good. I'm ready. Shall we go then?"

Walking out into the hallway, while closing the door behind them, they passed a couple looking to have been on their honeymoon, laughing and smiling along the way. Looking back at them just as they had reached their room, Alex, too, smiled at the thought of his nephews and the women they have come to love so much.

"It'll happen for you," he heard Ted say.

"Yeah, well it could have if a certain blonde cop would have stayed out of it."

"Hey," Ted pulled Alex up to a stop, just before reaching the landing, "I got some news that just might be of some strong interest."

"Oh? Let's have it then!"

Making sure the coast was clear, in a very hushed-like tone, Ted began, "You asked just how Delgado knew about our lady here!"

"Yeah, what did you come up with?"

"You're going to flip when you hear this, but we got an anonymous tip the other night, that Delgado has an inside man reporting to him on every move you've been making."

"As in, someone still working on the force?"

"Yes. And no, he isn't one of the guys working out here, but the Commander is wanting to know who."

"There's one way to find out. Get the guys together once we get Jarred up here."

"And?"

"Let's see who they have been talking to, and once we narrow it down, let's get the Commander to run a check on their bank accounts."

"Good thinking!" he agreed, walking on out to the front porch to find everyone sitting at the far end with a few of Alex's men not far away.

CHAPTER EIGHTEEN

BY THE TIME THE DAY was nearly over, Jodi had no more than gotten caught up on her work, that all she could think about then was Jarred, and the night they had almost made love. *'Oh, Jarred, I do love you,'* she thought, tiredly, while wrapping things up, when there came a knock at the door. "Come in!" she called out, closing her briefcase.

Opening it, Beth walked in with a warm smile on her face. "Jodi?"

"Hey, there! What's up?"

"Alex told me that he wants me back in the kitchen to help Annie."

"How do you feel about that?" she asked, while leaning back in her chair.

"I love it!" she smiled, while going over to the window to look out. "It's just like it was before! I get to have fun cooking with Annie again!"

"Well then, let's go and see Annie!" she announced, when getting up to walk over to the door. "She'll be happy to know you'll be in the kitchen with her again."

"Oh, but she already knows!" She turned back and smiled.

"Let me guess. Alex?"

"No," she blushed. "I couldn't wait to tell her myself."

"That's all right! But still, how about we go and see her anyway. I want to see if she has anything I might be able to take down with me, since I had to work right through dinner."

Agreeing, the two headed out of the office, shutting off the lights on their way.

Reaching the kitchen to find Annie putting together a few things for Jodi and her girls, Jodi smiled tiredly, "Thanks a million, Annie, I'm sure the girls and I will enjoy this."

"Anything for our Ms. Jessi's favorite cousin!" she smiled warmly, while handing her the basket with her favorite foods in it.

Turning to take her leave, Jodi headed out of the kitchen to take the food down to her girls, when she bumped into Alex.

"Hold up there," he spoke up, taking the basket from her, "there's something I want to show you."

"Alex…" she cried tiredly, "can't this wait until tomorrow?"

"No, it can't. I need your opinion on some changes I've made to Beth's quarters, since the last time she was here. I want you to tell me what you think!"

"All right, but then I'm going to bed!" she complained, while going up to see Beth's old room, which was up in the finished out attic.

Getting there, he turned to Jodi upon opening the door. "Well, what do you think? Do you think she would like it?"

"Alex, this looks real nice. However, why would you really care how it looks?"

"Well, because she deserves it!" he exclaimed, with that sheepish smile of his.

"Why, Alex, you do still care about her, don't you?" she teased, catching him off guard.

"And what do you know about that?"

"Enough! Something to do with departmental rules, I believe."

"Yeah, well if you weren't such a lady, I'd tell you just what I think about their…"

"Damn rules?" she came back frowning. "I know, it…"

"Sucks?" he then laughed, while turning to leave the attic.

Stopping, she turned back in the small amount of space the stairwell had to offer, "Let me ask you this, since you had asked me a similar question earlier, do you still love her?"

With a heavy sigh, he did not answer. Though the look she was able to see, from what little light there was, said what she wanted to know.

"Okay, that's all I needed to know," she smiled, while running a hand over his masculine arm, before turning to head back downstairs, where at that moment, Beth was coming out of the kitchen.

"Alex! Jodi!" she smiled sweetly, while giving him a silent nod of her head to something he had only to ask with his eyes, as he looked toward Jessi's quarters.

"Beth," Jodi spoke up, while taking the basket back from Alex, "Alex has something to show you."

"You going on down to get ready for bed now?" he asked mischievously.

"Yes, so if the two of you will excuse me, I'll just say my goodnights and leave you now to get some sleep."

Smiling at one another, both Alex and Beth said their goodnights to Jodi, while watching her head for the door to her cousin's quarters.

Coming shy of reaching the bottom step, she found the lights turned down low, with the exception of a few candles and the light of the fireplace to illuminate the room. Adding to that was the heavenly aroma of food cooking, along with the sound of soft music playing in the background.

"What is this?" she asked, while going on down to stand poised in front of the fireplace.

It was then she heard the familiar voice coming up behind her, while she continued to look around. "May I have this dance?" he asked, taking the basket from her to set it down.

"Jarred...?" she cried softly, while turning to see him standing there, looking all so handsome in his tux, and his nicely trimmed beard and mustache, and thick wavy hair, that barely touched his collar.

Meeting her gaze with his, he slid an arm around her waist, while taking her hand in his, and began to dance.

"This has to be a dream...!"

"No, it's not a dream. I'm real. And I'm here. And I'm not going anywhere," he said with a hint of certainty in his voice, as their eyes continued to hold each other, until he leaned down to claim her lips. "I love you, Jodi Tate," he whispered. "I have for so... long, and I don't want to spend one more day without you in it."

"Oh, Jarred..." she cried, hearing those words. "I love you, too, but how...?" she asked, seeing everything laid out around her.

Placing a finger to her lips, he led her over to the table that was set up near the patio door. "How about we get something to eat, while I tell you?"

Smiling tearfully, after taking her seat, he went on to wait on her, while telling her all about the heated conversation, between him and his uncle, the night before. "I told him I was tired of hiding out from Delgado, and that I wanted my life back."

"So that's what he meant, when he said you were putting your life on the line for me." Shaking her head, she looked away to hide the tears she was no longer able to hold back. "You told him you were going to come up here to be with me, didn't you?"

"Yes. He said you needed help on your paperwork. Funny thing is I just happened to have mastered in accounting with his help!"

"What?" she shot back around to face him. "You're the new help he was talking about?"

"Yes. That, and..."

"You couldn't bear to be a part from me any longer? Oh, Jarred..." she cried, reaching out to him.

"Then you're happy to see me?"

"Happy...?" she was saying, when hearing one of her girls coming in to get something to drink.

"Hi, Mom..." Kyleigh greeted with a big smile on her face, when going over to pat Jarred on the shoulder.

Seeing the look on her daughter's face, she laughed, "You knew about this...?"

"Of course!"

Getting up to pull out a few more chairs, Jarred asked thoughtfully, "Why don't you and your sister join us?"

"No," Madison replied, walking into the living room, then, smiling, "the two of you need some time together. We'll see you in the morning at breakfast."

"You think so?" Jodi asked, wondering what all they knew about this man.

"Sure!" Kyleigh said, seeing her mother's baffled expression, when she came back with something to drink for the both of them. "It's okay, Mom, we know who he is. Alex told us!"

"Alex again, I see?" she grinned, shaking her head.

Laughing, the two said their goodnights, and headed back to their cousins room.

Hearing them laugh on their way down the hall, she said her goodnights as the door closed behind them.

"They're good kids!" he commented with a broad grin, as he too heard their laughter even with the door closed.

"Yes, they are."

"What of their father?"

Turning slowly to look down at her plate, he saw the saddened look mixed with anger.

"He sees them from time to time, but not as often as he should?" he asked, not waiting for her answer. He had to wonder if she didn't still harbor some feelings for the man.

Looking up to see the questioning look on his face, she groaned quickly, "Oh Lord, no, that boat sailed a long time ago, when he went off with that other woman."

"That couldn't have been easy for you, leaving you with two girls to raise alone."

"I had my granny at the time, and Jessi, to lend moral support."

"Not to mention, your friends and other family members!"

"You're right about that! I would have been lost without them."

Seeing how this was beginning to bother her, he dropped the subject, while they went on eating.

"Did you do all of this?" she asked, while quietly poking her fork at her broccoli.

"Mmmm… mostly. But I did have some help."

"Oh…?"

"Like I said," he grinned, looking over into her warm, loving face, "they're great girls!"

"Oh, my…" she smiled even more, "the girls…?"

"Yep!"

After eating, he got to his feet to pull her up into his arms so they could continue dancing. In doing so, he went to lay kisses along the soft curve of her neck, causing her to let out a soft, but very quiet moan.

"Oh, Jarred, you know if you keep this up, I may not be responsible for what'll happen next."

"Oh…?" he questioned, while the two continued their dance more nearer to the fireplace.

Soon a love song began to play. When it did, the magic of it started to do its work, as his lips found their way down to the soft curve of her neck once again.

"Mmmm…" she whimpered, running her fingers through his hair at the back of his neck, "Jarred…!"

Pulling back, he looked into her sultry eyes. "Jodi, I want you, but not if you think it's still too soon."

"I wish it were all that easy, but…" she hesitated, while feeling the heat of her own blood rising, as she looked over to the bottle of wine that he had sitting in a small tub of ice, chilling.

Sensing her hesitation, he pulled away to go over and pour them both a glass, while leaving her to stand there and feeling bad for putting him off, yet again.

"Jarred, I'm sorry," she replied sadly, while looking at the outline of his broad shoulders, when he went to pick up the glasses.

"No, don't be," he returned, handing her a glass.

"I do want you," she replied, taking it. "God knows, I do, but it isn't easy for me to give myself to another man totally, after what my ex-husband put me through."

Finally he knew why she was so hesitant, but was there more to it?

"I can't imagine how he could have done that to you. What happened to cause him to leave you, like he did?"

Taking a sip, she began, "He couldn't handle being a father, again, after our first child was born."

"Funny you would say that," he laughed bitterly, while looking into his own glass.

"Why?"

"Marriage and fatherhood is all I had ever dreamed of."

"Then why…"

"Why haven't I ever married?" he asked, looking into her eyes, knowing the answer was right in front of him.

"Jarred…"

"If your grandmother hadn't stopped me from asking you out, we could have been together a long time ago."

"How do you know that it would have worked out that way?"

"I just know," he responded sadly, while feeling the hurt of seeing her going on with her life when marrying a man that eventually left her for someone else.

"I had no idea you felt that way toward me."

"How could you, your grandmother stopped me every time I saw you in her shop! Then one day…" He finally had to tell her.

"One day, what?"

"One day, a few months later, you were coming out of the newspaper office. I started to approach you then, to ask if you would like to have dinner with me."

Not remembering that day, she asked, "Why didn't you?"

"I overheard your friend, Karen say your wedding was going to be perfect."

"Ouch," she cringed, recalling Karen's comment. "That had to have hurt hearing that."

"It was quite a blow!" he said, shaking his head, while taking in a rather large sip of his wine.

"What happened then?" she asked, seeing his anguish.

Turning to look into the fire, he inadvertently squeezed his glass a little too hard, when he told her how he went on with his life. At that moment, the glass shattered, surprisingly not cutting him. "Damn!" he swore, sharply.

"Jarred, are you all right?" she asked, feeling a little stunned at what had just happened.

"Yeah. What about you? Did you…"

"No," she cut him off, as she went to set her glass down to have a look at his hand.

"No, really, I'm fine!"

"Jarred… you could have really hurt yourself. What were you just thinking anyway?"

"I…" he started, but stopped, not wanting her to know that he had seen her husband with countless, number of women.

"You are so lucky, the glass didn't cut you."

"And you?" he asked, again, while looking her over carefully. "I didn't hurt you, did I?"

"No, I'm fine! Really! But I have to ask, what were you thinking to have caused you to do that?"

"I'd rather not say if you don't mind," he concluded, while getting down on one knee to pick up the pieces of glass.

"Fine!" she conceited, as she went to give him a hand. "We can talk about something else!"

"No," he smiled warmly, while taking her hands to stop her, "I'll get this, but you can get me something to put it in!"

"Sure! I can do that!" she smiled, while getting to her feet to go off into the kitchen.

"Later, after years of working on the force as a cop, I had decided to join ranks along with my uncle, and became a Detective. That, of course, meant going through some rather intense training. Afterwhich, I became his new partner, when Ted went off to handle another assignment with a new partner of his own."

"But if Ted was originally Alex's partner, why break them up?" she asked, coming back in with a small trashcan.

"To train others like us."

"Like you?"

"We deal with a lot of drug cartels both in and around Chicago and other outlaying areas. And with a few other good people, we go after other bad guys, as well. Heck, aside from your grandmother passing away, I never knew you had been divorced!"

"Until that morning in your living room?" she smiled embarrassingly.

"Yes," he laughed. "And am I ever glad that that had happened!"

With that, he went to get himself another glass, while she went to set the trashcan back in its spot, alongside the furnace room door.

Coming back into the living room, with a sheepish grin, and a dishcloth, he filled their glasses, after wiping up the mess.

"To the angel who had walked back into my life," he offered in a toast, as he turned to hand her, her glass, before holding his up.

"Forever...?" she asked questioningly, while looking up into his beautiful blue eyes.

"Yes, Jo, forever," he replied, but then stopped to look even deeper into her wondering eyes. "After finding you again, I can never let you go, not ever."

At that moment, taking her glass with his, he set them down on the table, and then turned back to look into her beautiful blue-green eyes again, only this time with so much more love in his own. Swallowing hard at what he was about to do, he began, "Jodi, I wasn't planning on asking you this quite so soon, but I love you so much."

"Jarred... I..." she started to stop him.

"No. Please let me finish," he begged, holding up a finger, and praying that she wouldn't turn him down, not now, not after all this time.

Looking on fondly, she too swallowed hard at what she felt was going to sweep her off her feet.

Then it came.

CHAPTER NINETEEN

"Jo…" HE BEGAN, WITH TEARS welling up in his own eyes, "w…will you marry me?" he asked, holding her close in his arms.

Quickly her tears began to fall. "Oh, Jarred, I do love you, but…" Hesitating a moment, while he looked on hopefully, she knew if she were to say no her whole world would be lonely without him in it. "Oh…! Yes," she whispered, while going up on tiptoes to kiss his warm and gentle lips. "Yes, I'll marry you."

"Yes…?"

"Yes," she cried, as he went to claim her lips excitedly.

Feeling the heat rising up again between them, while wearing a soft, yellow, summer dress, she felt the warmth of his hand finding its way down to where her buttons were and began to unfasten them one by one.

"Mmmm…" she murmured, while unable to control the heat that was building out of control.

Then suddenly, feeling his lips trail down to where he had stopped with her buttons, only to find the voluptuous swell of one of her breasts, she bulked at the realization of what was about to take place in her own cousin's living room.

Pulling away to study her apprehension to their passion, he saw the blush come to her cheeks. "I can wait a little while longer. I don't want to rush you."

"Thanks, but it's more, than, just what he did to me. It's my kids too! This isn't right, before we're to get married. And if they were to…"

He pressed a finger to her lips to stop her. "I know."

Turning to leave her for the night, Jodi looked slightly alarmed.

"It's all right. Alex has a room for me next to his!"

"I'm glad! Then I'll see you in the morning?"

"You sure will!" he smiled, and leaned down to kiss her goodnight. "See you at breakfast!"

"Mmmm hummm…!"

Giving her one last kiss, he was off to his own room.

After seeing him go, she had decided at the last minute not to clean up after them or to take her hot bath. "It can wait," she uttered out, smiling, while heading straight to bed. And instead of the usual bad dreams, for some reason, it was as if they had never existed. The fears were fading away, now that Jarred was here at the Inn.

The next morning came, and with it was a soft knock on her bedroom door. Looking up, she saw a freshly dressed Jarred standing in the open doorway, wearing a comfortable pair of fitted jeans, enhancing his beautifully long, masculine legs, along with a plaid snap down, long sleeved shirt, opened at the neck, with the sleeves rolled up just beneath his elbows.

"Good morning," he greeted, coming in to stand at her bedside. "The girls are up!"

"Mmmm, I heard them," she groaned, lifting a hand to run over his arm, while looking up into his warm and smiling face, when then, there came another knock.

Turning, Jarred teased, seeing his uncle standing there, "What do you want?" he snapped playfully. "Don't you see I'm trying to talk to my fiancée?"

At that, they both began to laugh, as she got out of bed in her oversized t-shirt, to go off into the bathroom, to get washed.

Stopping first at the door, she smiled at Alex, "Good morning, Alex," she laughed lightly.

"Good morning to you too!" he returned with an ornery grin, while she went on into the bathroom, closing the door behind her. Turning back to his nephew, he continued grinning, "I came down to see if you were ready for a busy day."

"Sure! Right after breakfast, though."

"Speaking of breakfast, Beth and Annie are bringing it down right now. We thought the two of you would like some time to yourselves, before taking on the heavy work load."

"Thanks. I'm sure she would like that."

"All right, just let me know when the two of you are on your way up," he advised, while turning to leave. "Oh, and yes, congratulations, she's a great girl!"

"She sure is!" he smiled, looking at the bathroom door.

After getting through with her shower, Jodi walked out into the living room wearing a soft blue summer dress. "Is everything okay upstairs?" she asked, seeing the breakfast laid out on the table near the fireplace, where the previous night's dinner had already been cleared away.

"Yes. He came down to let us know Beth and Annie were bringing this down for us."

"It looks good! Has the girls already eaten?"

"Yes. They're up helping out at the front desk, now."

"Mmmm... good, Jessi would appreciate that," she cooed, taking a bite of Annie's fine cooking.

Meanwhile, upstairs, all was going quietly. Room four was about to checkout, and Alex's alter ego, Jake, was acting out his part well by carrying out their luggage for them.

"Thank you," the couple replied, while handing him a five dollar bill to show their appreciation.

"No, that's okay," he grinned, while trying to hand it back.

But they wouldn't hear of it, and left with him standing there, shaking his head.

"What was that about?" Ted asked, coming out to get himself some coffee.

"My first tip!" he laughed, holding it up for his friend to see, while heading back up onto the porch.

"Well, keep that up and maybe you'll be able to retire someday."

"Yeah, right, and I'll be a whole lot older, and even more grayer, before that happens."

"Well, older at least," he grinned, handing him a cup.

"Yeah, I got your older," Alex was just saying, when hearing what sounded like gunfire, going off out along the roadway, to the left of the Inn.

Looking back first to see the girls were still inside, the two dropped their cups, spilling the coffee everywhere, before taking evasive maneuvers to wait out what they thought was sure to come.

Just then, one of Alex's men called out over his walkie-talkie.

"Marcose," Alex called back hurriedly, "what was that?"

"Just an old farm truck backfiring," he announced. "It's okay!"

Seeing the old, green, truck for themselves, as it passed by, they relaxed their hands from around their service revolvers, and began to stand back up.

"Damn!" Alex groaned at the very moment Beth came out to join them.

"Is everything all right?" she asked, putting her own revolver away, while watching the old truck rattle and chug on down the road.

"Yes. Just an old farmer, is all," Ted replied, while brushing himself off.

"Yeah, well let's just hope that's all it was," Alex growled, while going over to get out some towels from beneath the coffee cart to clean up their mess, before getting them another cup.

"You don't think…" Beth began.

"Delgado?" he asked, looking even more angered at that moment.

"What do you think," Ted added, "checking us out?"

"Yeah, just maybe," Alex returned, while keeping an eye on the road, where the truck had gone, before disappearing. "Just maybe." But then more to himself, as he finished refilling his cup, he went over to stand at the porch post to think over what had just happened. *'Damn you, Delgado,'* he glared hard at the road, off in the distance, *'I wouldn't put it passed you to do something like that in order to checkout who is all here.'*

Meanwhile, after finishing up with their breakfast, Jarred called Alex to let him know they were on their way.

"Good, but first I have to ask, did either of you hear anything a few minutes ago?"

"Like what?"

Telling him what happened, Jarred was glad they hadn't heard the noise, for Jodi's sake.

"Well, if the two of you are coming, I'll be waiting for you in the office."

"All right," Jarred replied, hanging up on his end. Turning to Jodi, he saw her puzzlement, and smiled. "It's nothing. Shall we go?" he asked, while putting his phone back onto his belt, before taking her hand to lead the way.

"Yes."

Heading up the stairs, he kept what he was told to himself, knowing though that it was only a matter of time before she would pick up on it.

As for Jodi, deciding not to push it, she didn't want to lose the beautiful moment they had shared the evening before. So instead, she just held warmly to his hand as they went up in silence.

Upon reaching the office, they found Alex looking out the front windows, when he turned away, as they walked in to go over to the desk.

"Well," Jodi said, reaching up to give Jarred a kiss, "if you don't mind, I think I'll go and see what the others are doing, while the two of you talk."

"All right," he smiled, returning it. "You will be back, won't you?"

"Would I leave you to deal with all this alone?" she laughed, while turning to walk over to the door. "Just have one of the girls come and get me when you're ready to get started."

"I'll do that," he grinned.

"Alex!" she nodded pleasantly, just before closing the door.

"Jodi!" he returned.

Leaving the office, she went across the foyer to the Boutique, where she saw her cousin's two friends hustling around to get ready for another long day.

"Well, if it isn't Jodi!" the two called out teasingly, when seeing her walk in.

"Hello you two!" she greeted, while going over to get herself a cup of coffee, before taking a seat to look through some catalogs.

"Hey, whatchya looking for?" Ashley asked, while walking over to join her.

"Oh… just a wedding dress!" she smiled calmly.

"What…?" Ashley asked, sounding surprised.

"For who?" Renee asked from across the room.

"For me!"

"No…!" they both cried.

"Don't tell me," Ashley grinned. "Alex's nephew?"

"Yes…! And would you like to meet him?"

"Of course we would! Where is he?" Renee asked, coming over to the table.

"In the office! Alex brought him up to help me work on some paperwork."

"Well let's go see this guy!" Ashley suggested, eagerly.

"We will! But first I think Alex is wanting to talk to him about what's been going on."

"Sure!" they agreed, not mentioning the backfire they heard earlier.

Taking a seat once things were ready for that day, the three started flipping through a few catalogs and exchanging their own views on all the different styles of dresses they came across, until Madison came in to let her mother know that Jarred was ready for her to return.

"Okay, sweetie!" she smiled, while getting up to lead the way. "And while we're in talking, please keep an eye on things out here for me, will you?"

"Sure! And if anyone comes in…"

"Let us know," she smiled.

"All right," they replied, as she went to tap lightly on the door.

Sticking her head in, she asked if it were safe to come in.

"Sure. We can talk more later," Alex grinned, while turning to leave.

"Yeah, later," Jarred agreed, as his uncle closed the door behind him.

Speaking up first to introduce herself to the good looking man seated behind the desk, Renee smiled warmly, "Hello! We're Jodi's, cousin's, nosy friends from the Boutique!"

"Oh?" he smiled back, while getting up to come around to shake their hands. "Well, of course, I kind a remember seeing the two of you at the shindig Jessi held!" he grinned, seeing their surprised expression at how tall he was.

"Sure! Now I remember!" Ashley laughed. "You guys had gotten into that baseball game and beat the tar out of the other team!"

Seeing Jodi's expression, he laughed, "You also missed out on a good game."

"Well, I guess!"

"Wow, Jo…" Renee cried, "I can see just why you want to marry him, he's so tall!" she laughed, looking up at him from her measly five foot three height, while she and the others continued to laugh.

"Have you two decided on when all this is going to take place?" Ashley asked.

"No, not yet," she replied, standing next to her man, smiling.

"Are we talking about the wedding?" he asked, putting an arm around her shoulder.

"Uh huh!"

"We haven't had time to talk about it, but soon I hope."

"You are going to wait for the others to get back, aren't you?" Ashley asked.

"Sure! But I have no idea when that's going to be. Do any of you?"

"Soon, I would imagine," Ashley returned, recalled talking over their plans with Jessi just before she and Craig left for their honeymoon.

Just then, there came a knock at the door, when Madison stuck her head in, "Jarred you have company!"

"Oh?" Jodi asked, when a worried look came over her face, just then.

"It's okay," he replied, expecting his parents, when going out to see them standing at the front desk. "Mom…! Dad…! I'm glad to see you made it!" he laughed, going up to give them a warm hug.

"Well, son, what is it that you just had to tell us?" his father asked, puzzledly.

"Well, Dad, Mom, I'm getting married," he announced, taking Jodi's hand in one, and placing the other around her waist, "to this wonderful lady standing here next to me."

"Jarred…" his mother cried out, excitedly, as she went back to give her son another hug, along with Jodi, "that's wonderful!"

"Same here, son," his father replied, shaking his hand, before going around to congratulate the newcomer to the family.

"Hey now, what do we have here?" Alex asked, laughing, when coming up to join them. "Hey, sis!"

"Hey, yourself!" the fairly tall woman, in her late fifties, smiled back. "You didn't tell us he was getting married, too!"

"I just learned about it, myself," he returned, gladly, while still keeping an eye on the front door. "Hey, how about we take this somewhere else and free up the foyer. What do you say?"

"I have a suggestion!" Jodi spoke up. "How about us ladies go over to the Boutique to talk things over, while the men go on into the office?"

"Sure!" they all agreed, taking their leave.

Once back in the Boutique, Jarred's mother, Donna, spoke up, wondering if this was the girl her son had been so crazy about years ago, when she finally asked, "Jodi, are you the one who's grandmother owned an antique shop?"

"Yes, I am," she replied, looking away, wondering what Jarred had told her.

"Hun," the woman with her graying brown hair and pale blue eyes, smiled, when seeing Jodi's apprehension over her question, "it's all right, Jarred told me what had happened, and we knew he was hurting over something, but he wouldn't open up about it. That's when his father figured it had to be a girl."

"I'm sorry, I didn't mean for him to get hurt so bad."

"No, dear, we understand. We heard bits and pieces of what had happened over the years. We're just glad to see that it turned out so happily. Now, just when is this wedding going to take place?"

"We haven't talked about it yet, but he wants it to be soon!" she exclaimed, while getting up to go over and look at the sexy nighties, when the others got up to join her.

Picking out one for everyone to see, Donna grinned, "How's this one?" she asked, holding up a teal blue teddy. "This would go nicely with your eyes, don't you think?"

"It would," Jodi laughed, "but I would give it about three minutes."

"What? Three minutes?" she asked, laughing.

"Yes. One minute for him to come to after he faints, and another minute to focus again."

"And..." his father spoke up from the doorway, "what about the remaining time?" he asked innocently, upon their arrival.

"That, Mr. Stanton," she turned to see the men all standing there grinning, "is just the beginning of history in the makings." With that, she smiled, seeing Jarred's eyebrow shoot up.

"I heard that!" he teased, as everyone lit up the room with laughter.

"Well, it looks like my husband is wanting to leave," Donna announced.

"Yes, I have a lot of work at home waiting on me. We just stopped by to hear the news."

"No...! I wish you didn't have to go just yet!" Jodi went on, while giving them both a hug, "I could have had Annie fix us all something for lunch!"

"No, that's okay, we grabbed something on our way out," Donna returned, while going on to whisper something in her son's ear.

Agreeing, he smiled, while Jodi walked out onto the front porch with his father, so that he and his mother could exchange a few words amongst themselves.

"Son, I can see now just why you never wanted to marry anyone else."

"Mom, she's worth the wait."

"Yes, she is! And it's a shame you weren't aware of her divorce much sooner!" she grinned, smacking him on the arm.

"That's for sure," he grumbled, shaking his head, at all the lost time between them. "Unfortunately, I was too involved with the crimes going on around us to realize just how much time had passed by."

"A lot of years, dear?" she commented, shaking her head.

"Yeah, I know. That's why I don't want to wait another minute to have her as my wife."

Chapter Twenty

Later that afternoon, after working alongside Jarred on a lot of paperwork, Jodi got up to go out to the backyard to talk to Alex, who at the time was working on painting the gazebo.

"Jodi," He looked up to see her walking out to join him, "what is it? You look so serious."

"No, I'm sorry, Alex, I just wanted to thank you for letting Jarred be here with me. It means a great deal to the both of us," she explained, just before turning to leave him alone.

"Hey, hold up there a minute," he called out, putting the paint brush down, to wipe off his hands. "I didn't mean to sound so short just then. Do you want to talk about it?"

"No, that's all right. You look as though you have a lot on your mind already. I'll go and leave you to whatever is bothering you."

"No. Please!" he apologized, while pointing out a couple of chairs and a table with a pitcher and two glasses of iced tea sitting on it.

Taking a seat, she fumbled for the right words to say that best explained what she was feeling, while he refilled his glass.

"Care for some?" he asked.

"Sure, but how did she know to have two glasses out here?"

"Because Ted was out here earlier. But he didn't want any."

"Oh." Taking her glass, she took a sip, before sitting back in her chair to look over the freshly painted gazebo. "Looks good!"

"It will when it gets finished!" he returned, seeing how she was struggling to say what was on her mind. "Jodi, just spit it out."

"It's hard to."

"What?"

"Love. It's just that I never realized just how much I could really love someone. You know what I mean?"

"After your first love was killed?"

"Yes, and then after my failed marriage."

"I'm sorry to hear that. It sounds like you and your cousin have a great deal more in common than I thought!"

"We do!" she was saying, when Jarred walked out at that moment to join them.

Turning to look up at him, she smiled, when Alex interrupted their touching moment, "Well, as for the other night, did you have a nice time?"

"We sure did," Jarred replied, while smiling down at her.

"Good!" he grinned, while finishing off his iced tea, before turning back to his painting.

"Hey, what do you say we head back in? I have something to show you in one of your books."

"Sure!" she agreed, taking her glass with her.

"Alex, I'll see you later?" Jarred stated, before leaving him.

"All right," he returned, watching them head off to go back inside. But then suddenly recalling something he had left up front, going up to get it, he saw a man leaving the front porch in what seemed like a great hurry. Running up to catch him, he yelled for him to stop, while reaching out to grab his right arm, but grabbed onto his jacket instead, and spun him around. "What...?" he shouted, seeing who it was. "Harry...?"

"Hey...!" he yelled back nervously, when seeing Alex's alias. But then, looking at him a moment longer, a slight smile came to the stubbly fellows face. "Detective Storm...?" he whispered, while looking around nervously.

"What are you doing here?" he asked, but then seeing the way Harry was behaving, he became alarmed. "No...! Tell me you didn't."

"I...I just came to leave off something for Ms. Jessi to give you. Now, I gotta go...!" he cried, attempting to pull away.

"Why? Are you in trouble again?" he asked, holding tight to his jacket.

"Come on, Storm...! He's going to kill me if he sees me. And especially if he sees me talking to you!"

"Who? Delgado?" he asked, knowing the answer to that. "What did you do now, Harry?"

"You'll see," he cried, while still looking around. "Just let me go, before he finds me."

"No, I can't do that. Jessi would have my hide if something was to happen to you. She has come to liking you, you know?"

"Well, she sure was nice to me when I was here before, and all, but..."

"Just hold it," he ordered, pulling him off to the side of the Inn, and out of sight of the road, in case Delgado was watching them. Pulling out his radio, Alex called Marcose.

"Yeah," Marcose returned right away.

"Any sign of trouble?"

"No. None yet!"

"Good. Meet me back in the stables. I have a job for you and Ted."

"On my way."

"Storm_____!" Harry bulked some to try and get away again.

"Just hang tight another minute, Harry. I have a plan to get Delgado off of your case. But I need your cooperation to make it work."

"Like I did for Ms. Jessi?" He started to relax.

"Yes," he grinned at the memory of what she had done to pull off getting Tony back up to Craig's old room.

Meanwhile, back in the office, while sitting on the sofa, looking over an envelope she had just received, Jarred looked up to see the puzzlement on her face. "What do you have there?" he asked, shuffling through a hand full of receipts.

"An envelope someone had just left with my girls a few minutes ago. He told them I would know what to do with it when the time came. Yet, I can't help but feel this was intended to be given to Jessi!" Going on to open it, she stared down at its contents. "This is strange!"

"What?" he asked, getting up to join her.

"There's a letter in here for you, and one for Alex."

"What's for me?" Alex asked, walking in to join them, just then.

"This letter! It's from a man named Harry?" she replied, questioningly, while handing them both out.

Seeing it, Alex wondered if this was what Harry was talking about, when he went on to read it. "It says here that Delgado is planning to take me out along with you!" he said, looking to his nephew.

"Yes, but we already know that!" Jarred stated, while looking up from his. "Did he say just when, though?"

"Real soon, from the looks of it. And it says here, too, that Harry is also asking me to forgive him."

Just then, realizing there was a letter there for her, she cried, putting the letter down.

"What is it?" Jarred asked, taking the letter to read.

"What? What does it say?" Alex asked hurriedly, while putting down his own to listen.

"It says," he went to read out loud:

Dear Ms. Jodi

I know you are Ms. Jessi's cousin, and that you will make sure Storm and his nephew gets these papers. They will help them in what they've been

doing to clean up the department.

Tell 'em for me, that Delgado wants me to do another job for him, but I

said no. Now he's out to get me too. You see, Delgado hates Storm and his

nephew for puttin' him in jail two years ago, and again recently. I just wanted

to warn them that he isn't going to give up until they're both dead.

Tell 'em too, after what Storm had done for me on account of his other

nephew, I had to call 911 to save this one when Delgado shot him.

Tell Alex thanks for trying to help a guy like me, and tell Ms. Jessi, thanks too.

Harry

With great difficulty, Alex cleared his throat, while not mentioning his plans to help Harry get free of Delgado. "Jodi," he spoke up, trying to sound convincing, "I don't know quite how to tell you this," he hesitated, when looking over at his nephew, "but Harry was found shot to death, a short while ago, at his place."

"What…? No_____ " she cried, remembering now who he was, when Jarred took her into his arms to comfort her, "that can't be_____! These were just dropped off a short while ago_____!"

"Probably by messenger," he thought quickly to cover his tracks.

"No_____" she cried into his shoulder, "Jessi is going to be so upset when she hears this. She had told me all about Harry and how he hated what he was being made to do."

"Jodi," Alex's voice came out deep, but compassionate, "I'll get a hold of her and let her know what has happened," he offered, when suddenly, something caught his eye. "What's this?" he asked, taking the green notebook from her hand to open it.

Turning back, she wiped some tears away, before answering him, "I don't know! It was in with these letters!"

Seeing its contents, he swore heatedly, "Oh, hell____!"

"What is it?" Jarred asked, looking over at the notebook.

"This is what Tony thought David had, when he went after him over two years ago. Harry had it all along!"

"Harry had what all along?" Jodi asked.

"It's the list of bad cops, and a whole lot more!" he exclaimed.

"Before you tell anyone, you'd better read it first," Jarred suggested. "You don't know who we can trust right now."

Shaking his head, while looking over some of the names, Alex said in great disbelief, "I talk to these guys every day! Damn… why didn't I know this sooner?"

"What are you going to do now?" Jarred asked.

"I'll turn it over tomorrow to Internal Affairs. They'll handle it from there."

At that moment, Jodi got up to leave. "If you'll excuse me," she said, going to the door.

After closing it, Alex looked to his nephew.

"I've got to go to her, Alex."

"Wait!" he held out his hand to stop him.

"Alex, can't this wait?"

"No." The look on his face told Jarred it really couldn't.

"What is it? You look as though… Oh, no… You know something, don't you?"

"Yeah. I'm afraid so."

"Harry?"

"He's not dead. Just hidden well."

"Oh?"

"Yeah, he was just here to give Jessi something."

"But that letter had Jodi's name on it!"

"He changed it." Pulling a letter out of his own pocket, he gave it to Jarred. "This is the letter he had planned to leave for Jessi."

"Man!" he shook his head, reading the letter to himself. "He really felt bad for what all had happened."

"Yes, and he sure saved your butt, too!" He laughed sadly at what he had nearly lost. "Go to her," he returned, taking the letter back. "She needs you. But nothing of Harry's whereabouts," he suggested, while walking his nephew to the door.

"What are you going to do now?"

"Wait on Marcose and Ted."

Giving Alex his letter, he headed down to see Jodi.

Meanwhile, down in her cousin's quarters, having made up a pot of coffee, Jodi went into her cousin's room to cry it out, when Jarred walked in behind her.

"Jo..." he whispered after closing the door.

"Oh, Jarred... I am so... glad you're here. I couldn't stand it if Delgado would have killed you instead," she cried, clinging to him out of fear.

"I know, sweetie. I know," he whispered, while holding her close.

"We have to have a burial for him! Jessi would have preferred it that way. Do you think Alex will let us do that?" she asked, wiping away a few tears.

"I'll talk to him, and then get started on the arrangements myself."

"You will?"

"Yes. Heck, I can see now why Harry liked Jessi. You both have such kind spirits."

"From what she told me, he wasn't such a bad guy. He saved your life!"

"I know that, now," he replied, shaking his head, when she went to wrap her arms around him more.

"Oh, Jarred... please, just hold me!" she cried into his shoulder.

Laying her down on her cousin's bed, he held her in his arms, until she quietly cried herself to sleep.

Meanwhile, the girls were being told of what had happened by Alex, while still waiting on word from his two men.

Sometime later, before either one of them had moved out of each other's arms, Jarred whispered her name upon hearing her moan.

"Mmmm...?"

"Are you all right?" he asked, looking down into her sleepy eyes.

"Uh huh...!"

"Hungry?"

"A little."

"What do you say we go up and join the others?"

"Mmmm, sure, all right!"

Rolling out of bed first, he reached over and flipped on a light for her to see by.

"What time is it?"

"Seven-thirty-eight!" he told her, when taking her hand to help her up, until she was able to stand on her own. "Are you sure you're all right?"

"Just numb over everything that's been happening!"

"I wish I could change it all, but..." he started, before turning to look sadly away.

Seeing how he was beginning to feel, she reached up to kiss his cheek. "I know," she half smiled. "I'm just glad to have you here with me. It makes it easier to deal with, knowing that you are all right."

"Same here!" he turned back to smile down on her. "Shall we go?"

With a nod of her head, she stopped just outside her cousin's room. "I should freshen up some, before going up."

Following her over to the bathroom, he stood at the door, while she did just that, and then ran a brush over her hair, when then stopping in mid stroke, as the tears returned.

Taking the brush from her hand, he finished brushing her hair for her. "Better?" he asked, standing just behind her to look into the mirror.

"Yes," she replied softly, as the two walked out, shutting off the light.

Upon reaching the dining room, all eyes were aimed at them when Alex was the first to speak up, when the two walked in hand in hand. "Well, they are still alive!" he said, while trying to lighten the situation.

"Are you two hungry?" Annie asked, while walking in with a few plates of food.

"Yes," Jarred answered for the two of them.

After taking their seats, the conversation went on around the table, as Jodi noticed the expression on Beth's face, when a statement was made to Alex about needing a girlfriend. Right away, she knew who that would be. However, she just had one problem, the departmental rules. *'I can't let that get in the way,'* she thought.

CHAPTER TWENTY-ONE

AFTER THEY FINISHED EATING, JODI turned to Beth on their way out of the dining room, "Will you come with us? I need to talk to you."

"Oh. Okay!" she replied, following Jodi and Jarred back to the office.

Once inside, after closing the door, Jarred went back over to the desk to get started on more paperwork that came in, while the other two sat on the sofa to talk.

"What is it you were wanting?" she asked quietly, while looking down at her hands.

"Beth," Jodi began, when sensing her sadness, "are you still in love with Alex?"

"Oh, no... of course not! It's strictly professional!" she fibbed to cover up her true feelings. "As I already told you, we're not allowed to get involved."

"Yes, right," she returned, not believing it, when Beth got up to walk over to the window. "But you would like it to be that away again, wouldn't you?"

"Jodi..." Jarred spoke up, just then, "are you thinking what I think you're thinking?"

"Why not? After all they had a past! Why not get it rekindled again!" she exclaimed, while getting up to go stand next to him. "Just look at her! She really does care for him. We just need to get passed that one little obstacle!"

It was plain to see that Beth still carried feelings for her Alex, when Jarred put the question to her, "Well Beth, how do you really feel about my uncle?"

Turning slowly to face them, she answered sadly, "I do care about him. I always will!"

"Beth...?" Jodi spoke up.

"He..." Beth began, "he's so..."

"Hot?" she asked brightly.

"Well, yes!" she replied, blushing at her admission.

"Beth, it's all right! That trait seems to run in their family," she laughed. "Just look at this incredibly handsome guy sitting next to me!" She smiled down at him.

"I can see why you love him! Not just because the two of you are so attracted to each other, but also because you have so much more in common!"

"Beth, you have something in common with Alex, too!" Jodi smiled.

"Yes, you're both police officers," Jarred added.

"And you both care about the same things!" At that point Jodi went over to put an arm around her shoulder. "Come on, how about you and I go over to the Boutique, while he works on the books? Would you mind?" she turned back to ask the man she loves.

"That's fine with me!" he smiled. "I'll still be here when you get through."

"Thanks," she continued to smile, while going over to lean down and give him a hug. "I owe you."

"Mmmm... and I can think of a way you can repay me too!" he smiled back, with one raised eyebrow.

"I just bet you could!" she grinned, while going over to the door to leave.

With that, they walked out, leaving Jarred to his work.

"Did you bring any dress clothes with you?" Jodi asked, walking over to the Boutique.

"No, I didn't think I would need any!"

"Well, we'll just have to see what Ashley and Renee have over here," she announced, walking in to greet Jessi's friends again.

Spotting Ashley over at the coffee bar, pouring herself a cup, Jodi went over to join her. "Ashley?"

"Huh?" she answered, while setting down her spoon.

"Do you have anything here that Beth could possibly wear to dinner tomorrow night?"

"Sure!" she exclaimed, going over to a rack to get a beautiful gauze, peach colored, low- neck, summer dress off it. "We just got it in this morning! What do you think?"

With a look of surprise, Beth cried, "Oh, my... it's so beautiful."

"Why don't you try it on," Ashley suggested, handing her the dress.

"Oh, I don't know..."

"Go ahead, try it on," Jodi prompted.

"Right now?"

"Sure! They have that enclosed area there behind the coffee bar you can use. So go, see how it looks on you."

"All right...!"

While going in to change, Jodi went on to tell the others of her plans.

"And Alex doesn't know?" Renee asked, softly.

"No," she smiled.

In a matter of minutes, Beth emerged from the little dressing room. It was like looking at a completely different woman, when the trio cried out, as she turned in front of the full-length mirror. And yet, her figure was small, still it filled the dress out in all the right places. Especially in the breast department, which would surely to get Alex's attention, when he sees the ample size of her bosoms, as they more than fill out the top.

"Beth," Jodi continued to cry. "You look great in that."

"You really think so?" she blushed.

"Oh, yes," Ashley agreed, while leaning over to whisper something in Jodi's ear, "I think Alex will really love what he sees here."

"For sure!" she agreed, telling Ashley to wrap it up. Afterword, she excused herself. "Girls, I need to get back over to the office so Jarred doesn't work too late," she explained, turning to Beth, "I'll see you in the morning so that we can go over the dinner plans together."

"All right." Just as Jodi started for the door, Beth called out, "Jodi! Thank you for what you and Lt. Stanton are doing for me."

"We're doing it for the both of you," she explained. "Jessi told me,

Alex deserves to have some happiness in his life after everything he has been through, and so do you!"

"I really do care about him!"

"I know you do," she returned with a smile, before turning to see Jarred coming out into the foyer.

"Ready?" he asked, coming up to put an arm around her.

"Sure am!"

Having gone down to her cousin's quarters, Jarred stayed long enough to visit with her and her girls, before going back up to his own room

"You know, with the paperwork nearly caught up, what would you guys like to do in the next few days?"

"Horseback riding!' one called out, when the other suggested a picnic near the lake.

"Well, Mom, what do you think?" he asked, looking to Jodi.

"They both sound pretty good!" she returned, looking at the three of them.

"Then that's what we'll do!" he laughed. "I'll just talk it over with Alex first."

"Hey, maybe we can all go riding and have a picnic, " she suggested, while still thinking of ways to put Beth and Alex together, while one plan was being thought out for the following day.

"Who else did you have in mind?" he asked, interrupting her thoughts.

"Oh, no one else that I can think of!" she smiled, not letting on about the rest of her plan, just yet.

Soon the time came to walk him back up to the main floor. After getting there, the two gave each other a loving kiss goodnight, before leaving him, when seeing Ted at the front desk.

"He'll be fine going up to his room from here," he assured her.

"Thanks, Ted," she smiled, tiredly, while leaving Alex's friend to watch over the Inn, while she went back down to go to bed.

By the next morning, Jodi ran into Alex, as she was about to head into the kitchen to talk to Annie. "Good morning, Alex. You look rested!"

"I am. Ted stayed up most of the night, keeping an eye on things, while I slept in."

"Good!"

"You know, I was wanting to tell you how lucky I thought Jarred was, having someone like you in his life."

"Really?"

"Yes. Perhaps, someday, I'll finally be able to settle down and be just as happy as my nephews are."

"Oh, I have a feeling it'll happen a lot sooner than you think," she smiled to herself. "And now, if you'll excuse me, I really need to see Annie about a few things for today," she replied, while not giving him a chance to ask what she had meant by her comment, when turning to go into the kitchen.

Smiling, he headed for the office to see what Jarred wanted the other night, while at the same time, in the kitchen, Jodi went over to call Jarred on the house phone, to remind him about her plans for that evening.

"Sounds good! I'll tell him," he laughed, seeing Alex's expression when he walked in.

"Tell me what?" he asked, sounding a little confused, when Jarred hung up the phone.

"If you only knew," he thought humorously, while sitting back in his chair to study his uncle for a moment longer. "Why don't you have a seat and I'll fill you in," he suggested, while leaving out the fact it was all a setup.

Meanwhile, back in the kitchen, Annie turned to Jodi, while sitting a hot tray of freshly baked cookies down on the counter. "Now what is this I've been hearing? Something about a dinner tonight?"

"Yes, well we're attempting to do a little matchmaking, too, by reuniting Alex and Beth, after how the Department had separated them a few years back."

"Does he know about this?"

"No. It's supposed to be a secret," she explained, while going over to snatch one of the cookies from off the tray.

"Jodi…" Annie hollered, while swatting at her hand playfully.

"Oops…" she laughed at Annie's motherly expression.

"You're just like your cousin. Can't wait on things to cool."

"I suppose not. But back to Alex, don't you think it would be a good idea to get the two of them back together?"

"Yes, of course, I do! And it's about time someone helps that poor boy out. He has so much to offer her. And I would really hate to see it all go to waste. Besides, I think Jessi would love to see what the two of you are doing for them."

"I know she would," she agreed, while going over to have a seat on a stool, next to the sink, "I just can't wait until she gets back."

"She'll be back soon, just be patient."

"Patient..." Jodi was just saying, when Beth walked in.

"Jodi," she asked, "what are you wanting to do?"

"I'll have to fill you in later," she said, remembering something she had to do downstairs first. "Annie, I'll see you later about what to fix."

"Sure, dear," she nodded, seeing the look of secrecy on her face, when she left.

Feeling baffled over what was going on, Beth turned to Annie after watching Jodi exit the kitchen. "Annie...?"

"Sorry!" she shrugged, while turning back to work on her cookies.

Meanwhile, after leaving the kitchen in a hurry, Jodi ran downstairs to call her cousin, while back in the office, Alex and Jarred where talking over Harry's funeral arrangements.

"Jodi feels pretty strongly about this, Alex. Even though he isn't really dead, he deserves to have something done for him, for what all he had sacrificed for us."

"I don't have a problem with that, it's just making sure it doesn't turn into a multiple funeral that I'm concerned about."

"It'll work," she explained with such confidents in her voice, when walking in, while closing the door behind her.

"Jodi?" The two turned back to see her standing there.

Not taking nearly as long on her phone call, as she had thought, she walked over to stand next to her man. "Alex, it will work. I just know it."

"And just how do you know that?" he asked, looking at her critically.

"Trust me. I just do!"

"I wish it were that simple, but it isn't," he growled, shaking his head.

"Alex," she began, when seeing how his expression was full of concern over the whole ordeal, "I'm not about to see the man who I have come to love so much, get killed."

"I know that," he stated, heavily, while going over to look out the window. "And I'm sorry if I seem to be having so much trouble seeing just how much you could think everything will simply work out. But it isn't all that easy!"

"Why don't we just hear her out?" Jarred suggested, when turning his attention to her, "Just what did you have in mind?"

Smiling down at him, she began, "Well, the men will be wearing their bullet proof vests, provided they do have those! And they do, don't they, Alex?" she asked, with a hint of sarcasm.

Glaring at her, he shook his head, thinking back to when Jessi use to stand her ground with him. "Okay, I suppose we could use them!" he laughed.

"Good," she smiled, "and as for the funeral, we'll just keep it short and simple."

"That sounds safe enough to me! Alex?" Jarred turned.

"Yeah, sure, you just might have something there," he conceded, while looking at Jodi with a twisted expression on his face. "Are you sure you weren't a cop in a previous life?" he laughed.

"You never know by the idea's she comes up with," Ted commented, walking in, after having taken care of a few phone calls of his own.

Turning to Jarred, Jodi asked, "Did you ask him?"

"Yes, and he said all right," he laughed, looking over at his uncle.

"Jarred…" Alex grumbled.

"Relax! It's just a simple dinner to help us all unwind a little!"

"Well, if you will excuse us," Jodi turned, taking Jarred's hand to leave, "I need to borrow these two for a little while. You don't mind, do you Alex?" she asked, with a hint of mischief.

"All right, be that way!" he laughed. "I'll just be in here taking care of a few last minute things for the funeral."

With that, she didn't say another word, while leading the way over to the Boutique so that they could discuss her plans for Alex and Beth's dinner party.

Upon walking in, Ted asked, "Now, is someone going to let me in on what's going on?"

"We're going to have a real nice dinner tonight, to help break the ice for a few people," Jodi explained, while going over to get herself a hot cup of tea to throw off a sudden chill.

"Jo… with this dinner, just who else, besides Alex and Beth, were you thinking about," Jarred asked, while pouring him and Ted a cup of coffee.

"Well…" she smiled coyly, "unlike our horseback riding, Annie and Hank! Not to mention, a couple of surprise guests of sorts."

"Guests…?" they both chimed in.

"Uh huh…!" she turned back to look at their puzzled expression, and then smiled even more. "Are you ready for this?"

"Jo… you're driving us crazy! Who else?"

Softly giggling, she told him, "Jessi and Craig!"

"What…?" he and Ted both asked, sounding surprised.

"When…?" Jarred asked, excitedly.

"Soon. This was really Jessi's idea. They should be getting in just in time to eat," she announced, looking down at her watch, before changing the subject about Harry's funeral arrangements.

"The Commander approved, as long as no one's life is put in danger," Ted interjected.

"When is it going to take place?" she asked, feeling the pangs of her tears building up.

"Day after tomorrow," Jarred explained, as he slowly went to place an arm around her shoulder.

Brushing his hand aside, "I'm sorry," she said, as she turned to leave all of a sudden, "I should go through my things and see what I…"

"Jo…" Jarred tried to stop her.

"No, I have to do this. I have to see what I have to wear. But first I need to see Annie and Hank about tonight."

"Jodi…!" Ashley called out, as she exited the Boutique in such a rush.

"Boy, this has really gotten to her, hasn't it?" Renee asked, hearing about Harry's death.

"Yeah," Jarred returned, looking to Ted.

"Go," he suggested thoughtfully.

And that, he did, while in the kitchen, after having just enough time to go over the meal plan with Annie, Jodi turned to Hank.

"What did you have in mind?" he asked, following her out of the kitchen and into the family room.

"Jessi would like to have the fireplace going, along with the furniture pushed back to clear a space in the middle of the floor."

"Sure thing! I'll get started on it right away."

"Thank you," she replied, as she was about to turn and leave the room. "J…Jarred…" she cried, seeing him standing there, while watching her admiringly, "h…how long have you been standing there?"

"Long enough to see the master at work," he smiled. "You handled that as though you were made for it!"

"I just want things to go well for tonight, is all."

"And it will. Are you ready to go downstairs now?"

"Yes," she replied, taking his hand, as he led the way.

After arriving down in her cousin's quarters, the two went into her room, closing the door behind them, when he went over to sit on the side of the bed, while she went through the closet to find the right dress to wear to the funeral.

"Ted is going to pick up our suits for us," he explained, while trying to make light of the conversation. "It's supposed to be a pretty day."

"I'm glad!" she spoke softly from the closet, while trying to suppress her tears. "I just hope Delgado will leave us all alone while we're there."

"We're all hoping that too! However, to make certain of it, Alex is planning on having some K-9's there and here as well, along with plenty of undercover officers to make sure of it."

"Oh?" she asked, turning tearfully from the closet to walk over to the bed. Getting there, she let out a shaky breath, as a tear made its way down her cheek.

"Jo…" he said, holding out a hand to her, "how about a nap, before dinner tonight?"

"Oh, if only you knew how wonderful that sounds about now. Would you stay with me?"

"Sure."

Getting in next to her, he groaned, "Oh, Jo, it feels so good just to hold you in my arms."

"Mmmm… it sure does," she agreed, feeling his heart beating just beneath her ear.

CHAPTER TWENTY-TWO

A FEW HOURS LATER, AFTER falling off to sleep, Annie knocked at the door to let her know dinner was almost ready.

"I'll let her know," Jarred quietly replied. "Oh, and Annie, how is the project going?"

"Just fine!" she offered uneasily. "As for Miss Beth, I'll be bringing her down pretty soon for Ms. Jodi to help get her ready."

"Thanks." Just before closing the door, seeing how uneasy she was, it hit him what she must be thinking. "Oh, no, Annie, it's not what you think."

"Of course, sir, but it's really none of my concern."

"But you were wondering, weren't you?"

"I know Ms. Jodi has been under a lot of emotional stress. So if having you here helps her through them, then I'm glad you're here for her."

"So am I," he whispered, looking back at Jodi, while resting quietly in bed. "She'll be up soon."

"Yes, sir," Annie nodded, as she went off to get Beth.

Turning back to go over to the bed, Jodi asked, "Was that Annie?"

"Yes. We need to be getting ready for dinner now," he explained, while turning on a dim light to help see by.

"Mmmm… all right," she replied, as he went across the hall to get her shower ready.

Hearing the water running, she pulled herself together and headed over with her change of clothes, while he headed back up to his own room to do the same.

Not taking as long as she had thought, she walked out into the living room to find Jessi standing at her patio doors, looking out at their girls.

"Jessi..." Jodi cried out, as her cousin turned to see her standing there, wearing a long cottony, teal blue dress, with its raised neckline and a gold cross to show of the swells of her breasts.

"Hi... Cuz'!" the tall, brunette smiled, as she went over to give her a warm hug, while wearing her favorite pink, gauze, buttoned down dress, with her hair pulled back at the sides.

"How long have you been here?" she asked, pulling back to look her over.

"Not long, I had just passed Jarred going up to his room!"

Smiling broadly, the two gave each other another warm welcoming hug, as the tears began to fall.

"Are you ready to talk about it?" she asked, knowing about her cousin's dreams, after having gotten a call from Alex.

"What is there to talk about? It's just like what you went through! Well, maybe not totally," she pulled back to try and smile, "but just as bad."

"Yes, but the inhabitant of the house you wound up in was alive!"

"And..." she laughed.

"Upstairs sleeping!" the two cried out laughing, so they thought.

"Hey, now that you're here, I had better be getting my things moved so you guys can have your room back."

"Yes, well why don't you just move them into the girl's room. They can sleep out here."

"What about your girls?"

"They can join them, when they get back. Which won't be long, now."

"Good, I can hardly wait. Nor can the girls. Have you seen them?"

"Yes, when we came in," she grinned, not telling her cousin where they had been for the most part of their honeymoon, before coming home.

Having decided not to wait to move her things, she had it done by time Annie and Beth arrived to get her ready.

Meanwhile, upstairs, having gotten ready, both Jarred and his uncle, wore a pair of tan khaki pants and a black smooth fitting t-shirt, along with a sports jacket, to exhibit just how broad their shoulders were. And like both nephews, Alex looked just as devastating with his long masculine legs and taut rear end.

Smiling, Alex asked, "Are we ready?"

"Yep!" Jarred smiled, knowing what was in store for his uncle, when they went downstairs to the office to wait on the others.

Once inside, seeing Hank standing off in a corner, Alex was surprised. But when turning to see who was standing near the front window, was a much bigger surprise, his other, tall, dark haired, nephew, Craig, who resembled Jarred, in a lot of ways, except his unique smile, being slightly crooked.

"Craig..." he called out, going over to give him a hug, "when did you get back?"

"Just got here!" he laughed, turning to see Jarred smiling, as he too went over to give his cousin a welcoming hug. "Jessi's down with Jodi now, getting ready, and Ted's out walking the ground, making sure this dinner goes off without a hitch. It's been pretty quiet so far."

"Yeah, let's hope it stays that way," Alex put in.

Meanwhile, back down in Jessi's quarters, Beth was getting quite nervous.

"Beth," Jessi laughed, "I can't believe how nervous you are. It's not as if you and Alex hadn't gone out with each other before."

"Well..." she cried, "I had never gone out with him wearing a dress! We had always done things that required wearing jeans or other slacks!"

"You mean..." Jodi started.

"Uh huh," she blushed, seeing how the dress accented her breasts, while looking into Jessi's full length mirror.

"Well, get ready then," Jodi and her cousin laughed, "Because he isn't going to know what hit him."

Gathering up the make-up and hairbrushes, Annie asked, "Shall I go and tell the men you are ready then?"

"Yes," Jessi turned and smiled.

Meanwhile, back up in her office, Jarred was looking down at his watch. "What could be taking them so long?" he asked.

"You ought to know better than ask that!" Craig laughed. "They have to have things just right!"

"Well, dear cousin, I haven't had the opportunity to find that out yet."

"No, of course not!" he shook his head. "Sorry, I had nearly forgotten."

"Jarred," Hank asked, looking totally clueless, "I don't understand, why am I even here?"

Smiling, before either he or Craig could say anything, there came a knock on the door.

"I'll get that," Jarred offered, before anyone could make a move.

Seeing Annie standing there, he asked, "Is it time?"

"Yes, sir. The ladies are waiting on you now, and the girls are down in Jessi's quarters having their meals there, while watching the movies you had brought over for them," she announced, not seeing Hank standing just inside the room, when she turned to take her leave.

As she did, Jessi called out, stopping her in the hallway, near the kitchen, "Annie, we have got to get rid of your apron!" she announced, as she and Jodi took Annie aside to give her a quick once-over.

"Now, you look great!" they both smiled.

"For what?" she asked, just as the men arrived in the dining room.

"For dinner," Jodi replied. "What else?" she and her cousin both smiled, while Beth remained looking nervous.

At that moment, Jarred walked over to take Jodi's arm, as Craig did the same.

"Hank," Jarred leaned over to whisper, "did I mention..." he began, when Craig cut in.

"Annie's your date for this evening," he smiled his crooked smile, when Hank stepped up, seeing how Annie looked all so pretty standing there.

"Ms. Annie, may I?" he grinned.

Turning back to look at Jessi, she blushed.

"Go for it," Jessi smiled.

And now, it had come down to Alex's turn. Anticipating the moment, everyone watched as he looked up to see Beth rounding the corner. But just when their eyes met, he swallowed hard at a sudden lump forming in his throat, as he slowly looked her over. However, when coming upon the fullness of her breasts, his eyes rested upon them, when catching a glimpse of their soft, sweet swells, just as the fabric parted when she took in a sudden breath, causing his mouth to almost drop, while an eyebrow shot up.

"I think we have a winner here!" the guys whispered.

At that, Jarred cleared his throat, "Uncle Alex, what are you waiting for?"

"B…Beth," his voice came out sounding broken up, when he finally found the words to say, "you look great! Shall we?" he asked, extending an arm out to her.

Taking it, she smiled sweetly up at him, "Yes, I'd love too."

At that moment the four cousins exchanged looks of success.

"Good job, sweetheart," Jarred grinned, giving Jodi a warm hug, while they all stood waiting for further instructions.

With a light clearing of her throat, Jodi spoke up, "Well, Jessi and I would like to thank each and every one of you for being here tonight. However, before we all sit down to eat, it would be nice to say a prayer to thank God for what we have here."

As they joined hands, she glanced over to her cousin, and with a warm, loving smile, Jessi bowed her head and began the prayer, "Thank you, Heavenly Father for watching over us during this time. May we all find true love in those near and dear to us, as we sit down to this wonderful meal for which Beth and Annie have prepared, and for what is to follow this evening. Through Jesus Christ we pray, amen."

That night, dinner was pretty lively, as the conversation went on until everyone had finished. At that time, Jarred and his cousin took their women and led the way into the family room, where the floor was cleared for dancing.

Going over to the stereo, Jarred put on some soft music to get things going. "Is this all right?" he turned to Jodi.

"Sure!" she replied, smiling at his selection, when he took her hand to lead her out onto the dance floor.

"Ms. Annie?" Hank turned to ask, when Craig and Jessi followed suit.

Turning to Beth, Alex asked, while taking her into his arms to dance, "Did you know what they were up to?"

"Not exactly!" she fibbed, feeling the heat of his hand at the small of her back.

Just then, he stopped, and really looked into her eyes for the first time that night, while feeling the heat of his own blood rising. "Look, I need some air, would you care to join me?"

"I…I'd like that," she replied, following him out onto the patio, where the moonlight shone beautifully overhead.

"Well, would you look at that," Jarred laughed quietly, while watching the two of them from just inside the doorway.

"I sure hope it works," Craig replied, while putting an arm around Jessi's shoulder.

"Us too," Jodi added.

Turning to Jarred, while the women went off to talk amongst themselves, Craig asked, "Have you heard anything?"

"No, thank God! We need this break, and Alex needs to take it easy," he explained, looking out on the moonlit patio, where the two were talking.

"He seems to be doing fine now!" he grinned his crooked grin, as he and Jarred went over to claim their women.

Meanwhile, while out on the patio, Alex was talking to Beth about his feelings. "You know this can't happen. We're not allowed to get involved with each other again. It's…"

"I know," she interrupted sadly, while turning away to walk out a little farther onto the lawn.

Seeing the saddened expression on her face, just before she turned away, he recalled that very expression, when they first had to breakup, years ago. Thinking of that moment in time, he had to fight the sudden urge to take her into his arms and comfort her. However, walking up, she unexpectedly turned to face him, when not realizing how close he was at that moment.

Meanwhile, nearly colliding into him, she stuttered out shyly, as she felt the heat of his body pressed up against hers, "I…I'm sorry! I…I didn't hear you come up!"

"No, I should have said something," he apologized, while looking into her baby blue eyes, when her lips parted just then. *'Oh, God,'* he groaned, finding he couldn't fight the urge any longer.

"Alex..." she cried, feeling his hands coming up to take her in his arms.

"Oh, God, Beth... why do you have to be so... beautiful?" he asked, while aching to have her back in his life again.

"Ale..." she cried again, only to be cut off, when he claimed her lips.

Feeling the heat raging between them, he groaned, "Oh, sweet, Beth, I've missed these lips."

"And I've missed yours!" she cried, wrapping her arms up around his shoulders, while the heat continued to consume them.

Then suddenly, feeling his hand come up to run lightly over one of her breasts, he pulled back to see what he had just done, while feeling it's nipple budding just beneath his caress. "Damn..." he groaned, hungering for its sweetness.

"A...Alex!" she swallowed hard, while feeling its wonderful sensation.

He laughed. "I just happened to think, we have never made love before."

"No, we..." She stopped to look away.

"Beth...?"

"Alex..." she began, but only to be cut off again, when he turned her back to face him.

"Beth," he went on, while unaware Jarred and Jodi had just walked out onto the patio.

Meanwhile, keeping their voices down, Jodi whispered, "I think we should leave them alone."

"Not a chance!" he laughed, clearing his throat to give his uncle a hard time. "Excuse us," he grinned, "but it's our turn now!"

Looking up slowly, Alex growled, "You guys need another hobby," he then laughed, taking Beth's hand to walk up to the patio.

Smiling at the two of them, Jarred offered an apology, "It's getting late and Jodi's having to call it a night."

"I should be saying goodnight, as well," Beth turned to Alex.

Not wanting the evening to end for them, he had to admit she was right. "I guess so," he replied, walking her back inside with the others. But then, getting there, he saw Ted walking in. "Ted?"

"Yeah?"

"Have you been through the house yet?"

"I'm getting ready to do that now. So why don't you get some rest, and I'll see you in the morning"

"All right," he replied, saying his goodnights, before walking Beth up to her room.

"I'll see you, as well," Jarred put in, giving Jodi a kiss, before heading into the office.

"Where you going?" she asked, suddenly feeling all alone, since Jessi and Craig had already turned in for the evening.

"Just into the office, I need to take care of a few things, before calling it a night."

"Oh, all right!"

Meanwhile, having just reached the top landing, Beth turned to look up into Alex's icy blue eyes. "I guess I'll see you tomorrow, as well?"

"Yeah, tomorrow," he grumbled, while watching her turn to head for the attic stairs. "Beth…" he called out, going after her, "wait…!"

Turning to see the urgency in his eyes, she swallowed hard once again, as he brought her back into his arms.

"I can't just let you go like this," he breathed so close to her face.

"But…"

"No, damn you!"

Scooping her up into his arms, he carried her up to her room, where he kicked the door closed with one booted heel, before taking her over to her bed.

"Alex…" she started to protest, when he cut her off by claiming her lips once again.

"Mmmm, no_____" she cried, fighting her own desire, "w…we c…can't_____!"

Ignoring her cry, he lowered her slowly to her bed, where, there, he captured the lushness of her breasts as he moved the material aside.

"Ahhh…" she cried out, feeling the sensation of his lips, as he began suckling even more, while attempting to remove his own things. And with her help, he had his shirt off in no time, before slipping her dress up over her head and onto the floor.

But then stopping at that moment, he caught what must have been the most beautiful sight ever. Her smoldering eyes, as she reached down to undo his kakis. "Beth," he smiled, while looking down upon her small trembling hands.

Giving her a hand, he slipped out of his slacks and black bikini briefs, as she blushed, and turned away, before seeing anything else.

It wasn't long after he rejoined her that she cried out feeling the pressure of his manliness pressing up into her innocence, once her panties had been removed.

"Beth…?" he pulled back to see the tears. "What is it?"

"I…I never…" she broke off, pushing him aside to jump up and run out of the room, and down the hall, into the attic bathroom.

Hearing her sobs, he became concerned and got up, pulling his briefs back on, before going down the hall to check on her. "Beth…" he called out through the closed door, "are you trying to tell me that you're a…" He stopped short. "Damn… what was I thinking?" Laying his head against the door, he shook it, *'Oh, God, of course she is… you idiot…'* he scolded himself for not thinking. "Oh, Beth, damn it, I'm sorry! I didn't think. Please come out so we can talk about this."

"I…I… can't…! I feel so…"

"No. Don't!" he stopped her. "Whatever you're feeling, we can get through it together. Please, just come out so we can talk. I promise, I won't think little of you. I just wasn't thinking, is all," he was saying, when hearing the door slowly open. Looking up, he saw her standing there with her arms crossed in front of her breasts, while her tears continued to fall. "Beth…?" Taking her back into his arms, he held her, lovingly. "It'll be all right!"

"H…how can you say that? I…I don't know what to do…!" she continued to sob.

"Then let me help you," he pulled back to gaze down into her tear-dampened face. "It'll be okay!" he grinned handsomely, while wiping a few of the tears away. "But hey, if you don't want to, we won't!"

"But I…I want to!" she whimpered.

"You sure?"

"Yes. Oh… yes," she returned, seeing his gorgeous grin, just before his lips found hers in the semi darkness of the hall.

Feeling all sorts of desires pouring through her, she cried, "Now, Alex, now_____!"

"Oh, Rookie_____!" he breathed against her cheek.

Not able to contain his desire any longer, he swept her back up into his arms again and carried her back into her room, closing the door behind him once again.

As the scene before them began to slowly unfold, going over to lie her down, he slipped back out of his briefs, before going on to remove her white lacy panties. There, he continued to caress her, first starting with her neck, as he went to lower himself onto the bed next to her, and then down to the swells of her breasts, taking one by one to nibble at their blossoming buds, until she wrapped her arms around his shoulders to bring herself up into his hungering lips.

And then it hit, finding she couldn't take the torture on her innocence any longer. "Alex...!" she cried, needing him, wanting him, having to have him, and now, she cried on hungeringly, until he slid on top her, while placing her hands just above her head.

"This may hurt some!" he warned, while looking deep into her eyes. "If it does, I'll stop."

"No..." she cried, "I don't want you to stop. I want this. I want you!" she moaned.

"Are you certain of this?" he asked thoughtfully. "I don't want to hurt you."

"Oh, Alex, I've waited for this, for you, for so... long! Please..." she went on, while pulling a hand free to bring his lips back down to meet hers.

"Oh, Beth..." he groaned, pressing forth his heated passion into her a little each time.

Feeling its abnormity, she tightened up unexpectedly, when unaware of doing so, would cause the pain to increase.

"Relax..." he cooed softly in her ear, while feeling her tears against his face.

Soon, his journey was complete when feeling the sensation of her innocence pop. At that time, they both were able to start anew, as she loosened up and began arching up into his needs by meeting each and every beat of his drum. In doing so, she poured herself into making him totally blissful, as their fire continued to burn for what had seemed like eternity, until he rolled over onto his side, bringing her with him. There they continued to lie in each other's arms after he had covered them both up, before going off to sleep.

Chapter Twenty-Three

Meanwhile, downstairs, having bumped into Jodi, in the kitchen, while making his rounds, he asked her, "Where's Jarred?"

"In the office, finishing on some paperwork, before going up to bed," she replied, while putting the last of the dirty glasses into the dishwasher.

"Okay. I'll be up front, keeping an eye on things, if anyone needs me," he returned, walking out of the kitchen.

"Thanks," she smiled, while walking out behind him, "I'll probably just go on in and keep him company, until he gets through with what he is doing."

"All right. Goodnight then."

"Goodnight," she returned, going into the office.

"Hey, there!" Jarred greeted, puzzledly. "I thought you would've gone onto bed by now."

"I was heading that way," she returned, while going over to join him, "but decided to see how you were doing first."

"Mmmm... I kinda like that!" he smiled, while reaching up to pull her over onto his lap. "Has Alex turned in already?"

"Uh huh! I saw him go up a little while ago with Beth."

"Good! So what do you say we call it a night, too? The rest of this can wait till morning."

"I thought you would have been through already."

"I was thinking of another way of doing this. Perhaps condensing a few of the things down a bit."

"Sure, if you think you can find away!" she agreed, getting to her feet.

"I just may have. I'll know more tomorrow. Tonight though, has been a long one. Not to mention, a pretty good one at that, wouldn't you say?"

"Mmmm… it sure was!" she said, turning to look up into his smiling face, when he went to hold her. Seeing his apprehension, she asked, "What is it? Is something wrong?"

"No, just wondering what's going to come of this once everything is over."

"With Alex and Beth?" she asked, while they headed for the door.

"Yes," he explained. "Rules are made for a reason."

"Yes, but it sounds like you don't want them to be together!"

"It's not that, Jo," he groaned, walking out into the foyer, when seeing Ted standing out on the front porch.

"Then what?" she asked, turning him back to face her. "Jarred…?"

"Those two were once very much in love. It had nearly torn them up when they had to end it. And then to make matters worse…"

"Craig's shooting?"

"Yes. Alex had nearly gone over the edge over that."

"Which brings us back to your own shooting," she added, seeing the look on Ted's face at hearing that.

Turning back to see it too, Jarred shook his head.

"Alex was beside himself that day," Ted added, when coming in to stand just inside the doorway.

"I'm glad this, Harry person decided to call 911, or I would've been…" He stopped to see the look of anguish come over her face. "I'm sorry," he groaned, holding her close, "I had never meant for that to come out the way it did."

"I know!" she cried, feeling his heart beating once again beneath her ear. "Jarred…" she pulled back to look up at him, "we have to come up with something! About Alex and Beth, I mean!"

"Yes, but what?"

"I haven't thought that far ahead, but something has to come of this!" she exclaimed, while looking up to see the tired expression on his face. "For now," she reached up to kiss him on the chin, "we'll just sleep on it," she smiled.

"We sure will."

"I love you!" she called out after him, as he turned to head up to his room.

Stopping on the stairs, he looked back on her, "I love you, too," he smiled warmly. "God, I love you, too," he repeated, as she placed two fingers to her lips, then waved goodnight.

Upon reaching the bedroom, belonging to Jessi's girls, Jodi went in to get changed out of her things and into a pair of pajamas, before going back out into the kitchen to get a drink.

"Hi there!" her cousin spoke up, when she walked in on her getting a bottle of juice out of the refrigerator.

"I thought you would have already been in bed!"

"I was just heading that way, but I got thirsty. What about you?"

"I was just coming in to get some ice water."

"Got some in the refrigerator if you would prefer?"

"Sure!" she returned, heading over to get a glass out first for herself. "Hey, before I forget, would you and Craig like to join us for a picnic after the funeral?"

"Sure!" she returned, giving her cousin a warm hug goodnight. "That'll give us time to have our heart-to-heart talk, before we go!"

"If it's about the dreams, I haven't had any more, since Jarred has been here."

"Good, and now what do you say we save the rest for tomorrow and get some sleep?"

"Sounds good to me," she smiled, while heading down the hall with her cousin. "Jessi?"

"Yes?" she turned back to see Jodi's tears.

"I'm sure glad you're back, Cuz'!"

"Me too!" she went to give her a heartfelt hug, before going on into her own room to join her husband.

By the time the funeral came around, the women were busy getting themselves ready, while talking over Jodi's upcoming wedding.

"Hey," Jessi began laughing, "I know what you two would like for a wedding present," she announced, while brushing out her long brown hair.

"Yes," Beth called out from across the room, "Vince Delgado's butt in prison?"

"You're right about that!" Jodi laughed along with everyone else in the room.

"Mom?" Kyleigh called out from just out on the patio.

"Yes, sweetie?"

"How long will you all be gone?"

"An hour at most. While we're out I want you girls to stay inside."

"Do we have to?" Madison asked, not liking to be closed up for long.

"Yes," Jessi came back sternly. "If you get frightened for any reason, Alex has a few of his men staying behind to make sure you girls will all be safe. And Hank will be by to check in on you from time to time," she added, reassuringly.

"I'll be glad when all this is over," Jodi heard her eldest daughter comment, while Jessi went into the kitchen to get some lemonade.

Turning to look back, she too heard the comment and looked to Jodi.

"What can I say?" she shrugged, helplessly.

"Well, I for one," she began, while going on to get everyone something to drink, "would have to agree. I wouldn't want something like that getting in the way again after having already gone through it myself."

"That's for sure," they all agreed, while she began to fill their glasses.

But then, seeing the expression in Beth's eyes, as she came over to sit down, she started to fumble with a napkin that Jodi had left out on the table.

"Beth," Jessi looked in on her from the kitchen, as she was just about to carry in their drinks on a tray, "why so gloomy? Has something else happened that we don't know about?"

"No. Well, not exactly."

"Which is it?" they asked.

"Well... there is something that I've been wanting to tell the two of you, but..." she began, while biting on her lower lip.

"What is it?" Jodi asked, worriedly.

"Is it Alex?" Jessi asked. "Has he..."

"Oh, no... I just wanted to thank you both for doing what you did to help us! As for Alex, he has really been wonderful lately!" she replied, as a small blush came to her cheeks.

"Beth...?" the two looked to each other.

But then it was Jodi who asked the next question that was sure to be on everyone's mind, "Hon, are you telling us that you and Alex..."

"Well...!"

"Oh...?"

"Then why the sad face?" Jessi asked.

"It's because I had never..." she broke off, turning away to fight back the tears.

"You're still...?" Jodi asked. *'Of course, Jessi said she had grown up in a convent!'* she goaded herself.

"Yes," she cried, just as the two went to comfort her.

Just then, they all heard the sound of the upstairs door open to Jessi's quarters, when soon after they saw her girls come running down the stairs at hearing that their cousins were there.

"Mom..." Cassi called out excitedly.

"Cass..." Jessi got up to hug the two of them, before they turned to gang up on Jodi.

"Hi, girls!" she cried.

"Madison...? Kyleigh...?" Cassi cried, when hearing Madison cry out over the sound of their phone ringing.

"Hey!" Jessi called out, getting their attention after getting off the phone. "That was Alex. He said we have to be going. You know what to do. Alex and Ted have both been over it with you," both Jessi and Jodi instructed, while giving their girls a hug.

"Yes, and so did Jarred last night and again this morning at breakfast," Kyleigh announced, pulling away.

"Well," Jessi replied, "he just wants you all to be safe."

"We will!" Lora, Jessi's oldest, laughed.

"Yeah, her boyfriend is staying behind to watch over us!" Cassi teased.

"Cassi, what did I tell you?" her sister groaned, while shooting her a mean look.

"Hey, enough," Jessi corrected, when seeing Baker walking down the stairs, looking quite handsome. "Baker…" she turned, "behave, or you will be hearing it from your Commander!" she warned, knowing he had taken a liking to her seventeen year old.

"Yes, Ma'am," he smiled.

"Yeah," she and her cousin both laughed, while leading the way up the stairs.

Getting to the top, just before going out to meet their men, Jodi stopped to ask Beth quietly what had happened.

"He slowed down and took his time," she smiled, seeing how the girls weren't able to catch what was being said.

"And then…?" they asked teasingly.

"He held me the rest of the night."

"Aww… Beth, that's wonderful," they both cried.

"Then you're happy for me?" she asked tearfully, looking to Jessi first, and then Jodi, while Jessi went on to open the door.

"Of course we are! You're perfect for him!" Jodi answered first.

"Beth," Jessi offered, "he's a good and honorable man. And from what Craig told me, he doesn't just jump into bed with anyone. He has to feel something for her."

"I know," she returned. "I also know he still cares for you, Jessi. And he probably always will!"

"Yes, we did get close while he was going after Tony for what he had done. But that was then, and our relationship was unique," she smiled, thinking back on those days, when walking in to greet the guys.

Still blessed with the gift of telepathy from Craig's tragic accident, which had brought them together, Jessi looked to her husband, as he picked up on her thoughts, when walking in. *"Are you all right?"* he asked.

Smiling, now that they had all arrived in the foyer, she nodded her head, as Jodi smiled, too, seeing the men all standing there in their black suits, and black turtle neck sweaters.

But then, they both felt the sudden impact of desire stirring in their blood, when Jodi first thought how Jarred looked so handsome standing there, wearing his sun glasses, while admiring his brilliant smile, when she walked up to hug him.

"Oh, how you look so… incredibly handsome standing here," she whispered.

"Look who's talking!" he remarked, taking in her beautifully long black, sleek dress, with its high neck line, accented with her gold cross necklace.

"Well, folks," Alex spoke up, heading for the door, "with what few men I left out walking the grounds, and Baker downstairs with the girls, shall we go?" he asked. "I took the liberty of borrowing a limousine so that we can all go together."

"Great!" everyone exclaimed, walking out to the car.

Thankful, Jarred and the others wore their sunglasses, as the sun was so bright the women had to use their hands to shield their eyes so they could see where they were walking, as the men took them by the arm to guide them.

"It's sure is a beautiful day to have a funeral," Jodi commented, while sliding in next to her cousin, whereas, Alex and Beth got in just in front of them.

Seeing the warm look he was giving her, made the others appreciate the effort they had put into making this work.

"What do you think?" Jarred asked in a whisper-like voice to the others.

"I think their feelings for each other are still yet very strong," Jessi smiled.

"No doubt," Jodi whispered.

CHAPTER TWENTY-FOUR

AFTER THE FUNERAL EVERYONE WENT back to the Inn for dinner, and to discuss what would be going on for the next few days.

"I just heard from the Commander," Ted announced, while sitting back in his chair, at the table.

"What did he have to say?" Alex asked.

"He feels since Delgado hasn't been seen around here for awhile, now, we won't be needing as many men on this case."

"Oh? Who's staying on then?" Jarred asked, getting up to get him and Jodi a refill, when seeing how her glass was nearly empty.

"Alex of course, Beth, and myself. The others are to go back to the station in the morning for their new assignments."

"Does that mean they'll be leaving tonight?" Beth asked.

"No," Ted offered.

Surprised at what he had just heard, Alex abruptly sat upright in his chair, "What?"

"Most of them have elected to stay on tonight," Ted grinned.

"And why is that?"

"After hearing from the Commander," Ted went on, "I ran into Marcose just before coming in here. He said he has a bad feeling Delgado would be showing up."

"Alex," Jarred turned, "that would make sense, since it's been so quiet around here."

"Yeah, too quiet," Alex thought out to himself. Thinking for a moment longer, he had to agree. "Okay, you're right. And it is probably for the best. So, Ted," he turned, while getting up, "keep an eye on things up front?"

"Where you going to be?" some of them asked.

"Out on the side porch to get some fresh air. Jarred, join me, won't you?" he asked, while his nephew was just setting Jodi's glass down in front of her.

"Sure!"

Taking their leave, the others went on into the family room to talk.

Once outside, Alex looked out over the side yard, where Marcose was crouched down, hiding amongst some bushes.

Standing next to Alex, seeing the same thing, Jarred turned to his uncle with a huge grin on his face.

"What?" Alex turned to see it. "What's so funny?"

"Well, as it seems, I'm going to be needing a favor from you soon."

"Oh? What's that?" he asked, looking back over the yard.

"Well, for some reason Jodi seems to think I need a best man. By any chance do you know where I can find one?" he asked, laughing, when his uncle turned back to look at him.

"Yeah," he laughed, patting his nephew on the back. "I just might!"

"Good. Because you were my first choice!"

"Oh, but why me? Why not Craig? And who, if I really need to ask, is standing up for Jodi?"

"As for Craig, I thought of him. But you and I have gone through a lot lately. And Jo…" he was about to say, when she came out to find them, after asking her cousin to stand up for her, with a smile on her face.

"Sorry to interrupt you two, but the others want to get a card game going. And, well…, Craig put me up to coming out to get you."

Looking at his uncle, Jarred knew how he loved to get in the middle of a good game, before he even had to ask.

"Sure!" Alex laughed, turning to go back inside with the two of them.

"Well, did you ask her?" Jarred asked Jodi with a grin.

"Yes! As if I even had to!"

"And…?"

"Oh, but of course!"

With the girls out back playing, the others got into a friendly game of 'Spades' while sitting in the dining room.

"Hey, I just heard from a building contractor," Craig announced, over their plans to have some cabins built soon, so to add to the size of the Inn.

"Oh, how is that going?" Alex asked, having been told about their plans, before Craig and Jessi had gotten married.

"Pretty good! Jessi's nearly finished with the plans. And from what she has told me, the two of you ought to see them!"

"What?" Alex asked, looking to Jessi. "But I thought you were having Craig draw them up."

"Well…" she grinned, seeing Craig's look of admiration.

"Alex," he said proudly, "it seems that she and her cousin have been working on them, before I came along. But here's the good news! It seems after talking with this Mr. Anderson and his son, he's interested in knowing where the two of them came up with the idea of circling the cabins around a cabin store."

"We both thought that one up," Jessi replied, proudly, looking at her cousin.

"And that's just what I told him!" he exclaimed, while trying hard not to burst out laughing.

"And…?" Alex asked impatiently, as Craig took his sweet ole time telling them.

Unable to hold back any longer, he let loose a roar. "He wants the two of them to consider designing more cabin resorts like it."

"He what…?" Alex asked, while the others laughed. "What did you tell him?"

"I told him," he replied with that unique grin of his, "that we would have to think about it, and let him know later."

"Well, I'll be," Alex grinned, with a look of amazement. "Where are these so called plans now?"

"In the office safe," Jessi replied, while getting up to go and show them. "Come on, I'll show you."

"You all might as well come," Craig put in, following her. "You too, Jarred, if you hadn't already seen them. You will love them, too!" he gleamed.

Going into the office, everyone gathered around the desk, while Craig insisted on going over to pull them out.

"As I was saying," he went on, "Jessi had been telling me that Jodi has been helping her quite a bit on these, before I came along."

"Craig did too! Don't let him fool you. He's been taking care of the finer details," Jessi spoke up on his behalf, while he took the plans over to lie out on the coffee table.

"Yes, well," he grinned modestly of his part in it, while everyone gathered around to look closely at the room sizes and the space between each cabin. "The cabin store, itself, is large enough to accommodate a fireplace and pool table. We had also added a basement in, in case, God forbid, a tornado was to hit. That was also their idea," he smiled, while looking up at his wife.

"And a darn good one at that," Jarred added.

"Yeah, well this sure looks pretty good, for amateurs!" Alex agreed, while going over the rest of the plans with both his nephews.

"I can hardly wait to see it happen," Jodi cried. "We have been at this for a long time."

"That's for sure!" Jessi laughed.

"Just one question," Beth spoke up meekly, when everyone turned to her, "since you are making plans to have the cabins built, why not a main floor guest room and eventually a Master suit for when the girls get to the point where one or both move out?"

"Or, seeing how big they're getting, they may want a room of their own?" Jodi suggested, knowing Jessi has been contemplating the idea.

Looking to Craig, Jessi knew they each had a point. "They're right, and they are getting too big for that one bedroom! Besides, I knew when we got the place it would only be temporary. I had even thought about the attic at one time, until…"

"The odd feeling you had about the back left corner?" Alex laughed, recalling the day she took him up to show him the extra two bedrooms for his female officers to use, while he handled the Belaro case.

"Yes," she blushed.

"So what are you thinking?" Craig asked.

"Putting Lora up in the extra attic bedroom for now, being that she's the oldest, and then later, Cassi, when Lora goes off and gets married."

"Yes, and at that point," Beth added, "the two of you can move into the Master suite, once it's built."

"Well…?" she asked, though, not really all that sure, since the basement has always been their home from the start. She knew it would be a difficult adjustment at first.

Sensing her uncertainty, while not giving any thought to the possibility of having any more kids at their age, he too agree, while running a hand over her back, thoughtfully. "But then again, we don't have to be in any kind of hurry to move either, if you don't want to!"

"No, I really don't, at least not at this moment. But at least having the suite built and ready for when we do want to move, is fine too."

"Sure!" he smiled, lovingly.

Not saying anything, Alex had his own sentimental reason about the basement, after all the time he had spent there.

"Question," Jarred spoke up. "What are you going to do with the basement when you move out of it?"

Thinking about Annie, Jessi smiled, but then thought, *"Why not set her up in one of the cabins so she doesn't have to keep driving in every morning?"*

"Sounds like a good idea!" Craig put in, grinning. *"But then what about Hank, with his bad back? Soon it will be his knees giving him trouble."*

"You're right. He's not going to be able to handle his room above the stables for much longer," she smiled back.

Seeing this, those who knew about their ongoing gifts, laughed.

"Yes," Alex grinned, interrupting them, "now all you have to do is wait, and get all the permits together to have everything built!"

"That won't take long," Craig laughed at his uncle, knowing they had been caught talking between themselves, while rolling the plans up to put back in the tube.

"It still never ceases to amaze me, when I see the two of you doing that," Alex grinned, shaking his head.

"Jessi and I were talking about that, back at my old place, that night, after the cookout. It really had us surprised that we still had the capability! I mean…" He shook his head in disbelief.

"Are we talking about our gifts?" Jessi laughed, while going on to close the safe door and lock it.

"Yes," Alex commented. "How is that possible anyhow? He didn't have it before hand! Why now?"

Seeing how the others were interested in hearing about it, she smiled. "Do you want to answer that? Or me?" she asked her husband, smiling.

"We think it's Gideon's why of telling me that I, or we," He looked on at his wife, "are to continue to help others through their troubles, when we encounter more like us," he grinned, knowing those around them were going to flip at hearing that.

"What...?" Alex growled, laughing.

"Yes, and who is this Gideon?" Jarred asked.

"An angel?" Beth smiled.

"Oh, but not just any angel," Jessi corrected, while looking to her man.

"No. Gideon was the one who helped me from the beginning, and told me how to get someone with Jessi's gift to perceive me. I owe it to him, to God, to do this. And I'm sure as heck glad to have had her by my side to get through it all."

"That goes for all of us here," Alex smiled, near tearfully.

"Yes, and now let's get back to what we were doing, before seeing those plans," Jarred laughed, just as he was about to head for the door.

When he did, they all heard a combination of Alex's walkie-talkie going off, and a loud screeching sound coming from out front, after Marcose had called them.

Instinctively, Alex, Jarred and Beth reached for their service revolver, and with the exception of Beth, headed over to the door, where out in the foyer Ted was already waiting.

Stopping, Alex turned back to Craig.

"I'll stay with the women," Craig returned, looking to Jessi.

Turning then to Beth, with a look of concern in his eyes, he saw that she was already standing guard alongside the front window, when she turned to give him a reassuring smile. With that he nodded his head.

Taking that time, too, looking back at Jodi, Jarred saw the frightened look on her face, when forcing a smile on his own. "It'll be all right, you'll see."

"It had better be!" she cried, as Jessi went over to place an arm around her shoulder.

"Let's go," Alex ordered, leading the way.

Meanwhile, just outside the office, Ted stopped them short of the front desk.

"What's going on?" Alex asked, squatting down next to him.

"Our friend is back, making some noise."

"Great, that's all we needed with their kids here!" Jarred groaned, shaking his head. "And I thought, too, with having your Blazer hidden, he wouldn't think we were here anymore."

"Yes, but if you recall, we weren't able to find the leak in the department yet. They're still looking over the notebook of names to see who it might be."

"You didn't see a name that stuck out at you?" Jarred asked.

"No, but that's not to say the person isn't using an alias."

"And as far as the kids go," Ted offered, over his shoulder, while trying to keep an eye on their uninvited guess, "Delgado won't make a move if he knows they're here."

"How do you know that?" Jarred growled, kneeling down next to his uncle. "He didn't hesitate going after Jodi!"

"Because kids are one of his weaknesses," he explained, while easing up a little more to see where their guest had gone, when he happened to briefly take his eyes off the road.

"Where is he now?" Alex asked, going around to have a better look for himself.

"Just down the road a ways," he pointed.

"What's the game plan now?" Jarred asked, when the others came out to join them, after seeing that Delgado had moved on down the road a piece.

"We're going to have to keep watch around the clock," Alex explained. "I have a feeling he isn't going to far tonight."

"What do you think he's up to?" Beth asked, joining them at the door.

"Just guessing he knows we're all here," Alex began, while keeping an eye on the black pick-up, "I'd say he's waiting us out, before making a move."

Suddenly, remembering the girls were out back, Jodi looked down at Jarred, as her eyes widened with terror.

"What is it?" he asked, getting to his feet to take her arm.

"The girls_____!" she cried.

"They're fine!" Alex offered right away. "He won't hurt them."

"No____, it's not just that!"

"Then, what?" Jarred asked again, looking even more concerned.

"Oh, my, God____" Jessi added. "They're outside____!"

"What____?" Alex jumped up. "When____?"

"While we were about to play cards!" she exclaimed, while moving aside, when Alex, Jarred and Craig went running for the kitchen door.

"Ted____" Alex called back.

"Go. I'll keep an eye on things up here."

And go they did. Leaving Ted to keep an eye on Delgado's truck, the three ran through the kitchen, half scaring Annie, while clearing the short distance to the back door.

Rushing out onto the landing first, Jarred called out to the girls, when spotting them right away, tossing the tennis balls around for the two dogs to catch.

"Yeah?" Lora called back, as she turned to see the expression on their faces.

Pushing past his cousin, Craig went out after them, as Jarred started to follow.

"Jarred. Stop…!" Alex called out, grabbing his arm. "You don't know whether or not Delgado is still in his truck!"

"I know, but if something were to happen…" He stopped, when the two turned to see both Jessi and Jodi standing in the doorway.

"Jarred_____?" Jodi cried, looking even more frightened than before.

"Jodi, I'm sorry you heard that, but it's going to be okay. He won't go after them!"

"So I've heard, but still…"

"Jodi," Ted put in, joining them, "you may have not heard me telling Jarred, but it's a weakness of his, when it comes to kids. Delgado just won't touch them!"

"I wish I could believe that," she cried, "but they mean everything to me."

"You have to," he offered in a comforting tone.

"Ted?" Alex turned questioningly.

Seeing his concern. "It's okay, Marcose showed up just after you guys left. He's keeping watch at the front door now."

"Good!" he returned, when the girls ran up the steps to be with their mothers.

"Mom… what's going on?" Kyleigh asked, seeing the tears rolling down her cheeks.

Leaning over to hug her girls, while wiping them away, she replied, "It's that man we told you about."

"Is he back?" Madison asked, not having paid any attention to the noise up front.

"Yes," Jarred explained. "So what do you say, we go back inside?" he suggested, while ushering them in ahead of them.

Meanwhile, looking around, Alex asked, "Where's Beth?"

"Right here!" she called out, coming into the kitchen, while putting her revolver back into its holster, before announcing she had already been downstairs to lock up the patio doors.

"You what_____?" he yelled, glaring down at her. "You shouldn't have gone down there alone! What have I told you about having back up? Damn it, Beth, he could have been down there waiting on one of us to show up alone!"

"I wasn't alone!" she snapped back. "Max ran in with Maggi, when Craig came back up to the Inn!"

"Alex," Craig spoke up in her defense, "I ordered the dogs in through the patio doors, when I saw Beth coming down the steps. I didn't see anything suspicious on my way up. Had have I, you would have known."

"Fine. Just don't do it again," he growled, shaking his head, angrily, when going back into the foyer to check on Delgado's whereabouts.

"Beth…" Craig offered.

"No, he has his reasons," she returned, while going back up front with the others.

"Ted? Marcose?" Alex spoke up, joining them at the front door. "What's going on? Anything?"

"No, not yet," Marcose offered, holding up a pair of binoculars. "It looks to me like he's having himself a smoke."

"What?" he asked, taking the binoculars.

Just then, they heard Delgado's truck start up and pull slowly away.

"Looks like he's leaving," he announced, easing out onto the front porch.

"Good," Ted replied, when he and Beth followed out behind him.

"Ted," Alex turned. "Call the Commander and tell him we're going to need the guys a little while longer."

"Sure thing," he returned, while going into the office to make the call.

"Alex," Jessi spoke up from the doorway, "why don't we all go downstairs and try to relax. This whole thing has been a bad experience for everyone here."

"That's all we can do at this time," he put in, turning to Beth.

With the exception of the two of them, the others all went down to Jessi's quarters to try and get what had just happened off their minds.

Meanwhile, up in the foyer, taking Alex aside, Beth started to explain.

"Look, Beth…"

"Alex, no. You were only doing your job. I understand that, but…"

"But, nothing," he turned to pull her up into his arms. "God, Beth, if he had have been down there, you would've had to confront him alone."

"Yes, and I would have had to shoot him, too!" she smiled. "Oh, Alex, don't you know?"

"Know, what?" he asked puzzledly.

"That I love you! I have always loved you…" she cried. "Aside from that, I couldn't and wouldn't have let that scumbag ruin what we had the other night. And if he had…"

"Beth, no…" he began, only to be stopped, when she placed two fingers to his lips.

"Yes, Alex," she started out tearfully, "I…I would have gone knowing we had each other, even if only for the one night."

Holding her close, he fought hard to hold back his own raging tears, when Ted went to hang up, before coming back out to join them.

"Alex," he spoke up, seeing the display of emotions, "is everything all right?"

"Yeah," he said, pulling back to study Beth's baby blue eyes for a moment.

"The Commander is going to extend the use of the men."

"Good. Are they still out in the woods?"

"Yes," Marcose offered ahead of him.

"Looks like your hunch was right, except when Belaro caught you off guard that one time out at Craig's place?" Alex grinned, when seeing the man's expression turn ugly. Dropping the subject, Alex moved on. "Well, good work anyway," he said, patting him on the shoulder, "I wouldn't want anyone else on my team, but who I have here with me now." With that, he turned to take Beth's hand. "Ted?"

"Go on, we'll hang out here for awhile, and then walk the grounds, when it gets dark."

"Take one of the dogs with you," he informed his friend. "I've been working on them to learn Delgado's scent."

"All right."

Heading for Jessi's quarters, Alex stopped abruptly.

"Alex...?" Beth asked puzzledly.

"No, not yet," he groaned, taking her back into his arms. "God, Beth, after what had just happened out there, I do love you, damn it!"

"Oh, Alex..." she pulled away reluctantly to look up him, "I've waited so long to hear you say those words!"

"I just about did back then, but..." He stopped when his face turned beat red, while recalling who had reported their relationship to the Commander.

"Terri?" she whispered.

"She had no right doing that. She was a fellow officer, and a good one at that."

"Yes, but she wanted you for herself."

"Yeah, well she was never going to have me," he growled, looking back at the front door, where Ted and Marcose were still standing, watching the road.

"What?" she asked, running a hand up along his ridged back.

"I'm not ready to go down to playing cards just yet."

"Then what..." she began, when he turned back at her.

"Do we take another chance at keeping this quiet, or..." he turned away, hating what he was thinking.

"End it... now...?" she asked, as the tears began to fall.

"You know the rules!"

Shaking her head slowly, she began to back away, "No...!" she cried softly. "Alex, I...I can't go through that again. I..."

"You think I can____?" he asked, pulling her back into his arms, "Damn it to hell____" he growled, painfully, "why____? Why did I have to fall in love with you, Rookie____? Tell me that," he went on, while remembering what he had always called her.

"Say that again?" she pulled back.

"I...I love you, Rookie?" he groaned once again, while getting lost in those glistening eyes of hers, as he went to claim her lips to his even more passionately now, than before. Only this time the passion didn't stop there. Taking her hand, he looked back to see that both Ted and Marcose must have sensed they needed their privacy and went out onto the front porch, before making his next move.

"Alex...?"

Placing a finger to her lips, he simply looked into her eyes, wantingly, for at that moment, there was no need for words.

Taking her hand, they hurried up to his room, where he closed the door behind him, before taking her back into his arms, until they couldn't stand it anymore.

CHAPTER TWENTY-FIVE

DOWN IN JESSI'S QUARTERS, EVERYONE was busy getting themselves comfortable around the table, while the girls went over to pick out a movie to watch.

"Mom?" Cassi spoke up.

"Yes?"

"Are these more of the new movies you guys bought?"

Looking over to see what she was holding up, Jessi smiled at her husband. "Yes, we bought those while we were away!"

"There should be a couple more next to them," Craig added.

"Cool!" they replied, seeing the rest of the DVDs sitting aside.

"I wonder what's taking Alex and Beth?" Jarred teased.

"It's hard to say!" Jessi came back, smiling, but then got serious all of a sudden. "He was pretty upset that she came down here on her own. What if…"

"No," Craig stopped her, knowing what she was thinking, "she was safe. I saw to that, myself."

"Safe?" Jodi spoke up, fighting back an eerie shiver. "But for how long?"

Having been standing behind her, Jarred leaned down to wrap his arms securely around her shoulders, while giving her a gentle squeeze. "As long as it takes," he said softly in her ear.

'But for how long?' she thought quietly to herself.

Having been there herself, Jessi could only sit there and feel the pain her cousin was going through. Even Craig knew just how deep that was.

"You can't take it away, sweetheart," he conveyed through his unique gift to his wife. *"In time Jarred will be safe again, and this Vince Delgado will get caught."*

"Like Jo said, how much longer?"

"As long as it takes."

Giving her his brilliant smile, she laughed, shaking her head.

"Cuz?" Jodi turned, seeing her eyes light up.

"It's okay," she patted her hand.

"Oh?" she, too, laughed, seeing the look on Craig's face. "That thing you were telling us about. You two were…"

Cutting her off, Jessi looked to the girls and quietly nodded her head. "They don't know about it."

"But if you have it, wouldn't it go to…"

"When they grow up, maybe."

In the meantime, up in Alex's room, feeling her essence reaching its peak, he groaned, claiming her lips again, "Beth…"

"A…Alex…" she too responded in kind, while clenching her fingers in through his, as the moment arised.

When it had, and gone, he rolled over heavily onto his back out of pure exhaustion, "I'm getting too old for this," he laughed.

"Mmmm…" she cooed, "I doubt that!"

"Oh…?" he grinned, while coming back around to gaze into her eyes.

Not saying anything more, with a shy, but sweet smile, she turned into his arms, as he went to hold her.

"Mmmm… you know we should be getting back to the others," he groaned, feeling her breasts pressing up against him.

"Mmmm… yes, and soon, before they start wondering what happened to us."

However, before either of them could say another word, his radio went off. "Alex?" Ted's voice came over the other end.

"Ooops!" they both began laughing.

Rolling over to his other side, he reached for his radio to return his call. "Yes, what is it?"

"The others, they were asking for the two of you. What do you want me to tell them?"

"Tell em'…" he turned back to look at Beth, who by then sat up covering herself. "Tell them to get another hobby!" he laughed, shaking his head.

"Gotchya!" he laughed, as well.

Feeling as though they had just been caught in the act, Alex continued to laugh, while shaking his head. "Well, so much for getting back, before they start to wonder!"

"Uh huh! So what now?"

"Mmmm…" he groaned, pulling her back into his arms, if only for a moment, before having to get up.

"Alex…" she giggled.

"I know," he grumbled, laughing. "We best be getting up and grabbing a quick shower, before heading down to see what's going on."

"Yes," she blushed, getting up with him to grab their clothes, before slipping out of his room, making sure, first, the coast was clear.

Not long afterward, the two walked in to join the others.

Seeing their uncle's face turn red for the first time, since meeting Beth three years ago, Craig and Jarred both called out teasingly, "Hey, glad to see that you have decided to join us!"

"Yeah, yeah, yeah," he returned, shooting them both a warning look. "Meanwhile, what's going on?" he asked, seeing everyone sitting around the table with a deck of cards, while the girls were a few feet away watching a movie.

"We thought we would go on playing to help us relax," Craig explained, while getting up to get a refill on his tea.

"By the way," Jessi spoke up, shifting in her seat to pass out the cards, "we just heard on the news that we're going to be getting in some rain later tonight."

"That ought to be nice to sleep to!" Jodi replied, while getting up to refill her glass, as well.

"Yes, but what about the others?" Lora called out, while Beth took a seat. "Brandon told me he and some others would be out in the woods tonight."

"They'll be okay. They came prepared for anything," Alex offered, from the kitchen, while getting him some coffee to help keep awake.

"Good!" some of them commented.

After Alex took his seat next to Beth, Jarred leaned over to ask if he was all right.

"Sure, we just had a few things to talk over, is all."

"Oh...?" he smiled, pointing to his uncle's wet hair, and then to Beth's.

Seeing where his nephew was going with it, he looked up at everyone at the table, and grinned, "Didn't you get my message?"

"Oh, we got your message!" Craig grinned, while standing in the kitchen doorway, recalling what he and Jessi put him through awhile back. At that, coming back over to the table, before taking his seat, he patted his uncle on the back, right where he had been scratched. "In that case, you won't mind if I just ask how the back is doing?"

"I was just about to ask you that very same thing!" he returned with a friendly growl.

Grinning over at Jessi, she too smiled at the recollection, when Craig's spirit, back before 'given a second chance' had used Alex's body to be with her in one of the most intense loves ever known to man. And what a love it was.

Later that night, everyone was ready to call it quits, after staying up, playing cards, and talking until the wee hours of the morning. Even Jodi and Jessi's girls had crashed out on the living room floor, after their third movie and three bowls of popcorn.

"They'll be out for a long time," Jarred announced, grinning at the four occupied sleeping bags on the floor.

"You're right," Jodi laughed, while she, Jessi and Beth cleaned up the mess they made.

Laughing himself, Alex got up to get another pot of coffee going.

"Hey," Jarred spoke up, joining him, while Jessi went to hand him a filter, "are you going to try and get some sleep at all, before we go out riding later?"

"No, the coffee is going to have to keep me awake, while the others get some rest."

"Isn't there anyone else to stand in for them?" Craig asked.

"No, everyone else is busy covering their own areas. Which reminds me," he stopped to look at his watch, "I've got to get up there now and meet with them."

"What about the coffee?" Jessi asked, following him out of the kitchen.

"Bring it up when it gets done?"

"Sure!"

As a yawn escaped her lips, Jodi made her excuse and said goodnight, as she headed over all the piles of kids on the floor to go to her room, "I think I'll hit the sack. Jarred?" she called back tiredly.

"Yeah, right behind you," he returned, saying goodnight to the others, before walking her to her room.

Stopping just inside the doorway, she turned, "Will you stay with me?"

"Sure, but seeing how there are twin beds, how did you want to do this?" he asked, closing the door behind him.

"Slide them together!"

Once that was done, not bothering to change out of her things, they slipped under the blankets together, after turning off the light.

"Comfy?" he asked.

"Mmmm hmmm!" she replied, as even then, in the darkness, he could feel her shaking in his arms, as he went to hold her close. "Oh, Jarred, I can't pretend that I'm not scared. It's as if I can feel you slipping away!"

"No. Not a chance. You're stuck with me, lady, until…" He stopped, when realizing what he was about to say.

"Until death do we part?" she finished, while bringing her fingers up to trace his lips, before going up to kiss them.

"Oh, girl…" he groaned, when kissing her back.

"Mmmm…" she cried quietly, running her fingers through his thick hair, before the two gave into their passion.

"Are you sure?"

"Oh, yes!"

And with the soft sound of rain pouring outside the basement window, so did their love, as the hours slowly drifted by.

Later that morning, after the rain had cleared, everyone decided to stick to their plan to go horseback riding, while bringing the girls along too. With Craig and Jessi up front, Craig on his black stallion, Joe, and Jessi riding, Maggi. In the middle, along with Jodi and Jarred on their own horses, Titan and Lexis, were the packhorses, carrying the blankets and food. As for the girls, they rode with Alex and Beth at the rear on Girl Scout, Misty, Pop Corn and Jade, all of which are used by Jessi's guests of the Inn.

"Wow, what a day. And to think, Annie packed a large picnic basket for us, too!" Jessi was saying, while Jarred and Craig were busy watching the sky.

"That sounds good!" Jodi smiled, while reining her horse around to avoid a down branch from the night before. "What did she put into it?"

"Ham and cheese and turkey sandwiches!"

"Craig, what do you think?" Jarred asked, when pointing out some dark clouds that were moving in from across the lake.

"Yeah, I see them."

"It looks like they're moving this way."

"You're right, they are."

"Jarred...!" Jodi spoke up, nervously, seeing the same bad clouds.

Turning to see her expression, he figured she was afraid of the oncoming storm, as well as her cousin. "Thinking about the storm that brought you to my house?" he teased.

"Yes! I was terrified then, too!"

"I remember a similar storm, when I first met Craig!" Jessi called back, while looking at her husband, with that same worried look in her eyes.

"Why don't we take them to the old shack up ahead?" he suggested. "If we have too, we can take shelter there!"

"Sure!"

"What about an old shack?" Jarred asked, reining his horse around to hear him better.

"Jessi and I came across it while out riding awhile back."

"Where is it?"

"Not too far ahead!" Jessi announced.

At that moment, Jarred turned his horse to ride back and fill Alex in on their concern.

While doing so, Lora called out, "Hey, Mom! Our favorite spot is right up ahead! Are we going to stop there to eat?"

"Yes, you're right, it is!" she smiled, seeing the area located on a slight hill near the lakeshore, with trees scattered out around it. "Jodi, what do you think?"

Seeing the spot her cousin was pointing out, she had to agree, "You're right, from here it looks perfect."

"Oh, but it is!" she looked to Craig, and smiled, while remembering those nights, during their honeymoon, that they stayed out there, under the stars, talking, amongst other things.

Arriving at their favorite spot, her cousin smiled, while climbing down off their horses, when Craig walked up to take their reins, along with his own, to tie up at a tree.

"Uh huh," Jodi laughed, seeing the smile on her cousin's face. "Holding out on me, huh? This place is absolutely gorgeous! How is it that you had never brought me out here, huh?"

"We just never found the right time!" she replied, while gazing out over the water. "Every time we'd get together, we had only time for a short ride. Though the stable isn't that far from here."

"That's true," she sighed, while coming up to stand next to her.

"Alex…" Craig announced, while going over to get some blankets down off the packhorse, "we're going to set up here!"

"Sounds good!" he called back, giving Beth a hand with her mare.

"Just how many acres do you have here?" Jarred asked, after taking care of his, Jodi's and her girls' horses.

"About two hundred!" she replied, when turning to walk up to her husband, while Jodi and Beth went about setting out the food. "Craig," she spoke quietly, while looking back over her shoulder at their cousins, "have you said anything to Jarred about what we had talked about last night?"

"No, not yet, but I guess this would be just as a good a time as any to bring it up," he grinned, while turning to Jarred, as he walked over to snatch one of Annie's cookies out from beneath Jodi's watchful eye. "Hey, Cuz," Craig spoke up, looking back at his wife. "Jessi and I were just talking the other night about this wedding of yours. And well, how about letting us fix a spot out in the backyard for the ceremony?"

"Yes, and it's going to be a beautiful ceremony, too!" Jessi announced, while looking to her own cousin, smiling.

"Oh…" Jodi asked, seeing that all too familiar smile of hers, whenever her cousin is concocting something good, "and just what are you up to now, dear, cousin?" she smiled back.

"Oh… you'll see! And now," she turned to the others, "before it has time to rain, let's all enjoy this wonderful food while we still can."

"We'll second that!" the girls all called out, plopping themselves down on a blanket to eat.

As everyone started in on what Annie had packed for them, the men kept an eye on the clouds, as they continued rolling in, while at that same time, the wind began to pick up.

"Great!" the girls complained.

"It'll be all right," both sets of cousin's announced.

CHAPTER TWENTY-SIX

AFTER NEARLY AN HOUR OF laughter and conversation had gone by, everyone heard the first sounds of thunder, as the wind picked up even more.

"Well, we had better be getting back," Alex suggested, while getting to his feet.

"I don't think that's going to be possible," Jarred pointed. "The storm is moving in much too fast. There's no way we're going to make it back before it hits."

"What do you suggest?" the others asked, worriedly.

"Let's try and make it to this old shack Jessi and I found, before it hits!" Craig announced loudly over the wind and thunder. "We will be a lot safer there," he explained, while everyone gathered up their things.

"Craig…" Jessi shouted out over a loud clap of thunder. "We should call the Inn and let Annie know what's going on…!"

"You're right!" he agreed, pulling out his cell phone to make the call. "I'll have her tell Hank to drive the truck out later and check on us."

"Do you think he'll get through on his cell phone with this bad weather?" Beth asked worriedly.

"Yes, I don't see why not," Alex returned, while continuing to look overhead at the growing storm, "I haven't seen any lightning yet!"

After making a quick call, Craig hung up, nodding his head.

"Okay! Let's hit it!" Alex yelled out over another loud clap of thunder, when suddenly, Madison cried out.

"Mom…! The horses! They're scared!"

"Here," Jarred called back, after getting onto his own, to rein him around, "take my hand!" he offered, reaching out to her, while grabbing onto her horse's reins.

Taking his hand, she slid in behind him on his horse, and soon they were ready, while pulling her horse in behind his.

"All right, is everyone ready?" Alex called out over the high winds.

"We're ready!" Craig called back, after see to it everyone else was mounted.

"Good! Let's move it!"

Taking the ride to the old shack as smoothly as they could, it wasn't long before it came into sight.

"Craig," Alex called out, "Jarred and I are going on ahead to check out the place. How about staying behind with the others?"

"Don't worry about us, just hurry!" he shouted back over the wind, while trying to keep his own horse calm.

"Here, you had better stay with your mom while I go with Alex," Jarred suggested.

Climbing over onto her mother's horse, Jarred and Alex took the two other horses with them to make things easier for the others.

After seeing them off, Jodi saw the first sign of lightning streak across the sky. "I sure hope we'll be all right in that shack."

"I'm sure we will," Craig offered, while looking over to his wife, smiling. "I'm sure we will."

Soon they saw the two coming back to get them.

"I can't believe I never noticed it before with all the times I've gone out riding, I never came across it," Alex was saying, when riding up.

"You would think you would have!" Jarred commented, before turning to the others.

"Well how is it looking?" Craig asked, hiding his amusement.

"Well, it certainly looks a lot better than it does out here!" Jarred announced, riding up next to Jodi.

"I hope so!" Beth was now saying, when Alex rode up to her.

"Are you okay?" he asked, seeing her shiver, while the group started up for the shack in a hurry.

"Ye…yeah!"

"Sure you are!" he laughed, radioing ahead.

"What's up?" Jarred's voice came back.

"How is everyone up there?"

"They're getting a little cold! Why?"

"I was just wondering, does that wood burning stove up there work?"

"Sure does!" Craig exclaimed. "Jessi and I've been back here a few times using it!"

"When did you find time to do that?" Alex asked, puzzledly.

"Well we might as well tell them," Craig laughed.

"Yes, I guess so."

"Craig…?" Alex asked again.

"When everyone thought we were still on our Honeymoon!" he laughed, just as they arrived, when the rain started coming down.

Climbing down off their horses in a hurry, the guys went to help the women and girls off theirs.

"Jodi, us guys will put the horses up, can you ladies handle the rest?" Jarred asked.

"I don't know!" she turned to her cousin and laughed. "What do you think, can we do it?" she teased, not seeing her man coming up behind her to snake his free arm around her waist.

"Just you wait until we're alone," he warned, letting out a soft growl, "I'll teach you not to tease the man you love."

With a coy smile, she turned to whisper something in his ear, before he could get away, and then gave him that frustrated look of hers.

Grinning, he spotted his uncle and cousin walking by.

"Oh, Jarred…!" Alex teased. "You're just going to have to maintain yourself, until we get back to the Inn."

Adding a note of understanding, Craig stopped to kiss his wife. "Believe me, she has that same effect on me."

Laughing, Jodi added, "You just might say it runs in our family!"

"And don't you ever forget it, Matthews," Jessi teased.

Sometime after the guys went off to take care of the horses, Beth walked up to Jodi and her cousin in the shack that held a full size bed, and a table with four chairs around it.

Looking sad at the time, Jodi turned back to see her expression. "Beth… what's wrong?" she asked, when Jessi, too, turned, sensing her sadness.

"Seeing the two of you with your men, I just hope I can excite Alex the way you do with them."

Clearing his throat, after coming back inside, Alex walked up behind her.

"Alex…!" she cried, turning to look up at him.

"I heard what you said, and believe me, you have nothing to worry about."

"But…"

"But nothing. We have our own kind of magic, you and I."

"And that's all it really is!" Jodi smiled, as Jarred and his cousin came in, closing the door behind them, before going over to get the old wood stove going to warm it up in there. "Do we have everything?" she asked.

"It sure looks like it," Jarred returned, while going over to pull off his wet boots.

"And just in time, too," Alex added, while going back over to the window to look out. "That storm is really beginning to do its thing out there."

"Boy, you're not kidding!" the girls cried, going over to look out the window, as well.

"Here, this might help since it's starting to get a little dark in here," Jessi offered, while handing Alex a couple of old lanterns.

While going over to sit with Craig, Jessi asked, "How are the horses?"

Tugging off his last boot, Alex replied, "Mmmm, their out… back… under a lean-to!"

"Got it?" she asked, offering to give him a hand, smiling.

Laughing, he shook his head. "Thanks, but… when they get wet, they're… a mother to take off," he breathed a sigh of relief, having finally gotten the last one off. "Which reminds me, are you going to want these back?" he asked, looking to Craig.

"I don't know. They look fine on you now!" he grinned, looking to his uncle. "By the way, did you bring your deck of cards with you?"

"Sure did!"

"Great! Anyone want to play?" he called out, taking the cards from his uncle.

"Count me in!" Jarred called back, when he got up to set his boots down near the stove, while Jodi went over to look out the window.

While there, looking out at the raging storm, she had a concerned look on her face, when she shivered unexpectedly.

"Hey…" Jarred came up to hold her, "are you all right?" he asked, while quietly taking her back into his arms.

"Just thinking!" she exclaimed, when suddenly a streak of lightening hit close by, scaring her even more into his arms, as she turned to hold tightly to him.

"It's okay! You're safe in here."

"Jodi!" Jessi called out, seeing what had happened, when coming over to get her. "Come on over here with the rest of us, while the guys take care of the windows."

Looking up into his eyes, he smiled down at her. "Go on, we'll cover the window with something!"

"All right."

Just back off in the corner of the one room shack, while looking for something to cover the window with, Alex came across something hard and oblong, wrapped in an old rag. "Hey, guys! Take a look at this!" he called out, holding up an object he had found.

"What is it?" Jarred asked, seeing a black book in one hand and a large tattered rag in the other.

"It looks like a ledger!" Craig offered, while going over to check it out.

"And a pretty old one at that!" Alex was saying, when everyone else joined them at the table to see what he had.

"Can you make any of it out?" Beth asked.

"It's dated: August 27th. 1967," Craig explained, when looking over at Jessi.

"Does it say who may have written it?" she asked, when he turned to hand it to her.

"I don't know," he replied, while pulling out a chair for her, "but with this being your property and all, that would make the book yours, as well."

Just as she sat down, she began to read the first page.

August 27th, 1967:

It was a rainy Saturday morning. Just a typical morning so I had thought. My husband, after seven years, had just told me he was dying of Leukemia. We had our

*whole lives ahead of us. A beautiful little girl name Katie
Nicole, who is now five. How am I going to tell her that
her daddy has only a few weeks to live?*

"Wow, what a beginning!" Madison exclaimed, while Jessi went to turn the page.

"Go ahead," Jodi prompted, as her cousin went to clear her throat, before reading on.

At that time, everyone else found a comfortable place to sit. With Craig at his wife's side, Jarred and Jodi sat on the floor nearby with a blanket over them, while Alex and Beth had done the same, when the girls went over to sit on the bed.

August 30th, 1967: she continued,

*Sam was acting strange all day up in the attic, building
something, but what? He wouldn't tell me. Just that it
was for his little angel.*

September 3rd, 1967:

*When Sam came downstairs, we had a lobby full of
guests for Labor Day weekend. His face was flushed and
dripping with sweat. Wanting to know where his little
angel was, I left the front desk to our helper and went to
the kitchen where Katie was last seen, helping the cook
with her favorite cookies. Covered in flour when we
walked in, she had the cutest smile on her sweet little face
when she looked up to see her daddy standing there.*

"Hold up a minute," Jarred asked. "Is this someone who had lived up in your Inn?"

"I don't know! But there is something about the attic that does sound familiar in this story."

"Your right about that. From the first time you took me up there," Alex agreed. "But go on with the story and let's find out as you go." Finding her place, she went on.

Going over to pick her up, the three of us headed up to the attic to see what he had been working on for so long. And to my surprise, it was her very own special playroom that only she could play in.

Later that night, Sam slipped out of the Inn. No one knew where he had gone off to, not even me.

September 4th, 1967:

Oh, my, God...! No...! Sam...! He's gone...! He left me a note, telling me that he couldn't handle the pain anymore. We tried but couldn't find him anywhere.

Stopping all of a sudden, Jessi turned to Craig with tears welling up in her eyes. "I can't read anymore of this, it's so sad!"

"I'll read it," Jodi offered, reaching up to take the book, when she sat up more in Jarred's arms to get more comfortable, while the storm still carried on outside,

September 7th, 1967: she went on,

The local Sheriff, Samuel Mathis came to me with the worst news I could have ever imagined. They had found Sam down at the old shack, at the back of our... prop... erty...

She looked up all of a sudden.

"What...?" Jarred asked, looking over her shoulder.

"They found him here...?" Lora cried.

"According to this ledger, yes," Craig stated, after taking the book to have a look at it for himself.

Taking Craig off to the side, Alex asked, quietly, "If this book is telling the truth, and I'm not disputing it, wouldn't Jessi have picked up on Sam's spirit, like she did with yours?"

"Not necessarily, I called out to her. Sam obviously didn't!" he exclaimed, looking over at his wife, who had been there for him, when he really needed her.

Getting up to pour them all a drink with Jessi's help, Beth

commented, "It's so hard to believe that they're talking about this shack!"

"It sure is," Jodi agreed, when Beth handed her a cup of lemonade.

"Mom..." Cassi spoke up, "I hope it's not haunted here!" she cried, while going over to get closer to her mother.

"I don't think so," Jessi smiled, looking to her husband, "we would know it if it was."

"What is it?" Craig asked, picking up on her thoughts.

"I haven't noticed anything while we've been out here. Have you?"

"No."

"Mom," Kyleigh spoke up, "can we have something to eat, while we're listening to the story?"

"Sure," she replied, handing Jarred her cup to get up. "Are you hungry, too?"

"Yeah, sure, I could use another one of Annie's famous ham sandwiches about now!" he grinned, before taking his turn with the story.

While everyone got comfortable again, Alex stoked the wood stove to build up the fire.

"It looks here like she skipped a few months," he stated, as he began to read:

7:15pm, April 3rd, 1968:

It's Thursday evening now, and it looks like it could rain at anytime. Katie is outside playing with her favorite doll that her father had given her when she was a baby.

Oh, great! The power just gone out, and I can't see to write much in this light. I might as well go and check on her.

7:45pm April 3rd, 1968:

I brought Katie in and handed out candles to the guests. Katie was crying when I had gotten back to our living quarters. She had lost her doll outside when it began to rain. I'll have to go out tomorrow and find it for her, or she will continue to be upset over it.

April 4th, 1968:

It's 2am. Katie has a high temperature now because she had gotten herself wet while playing outside. I had to call the doctor, she was burning up while all along, crying for her doll.

April 4th, 1968:

It's now 9am. I tried real hard to find it for her. It's as if it had vanished. God help me, she has never been separated from her doll before. What am I going to do?

April 7th, 1968:

My baby is fading away quickly now. The doctor said there was nothing left he could do for her, she had picked up pneumonia and won't make it through the night.

Stopping, Jarred got up to put the book down on the table. "I can't go on. It's just too sad for even me to read," he said, shaking his head, while walking over to the door with Jodi, when she had gotten up along with him.

"I'll give it a try," Beth offered, while reaching out to get it. Picking up where he had left off, she sat back in her chair opposite of Alex.

Her last words that had been spoken were; 'Find my doll. I can't sleep without my doll!' I promised her, I would try.

April 8th, 1968:

Our little angel is now with her daddy in Heaven. However, at night I feel that I can still hear her little cries, asking for her doll.

Looking up, Beth commented, "She writes some other things here about her husband's dreams of having cabins built."

Just then, Jodi and Jarred both turned back from the door to look at Craig and Jessi.

"What did you just say?" Jodi asked.

"Her late husband had dreamt of building some cabins!" she explained. "Here! Here's a piece of paper!" she offered, handing it to Craig, when he and Jessi walked over to the table.

Opening it, he looked to Jessi. "I think you should see this." he suggested, handing it her.

Seeing the concerned look on his face, she took the paper. Looking at it for herself, her own hands started to shake.

"Jessi...?" Alex spoke up, when Craig took the paper back to hand to him, while taking Jessi into his arms.

After looking over the plans, Alex turned to Jessi. "It's just a coincidence that your plans looks like theirs," he commented, giving the paper over to Jarred, who laid it out on the table so that he, Craig and Alex could look it over more carefully, with Jessi and Jodi by their side.

"Their identical!" Jarred said, looking surprised.

"But how can that be?" Alex asked, when Beth joined them along with the girls.

"Jessi, did you by any chance have a dream about these cabins?" Beth asked thoughtfully.

"Come to think of it, yes!" she exclaimed, looking over at her cousin, then back to Beth.

"Do you remember what it was about?"

"In the dream, I had been out walking the grounds one foggy morning, back in April. When I came to the edge of the woods out near the garage. The fog had cleared away, and just inside of the woods I saw these cabins!"

"Beth, what does it mean?" Alex asked, while Jarred went looking around the shack for any other clues to their new mystery.

"Well, for starters, she has reopened the Inn!"

"Guys..." Jarred called out from off in the same corner, "take a look at this!"

"What is it?" Craig asked, going over to look at a piece of wood he was holding.

CHAPTER TWENTY-SEVEN

THE SERENI_____

"What do you make of that?" Jarred asked, looking to his cousin.

"It's been burnt!" he stated, while turning it over in his hands.

"Yes, but it looks like it s…" Jodi started, when Jessi let out a cry.

"Oh, my, gosh…! It looks as though it could have read 'The Serenity Inn'!"

"Yes, but that's the name you had thought of for years, before you ever won that money," Jodi explained.

"Yes, and by reopening the Inn," Beth went on, "Sam's dream was meant to be fulfilled!"

"Then why didn't his wife do it?" Jarred asked, pointing at the plans.

"She had to have been in too much grief to think about such things," Beth replied, turning to Jessi. "Your will was stronger, and your spirit was open to this place, like it was for Craig! Only in a different way."

"That explains why I was so drawn here," she replied, turning to look up into Craig's gentle smile.

"God knows our hearts," Beth explained with a sweet smile, as well.

"And yours too, Beth!" Jodi added, when a glow came over Beth's face, just then.

"How do you know these things?" Alex turned to her and asked, while still baffled over what he had just heard.

"While I was at the convent, I was trying to find myself, when an elderly nun came to me one night after Mass. She told me I wasn't going to be there much longer, God had a need for me on the outside. So I did some studying on the matter. It was a year later when I left the convent and joined the police force. You, Alex, were my instructor!"

"Yeah, don't remind me," he roared out laughing. "I didn't want any part of being the instructor at that time, but Jones was sick and the Commander was on a war path that day."

"I remember," Jarred laughed. "Alex said that he didn't want anything to do with babysitting a bunch of brats."

"Well, she was a brat!" he complained, as she smacked his arm.

"So... I have never held a gun before!" she explained, without thinking of what she had just said.

"Beth, Beth, Beth, what did I tell you about calling your weapon a gun?" he yelled, teasingly

"Oh, no...!" Jarred laughed.

"Alex...!" she yelled, laughing back at him, when he took her into his arms.

"Well, Uncle Alex," Craig spoke up, holding Jessi in his own arms, "looks to me like you have found your own angel," he laughed.

"Yeah, I sure have! We just have one small problem, though."

"Yes, it being against regulations," Jarred put in, shaking his head.

Turning to Jarred after Alex and Beth walked away, Jodi whispered sadly, "We can't let that get in their way. We have to come up with something."

"No," Jessi corrected, "*we all* have to come up with something. And I think I have just the solution."

"Well, let's hear it," Jodi insisted.

"You know how much she loves being here at the Inn with Annie. Why don't I just give her a job?"

"Of course, and Annie loves her!" Jodi returned excitedly. "Yes, why not?"

"Beth..." Jessi called out. "Can we have a word with you?"

"A...Alex...!" Beth hesitated.

"Go on," he nodded, before turning away to look out at the continuing storm.

Taking Beth's arm, Jessi and Jodi led her over to the other side of the room, while Craig and Jarred went over to keep Alex occupied.

"What is it?" she asked, looking back at Alex. Her own expression was saddened at the thought that their whole relationship may have been for nothing, once again.

"Beth, it's not over yet," Jodi said cheerfully.

"How can you say that? You heard him!" Her tears began to fall at that time.

Seeing them, Alex started over to her.

"No, Alex," Jarred stepped in to stop him. "Let them handle it from here. They just might have an idea that will turn things around for the two of you."

Watching the women talk, Craig laughed to himself, "Leave it to the two of them, they just might come up with anything!"

Meanwhile, telling Beth of their idea, Jessi asked, "So, what do you think?"

"Leave the force?" she cried quietly, while looking back, once again, at Alex.

"Jarred…!" Alex spoke up again, not liking what he was seeing.

"Hang in there just another minute longer!" he told him, as he and Craig were beginning to wonder themselves.

"Come on, Jess! Just what are you telling her?"

Before she could respond, Beth agreed.

"All right. I'll do it. I'll accept your offer."

"What offer?" Alex asked, walking up.

Turning quite suddenly, she didn't know what to say.

"Uh…" Jodi had to think quickly, "gee… the storm seems to have subsided a little. Why don't the two of you go out and talk amongst yourselves?"

"Beth…?" Alex extended his arm out to her.

After they left the shack, Jodi turned back to the others, "Do you think he'll agree with her decision?"

"He will, if he knows what's good for him!" Jarred and Craig groaned, while looking out at the two walking around in the light rain.

"You know, don't you?" Jessi asked, turning to her husband.

"Yes, he's her first!"

"Mom, what's going on?" Cassi asked.

"Alex and Beth, just need to be alone for awhile to talk things over," she explained, while looking back out at them.

"While they're doing that," Jarred spoke up, looking to Jessi, "I have a question for you!"

"All right, let's see if I can answer it."

"At any given time, did you know this place was here, let alone called 'The Serenity Inn'?"

"No. That, and during the time I have been here, in Langley, the place wasn't an Inn!"

"No, and come to think of it," Jodi added, "I don't even think the Realtor ever told you about the Inn."

"Yes, but something like that has to be disclosed in the sale of any property now," Craig added. "It's the law!"

"If it had," Jessi agreed, "I didn't think to look over the paper work, once everything was signed and turned over to me. After all, we weren't thinking to clearly back then. We were too excited over getting the place to think clearly. And as for the paperwork, it's back in my office in the filing cabinet. Oh, but wait, there was mention by the previous owner about a doll. I just don't recall what, though," she explained, while trying to place the conversation she had with the woman, when she stopped by right after the opening.

"No matter now," Jodi smiled.

"Then again, just maybe it will be mentioned in this ledger!" Lora teased.

Picking up the Ledger, while waiting on the other two, Jessi and Craig thumbed through it for a moment to see what they could find out.

Meanwhile, after what seemed like an eternity, Alex and Beth returned with warm smiles on their faces.

"Folks," Alex spoke up, while smiling down at the woman standing next to him, "we have an announcement to make," he smiled even more.

"Well...?" Jarred and his cousin both cried.

Laughing, he went on, "Beth has agreed to leave the police force, and..." He stopped.

"Well...?" they asked.

"She agreed to be my wife."

"What…?" they cried happily.

Leaving Beth's side to walk up to Jessi, he took her into his arms to thank her. "If it weren't for you and your cousin coming into our lives, I probably would have never realized what I could have lost out on."

"Alex," she replied, thoughtfully, "she's the right one for you, not me. And had had Craig not come back to us, well, you would have missed out on her had we… You know what I mean." She pulled back to gaze caringly into his warm loving eyes.

"You're right. I know that now," he grinned, turning to Craig, who had nearly left them forever. "And I'm really glad you did come back to us." He nearly broke down, when hugging his nephew.

"Me too!" he grinned, patting him on the back. "Me too!"

"Perhaps we can make this a double wedding?" Jarred suggested, looking to Jodi, just when she turned to look off toward the black ledger again.

"Jo…?" Jessi spoke up, thinking she may have seen her apprehension just then.

"Hey, what is it?" Jarred asked, sounding concerned, when he saw the look on her face, as well.

"Jo…?" Jessi called out again. But then she saw where Jodi's attention was going.

"Sweetheart?" he too saw it, just as she went over to pick it up.

Finding her thoughts drifting back to the story, she turned to look back at the others. "Jessi…, the doll…! It was never found!"

"Wait! That's it!"

"What's it?" they asked, puzzledly.

"The previous owner, that's what she came to tell me!" she replied, when looking to her cousin, and then to Craig. "That's if it was the same doll that had turned up, before I bought this place. And come to think of it, it wasn't the previous owner, but the Realtor who told me that the previous owner had found the doll."

"Where?" Most of them asked.

"Out in the old well, behind the Inn! After finding it, she took it in and cleaned it up, then laid it in one of the bedrooms upstairs!"

"Then she still has it!" the girls assumed.

"No. When she went back the next morning, it was gone!"

"What…?" Madison asked, wide-eyed.

"Mom…?" Lora asked, while listening in on the story.

"Jessi?" the others were asking too, wanting to know what had happened to it.

"Seeing Jessi's smile, Jodi, doing the same, while looking down at the ledger, replied, "I think I know!"

"What?" Jarred asked, while the girls went back to sit down.

"The little girl had come for it," Jessi, Jodi, and even Beth, who was getting in on it, announced.

"What____?" Alex asked, unable to believe what he had just heard. "Now you are stretching it a bit."

"No… really…!" Jodi cried, while flipping through the pages. "Just bear with me for a moment, while I look for something that I had seen earlier."

"What is it? What are you looking for?" Beth asked, as she and the others went to look over her shoulders.

"Here…!" she cried out excitedly. "I came across it while we were eating. It says here:

April 7th, 1978:

It's been ten years now since our angel went to be with her Father in Heaven. I can't take it anymore.

"Take what?" Cassi asked, when Jessi shushed her daughter. "Just listen to the story," she replied, as her cousin went on.

Hearing her cries at night from her playroom up in…

Jodi suddenly stopped.

"What?" the girls asked.

"Jo…!" Jessi spoke up, having sensed something sad had happened up there, when she and Alex were there awhile back.

"It says here, up in the far left corner of the attic! Cuz… wasn't that where you said you had a strange feeling coming from that particular spot? In fact, you had even kept the attic locked up because of it."

"Yes, I know!" she exclaimed, looking to Alex. "That's where you were wondering why that particular spot was so different from the rest of the attic."

"You're right! Not to mention, the reaction you had gotten when you picked up on something outside the attic bathroom door!"

"What…?" the girls cried.

"It," she began hesitantly, while looking at Beth. "Maybe I shouldn't say just now."

"Well, girls, let's just say," Alex offered, humorously, "that you couldn't tell by the way we ran out of there, that there was ever anything wrong."

"Oh…?" Beth looked to him, quizzically.

Seeing this, he went to give her a hug, while Jodi continued to read.

> *I had to have the room closed off,* she began. *And as for the Inn, I can't go on anymore. I have to close the Serenity Inn, as well. People are beginning to go elsewhere. As for me, I haven't been doing so well, myself, since the two most important people in my life have gone away.*
>
> *I just want to be with them!*

Turning the page, she went on.

> *September 14th, 1978:*
>
> *Dear God, forgive me for what I'm about to do. I need my loved ones. I have… no will… to go on… any… l o n… g e r_____*

"She must have written this out here, so that she could feel closer to Sam!" Jodi suggested.

"Then hid the ledger!" Madison commented.

"Oh, sure…!" Lora kidded. "And then committed suicide."

"No," Jessi spoke up. "She starved herself up in the attic, near the playroom, so that the last thing she would hear would be the cries of her little girl, for her doll. At least that's the feeling I'm getting from this," she explained, looking to Alex.

"You said that you felt a woman's spirit, though not of this time," he commented.

"Yes. It must have been hers!"

"But then," Kyleigh spoke up, "how…"

"Did the book get out here?" Jarred asked.

"Someone had to have brought it out here. But who?" Jessi asked, taking the book to close. "Craig?"

"When we get time, I would like to go up and open that room up. I want to see what's in there now. If you will help me."

"Sure!"

Just then Jessi's cell phone started to ring, when she went off to answer it.

"Wow, what a story!" the girls were saying.

"Sure was!" the rest agreed, while going around picking up after themselves.

Coming back after taking the call, she announced, "Hank is on his way with the truck."

"How are things up at the Inn?" Alex asked.

"Well, the storm had blown over some tables out front! So it looks like we have some work to do when we get back."

"Well, at least it wasn't too bad," her cousin offered.

"No. Other than, maybe a few shingles and some downed branches, everything else seems to be all right!"

"Jessi," Alex asked, changing the subject, "in all the time I've been here, I don't recall seeing an old well anywhere."

"That's because it had been sealed up!" Craig explained, grinning.

"Where was it?"

Grinning even more, Craig looked down at his wife. "Shall I?"

"Sure!"

"You've been standing on it plenty of times."

"What…?"

"In fact, I would say we all have," she laughed.

Still looking dumbfounded, Alex asked, "All right. Where?"

"The gazebo!" the two laughed whole-heartedly.

"What…?"

Still laughing, Jessi went to put a gentle hand on his shoulder. "Mr. Anderson and his son were called back after having learned that they were the ones who had closed off the attic room. The previous owners had them come back to seal off the well, too, and in place of it, they had built the gazebo!"

"Cool…!" the girls all chimed in.

"This place really takes the cake," Alex shook his head, grinning. "First, the playroom gets sealed off, and now the well? Anymore secrets you care to tell us about?" he laughed.

"No. Not that we know of!" Jessi conceded, while hearing Hank pulling up outside.

Walking in to see if everyone was all right, he shook his head with a hint of amusement. "Boy this place sure has taken a beating over the years," he laughed. "I'm surprised it's still standing after everything it has been through."

"What do you know about this old shack?" Jarred asked, taking a load out to the truck with Alex.

"Quite a bit! My father used to take me fishing out here."

"Then you would know what happened to Sam?" Alex asked.

"Sam?" Hank looked surprised.

"Yeah!"

"Wow, Sam Bishop…? He died of Leukemia!"

"So he didn't take his life?" the others asked, curiously.

"Goodness no…! Where did you hear that?"

"We found this ledger!" Jessi explained, while walking out to the truck with it in her hand.

"Bishop's Ledger?" he cried, seeing the old black book in her hand. "Ms. Jessi, you have got yourself a great piece of history there in that old book. Don't let go of it. People have been wanting to know the truth of what had happen to the woman of the Inn for years!"

"Great!" she laughed. "That's always nice to know!"

Changing the subject, Alex went to ask, "What about the horses? What are we going to do about them?"

"Well, what do you think, girls?" Craig turned and smiled. "Do we ride them back, or go in and get the trailer?"

"Mom?" Madison asked.

"Jarred?" Jodi turned.

"I promised you a ride! So let's ride them back!"

"All right…" the girls all cried.

"Okay," Craig smiled, while turning back to their stable hand, "Well, looks as though we will be seeing you back at the Inn!"

"Good enough! I'll let Annie know you'll be there soon. She'll probably want to have something hot on the table for everyone," he said, waving goodbye, while getting back into the truck to leave.

Meanwhile, having brought the horses around, everyone was on their way back, while laughing at what a day it had been.

"Yeah, what a day!" Alex agreed, looking over at Beth, with a smile on his face. "What a day!"

CHAPTER TWENTY-EIGHT

AFTER GETTING BACK TO THE Inn, Ted signaled Alex off to the side to talk to him privately.

"What's up?" he asked, going into the office.

"I have news for you on Delgado."

"Great! Let's have it."

Going to the door first, Ted looked out in the foyer to make sure their conversation wasn't going to be overheard. Afterwards, he closed the door behind him.

"Come on, out with it. What's going on?" Alex asked, impatiently.

"You may want to sit down first," he suggested, while trying to keep a straight face.

"Am I going to like this?"

"You might!" he grinned.

After a few more minutes, everyone in the Inn heard Alex yelling at the top of his lungs, just as the office door came flying open.

"It's all over!" he cried, coming out, smiling, as the others came running up to see what the commotion was. "It's finally over."

"What are you talking about?" Beth asked, arriving first.

"Vince Delgado is no longer a threat!"

"What...?" Jarred jumped in.

"Come on, I'll tell you all out here," he explained, leading the way out onto the front porch.

Getting there, Jarred turned even more impatient. "Come on, Alex, what's going on?"

"Vince, he was taken care of an hour ago, and being charged for your shooting, and a whole lot more, including your attack, Jodi's!" he gleamed with joy now that he and Jarred's lives were no longer in any danger.

Well at least not until the next case they get into!

"Wait, but I thought Jarred's shooting couldn't be proven without the man's name that called it in!" Jessi asked, having been told, by her cousin, prior to the funeral.

Alex looked to Jarred.

"Jess, we found that man," Alex explained.

"Harry?" Jodi spoke up, recalling the package he had left them. "Oh, but of course!"

"Yes, and with his written testimony Delgado can now be charged," Alex added, and then slowly started to smile at her changing expression, as it gladdened.

"Then it's really..."

"Over? Yes," Alex grinned, looking to his nephew, Jarred. "It's really over."

"Oh, but wait!" Craig asked. "Who caught him?"

"Our men...!" Ted boasted.

"What...?" most of them were asking.

"Once we had gotten the written testimony, Ted had the guys go out and set the whole thing up to look like a typical traffic violation, and snagged him right up. This way," Alex looked to his old friend. "This way there would be no risk of gun fire to hurt anyone one else." Turning back to the others, Alex went on. "And to beat all, I didn't even know it until we got back from our ride."

"But I would have thought that you would have wanted the honors of nabbing him yourself?" Jodi asked.

"You see, Jodi," Ted offered, "with Alex and Jarred's lives being in danger, we had to get them out of the way so we could move in. The horseback riding was the perfect answer, though I didn't know about it, at the time, until Alex came to me the other night to let me know he was going out with you guys."

"And like I said, Ted didn't even tell me that he and others were going to do it," Alex laughed.

"No. We saw the opportunity and went for it after you all had left. That and I knew he would have wanted to be there, but it would have been too risky."

"When Ted pulled me aside to tell me what happened, I was pretty pissed at first, until he convinced me that seeing me would have set Delgado off, and may have started something that innocent people could have gotten hurt over. Ted," Alex turned, proudly, "and Marcose, heck, even Baker, did a great job handling it on their own. Good job, buddy. You, and the guys."

"Yes, and now both you and your nephew are safe and able to get on with their lives, as Jarred is about to do with his own," Ted grinned.

"Thank, God…" Jessi cried. "Now we can really start making plans for both weddings."

"Both weddings?" Ted asked, looking confused.

Alex laughed. "Oh, yes. In all the excitement I never got around to tell you. Beth," he turned to the love of his life, "and I are getting married."

"What…? But…"

"We've taken care of that. She's leaving the department to come and work for Jessi just so we can be together."

"Well, congratulations the both of you!" Ted smiled, shaking Alex's hand, while patting him on the back, and going up to give Beth a hug.

"Yes, well…" Alex looked to Jarred.

"What?" Jodi and Jessi asked, seeing that look.

"There is one more detail we have to clear up first," Alex grinned.

"Alex…" Jessi asked. "What else is there?"

Holding up a hand, he pulled out his radio to call Marcose.

"Here," he replied.

"Are you out at the stables now?"

"Yes. What's the word?"

"Bring up our new groundskeeper, please!"

"We're on our way!"

"Alex… what's going on…?" Jessi asked again, while she and her cousin were both looking puzzled.

"I think it's time you met a new member of your staff," he grinned, apologetically.

"Jarred...?" Jodi turned, seeing the look on his face, now, as well. "You know something, don't you?"

"Yes, and I'm sorry I couldn't have said anything about it before, but..."

His comment was soon cut short, when Marcose, Hank and a man with reddish-brown hair and glasses showed up.

Looking at him, when they walked up onto the porch, neither Jessi nor Jodi recalled seeing him before.

"Ms. Jessi..." Alex put an arm around the new guy, "this is your new groundskeeper, Steve Hankins. Steve, your boss, Ms. Jessi, and her cousin, Jodi."

"Ma'am!" he exchanged hands with the both of them, and nodded his head politely.

The look on Jessi's face brightened into a smile at the familiararity in his voice. Then turning to Alex, she cried, smacking his arm, "You... big... jerk...!"

"Ouch...! Jessi...!" he began laughing, when the stinging sensation started to set in.

"Don't you even..." she yelled, controlling her humor at seeing Harry alive and well.

"Jessi...! But damn...!" he groaned again, thinking that he had seen the last of her temper.

Craig, however, grinned, knowing what his wife was up to, while seeing Harry standing there looking nervous.

"Steve is it?" she turned.

The man smiled.

"What?" Jodi asked, puzzledly.

"Jo," Jarred spoke up again, "this is what I couldn't tell you."

"You see, Jodi," Alex went on, "the day the package was dropped off, was when I saw Harry out front here. He looked as though his life was in danger, so once he had explained what he had done, we had to make it look like he had met up with a unfortunate accident, to get Delgado off his case."

"So, you're Harry?" she asked.

"Not anymore!" Harry smiled, more at ease now. "The name is Steve!"

Looking to Jessi, Alex asked, "Can he stay on for awhile? He's really good at his job, and well liked by the others."

"Besides," Hank spoke up, "he seems to have really shown an interest in turning over a new leaf. And I like him!"

"Harry," Jessi turned, "no more troubles? You'll keep your nose clean from here on in?"

"Oh, yes… Ma'am! Count on it."

"Good," she smiled, when going over to give him a hug. "I really hope so."

"And Harry," Alex added in, "we're all going to be keeping an eye on you. So don't make me regret giving you, yet, another chance. This is it for you. No more!"

"Yes, sir, you can count on me. No more mistakes," he promised.

After Hank and Harry left, the others all sat down to relax to a meal Annie had prepared. And while looking over to the love of his life, Jarred leaned over to whisper something in her ear.

"Sure!" she smiled warmly at his suggestion.

"Alex, after dinner Jodi and I are going to slip off for the night."

"Where you going?"

"Back to the house. We haven't had much time to be alone, since all this mess, and now with the wedding and all."

"Go for it," he smiled.

"Jessi?" Jodi turned, looking to her cousin.

"Don't worry about the girls, they'll be fine here with us," she offered, while leaning over to give her a well deserved hug.

"Thanks, cuz!" she smiled.

"Hey, that reminds me!" she went on. "Just when are the two of you getting married anyway?"

"We'll let you know when we get back in the morning," Jarred smiled. "And what about the two of you?" he turned to his uncle.

"We haven't talked much about it."

"If Jodi wouldn't mind, though," Beth spoke up questioningly, "it really would be fun…"

"To double up?" she asked, looking to Jarred, who then smiled his approval.

Loving his uncle the way he did, he laughed, "Sure. We would like that."

"Great!" both, Jessi and Beth laughed.

"Hold on, though," Craig spoke up. "If the four of you are doing that, who's going to be the Best Man then?"

Jarred turned back to look at him, and grinned, "Well, you of course!"

After dinner, the two cousins went down to Jessi's quarters to pack Jodi's suitcase for her stay at Jarred's, while the guys stayed upstairs.

"What are you two going to do while you're there?" Jessi asked.

"Catch up on all the time we had missed!" she smiled timidly.

"Oh...?"

"Jess...!" Jodi flushed, while turning to grab a fresh pair of jeans.

"Okay, but hey, I know what I can do, while you're gone."

"What would that be?" she asked, closing up her suitcase.

"Get started on the wedding plans! Craig thought it would be nice to have the ceremony out back in the gazebo."

"Oh, Jess, that would be great!"

"Then it's settled."

"Good. And call Karen to help out with it. I'll let you know when, when we get back."

"All right."

"Oh, and Jess! Thank you for being my Matron of Honor."

"I'm only too glad to be, after all we have been through over the years," she smiled, giving her a hug.

Gathering up her things to up to the foyer, Jarred met her halfway. "Ready? Alex had Marcose bring my truck up so we wouldn't have to figure out where to put your things for the ride there."

"Good!"

Leaving for his place, they were glad to finally be able to be alone.

Meanwhile, walking up to join his wife at the front door, Craig smiled, "Hey."

"Hmmm...?" she replied, while looking out at the evening sky.

"They'll be all right now that everything is over."

"Mmmm... just like us...?" she asked, feeling his arms cycling around her.

"Just like us. And now Alex, too!" he laughed, as she turned in his arms.

"And we are happy!" she returned in her special way, while they continued to hold each other.

Meanwhile, on the road back to his place, Jarred turned to see her looking off at all the trees they were passing by. "What are you thinking?"

"All the work in getting this wedding ready, which," she turned to study his expression, "you haven't exactly told me when you were wanting to get married!"

"Soon!" He smiled over at her. *'Real soon.'*

"Soon…? That's all you're going to tell me…! Uh, Jarred…!"

"You'll just have to wait!" he grinned.

"And for how long…?"

Not saying a word, he turned into his driveway, when they arrived.

With that look of mischief on his face, she knew if she wanted to get the information out of him, she was going to have to play dirty. And dirty she would.

After carrying her things in for her, he went over to start a fire to warm things up a little, since it had gotten somewhat chilly out.

"Hey, while you're doing that, I'll just be in getting changed if that's okay with you?"

"Sure!" he smiled up at her.

Smiling back, she went off into the bathroom with her suitcase to pull out a t-shirt that would surely drive him out of his mind, enough to tell her what she wanted to know.

Not realizing how long she had been there, Jarred began to get worried. "Jo…" he called in, from outside the door, "is everything all right?"

"Uh… yeah!" she called back, while stifling a snicker. "Everything is just fine! Be right out!" she laughed quietly, while listening for him to walk away.

"All right! Hey," he called back, just as he was about to turn away, "how about some hot chocolate while relaxing by the fire?"

"Yeah, sure…!"

Not sure what to make of it, he shook his head and smiled.

Hearing him walk away, she breathed a sigh of relief, while hurrying out of her clothes and into the white cottony t-shirt that barely covered her hips, while showing off just enough of the black lacy panties she had brought with her. "Well now," she gleamed, "no doubt, this will do it! He will surely tell me now when we are going to get married, hmmm!" Giving herself one last look in the mirror, she was ready. "Okay, girl, it's show time!" she smiled, on her way back out to the living room, to find him standing at the fireplace, holding two mugs of hot chocolate.

Turning back as she walked in, he nearly dropped the mugs, when seeing what she had on. "Damn..." he groaned, admiring the swells of her breasts as they pressed out against the material of her t-shirt.

"What is it, sweetheart? You look as though you saw a ghost!"

"No. No. Just a woman who looks as though she's about to put me into an early grave, is all."

"Oh...?" she smiled sweetly, while taking her mug.

"You know," he went on, while trying to keep his mind off her beautiful body, "tomorrow I could fix us breakfast on the open fire again, like it was the first time you were here!"

"That sounds wonderful! I hope you will still do that after we're married!"

"Sure, if you'd like!"

"Mmmm... I would like," she continued to tease, while going on to set her mug down on the mantle next to him.

"What are you up to?" he asked, watching her moves closely.

"Who? Me? Why, nothing!"

"Uh huh..." he laughed, seeing what she was doing. "You know," he began, while setting his own mug down next to hers, "two can play this game."

"Oh?" she smiled, as he went to pull off his shirt, to give it a toss onto the sofa. "Mmmm..." she grinned, gazing at his beautiful upper body. *'So it's gloves off, is it?'* she smiled. *'All right!'* Moaning, she turned to walk a few feet away, while lifting her hands up to run her fingers in through her hair. While doing that, she turned back to show what happens when her top slid up too.

'Oh, you are so... mean...' he thought, swallowing hard at the lump just at the back of his throat, when catching sight of her black lacy panties. Seeing the dark ringlets just beneath the surface, he knew he was about to lose control. "Oh, lady, you're not playing fair," he groaned, "but let's just see how long you can control yourself after I get rid of these!" he grinned, while slipping out of his jeans, only to reveal a pair of black bikini briefs, accenting his long, handsome, legs, and the swell that was beginning to make itself known just beneath the surface.

"No. Now that is mean...!" she laughed, backing out toward the entryway, where the stairs leading up to his room were located. "Oh, Jarred…!" she called back seductively, while going up a few steps at a time.

"Now what?" he asked himself quietly, while walking out into the entryway.

Looking up, he smiled, seeing her standing there.

"You know…," she smiled sweetly, while going on to slowly remove her t-shirt, "it's getting awfully warm in here. So I guess I won't be needing this any longer," she teased, while tossing the shirt at him.

"Oh, nuh huh…! You wouldn't dare!" he groaned, watching her take each step with the slightest of bounce to each one, while causing his mouth to water at how her movement would cause her voluptuous breast to bounce, as well. "Damn you…!" he groaned, taking each step two at a time, until he had caught up to her outside his room.

"Ahhh…" she cried, laughing, once he had her turned around, and pinned against the wall.

"This is totally unfair, you know that?" he growled, hungeringly, while picking her up.

"Uh huh…" she smiled, while bringing her arms up around his neck, right along with wrapping her legs around his narrow hips.

Taking her lips to his, he claimed them with so much passion, until neither one of them could bear the tension any longer. At that point, carrying her off into his room, he dropped her onto his bed, before slipping her panties off her, and then his own.

"Oh, Jo…" he groaned, taking her right then and there.

"Oh, yes…" she moaned, while he placing her hands up over her head to clench down on them tightly, when plunging forth their desire.

From that point on, they loved and gave love to each other for most of the night.

"You are so… hot. You know that?" he asked.

"Mmmm… and you too!" she breathed, running her tongue lightly over his sweat-drenched neck, before going on to suckle at the salty taste of it.

Feeling his hands running over her breasts, she cried in agony at its luster.

"Damn," he swore, aching to have them back in his mouth, yet again.

Chapter Twenty-Nine

AFTER ANOTHER HOUR OF REPEATED passion, they stopped long enough to rest up in each other's arms, before feeling the need to grab a shower.

"I feel like the luckiest man in the world right about now."

"Oh…? Then I guess you won't mind telling me just when we're getting married?"

"How about in three weeks. Will that give you ladies enough time to pull it all together?"

"Three weeks…!" she cried.

Laughing, he hugged her lovingly. "Mom said she and Aunt Sue would only be too happy to help."

"Good! Because we're going to need it and then some!" she laughed.

"You'll do fine," he laughed, pulling her up with him.

Going in to get their shower, it wasn't long before they were almost finished that he wanted to go downstairs to get their breakfast started, when hearing the birds chirping away outside.

"So early!" she groaned, enjoying the water. "I can't believe it's almost morning already."

"Well, 4:17 at least," he stated, looking at his watch, "and I'm starving. How about you?"

"Yeah, well, sure! But what about getting some sleep?"

"Sure, right after I fix us up some breakfast," he smiled down at her, when getting out to towel off. "Do you want me to bring your things up to you?"

"You had better in case we get company!"

"At this time of the morning! Who would that be?"

"Uh…, your uncle, maybe?"

"Alex? I would think he would be cuddled up with Beth, and if not sleeping, planning their honeymoon or something," he smiled, while going on to pull on his jeans.

"Honeymoon…? And just where are you planning to take me?"

"Can't tell you everything," he laughed, running out of the bathroom. "I'll be right back with your things, though!" he called back.

"All right, I shouldn't be too much longer after that."

"Take your time!" he called back.

Leaving her to think things through, Jarred just smiled even more at keeping her in the dark as to where they were going. But then again he wasn't all that clear either.

Meanwhile, after getting her things taken up to her, he went back down to get breakfast going, while she was getting finished in the bathroom.

"Mmmm…" she cooed, walking down, in a fresh pair of cotton pants, white sox, and a white t-shirt to sleep in, "something smells good!"

"Good! Because I sure hope you're hungry."

"Actually, I'm starving, now, thanks to you!"

"Oh? Then what do think about going for a walk after we eat?"

"Are you serious?"

"Yes!"

"Mmmm…Okay, just let me slip on a pair of tennis shoes, before we go."

Getting the plates and silverware out, she set up a place on his coffee table, while he went on cooking over the open fire.

After enjoying another one of his fireplace breakfasts', the two put on their shoes and went for an early morning walk, before getting some sleep.

"What do you think about it out here?" he asked, not knowing they were being watched, from the road.

Meanwhile, sitting amongst some trees, the dark sedan, with tented windows, sat quietly, before the rear window went down to expose the man inside. "So, Delgado missed you again, did he?" he laughed, while puffing on his expensive cigar. "Hmmm... just maybe I will have to keep you and your uncle around awhile longer? Until next time, Storm," Santose grinned, having liked something about Alex and is people. With that the window went up, with him repeating, "Until next time."

"Mr. Santose?" the driver spoke up, looking in the mirror.

"Yes. Drive on," he ordered with a superior wave of his hand. "We're done here, for now."

Not having heard anything, as the car went on down the road, their walk came to an end, when Jodi started yawning.

"Mmmm... this time together has been really nice," she murmured, against his shoulder, while walking back into the house.

"Mmmm... sure has," he agreed, while locking up.

Once upstairs, the two slipped off to sleep no sooner than their heads had hit the pillows.

By the time they had gotten up and ready to go, the others were already setting up at the Inn for another day.

"Jodi should be here at any moment," Jessi was saying, while walking in to greet her two friends "which at this moment I am waiting on a call from Karen."

"Good," Ashley put in, while getting their coffee poured. "Now, what do we have going with the gazebo?"

"Craig, Alex and Hank are working on that."

"What?" Renee cried. "Guys aren't any good on flowers and streamers!"

"No. They're making sure that the structure will be sound."

"Speaking of sound, what about it?" Ashley asked, taking her seat at the table. "Where is it going to go?"

"They're handling that too. And where, I haven't a clue. They chased me off, and said they will take care of it."

"Mom...?" Lora interrupted, "Karen's on the phone! She wants to know what the emergency is."

"You didn't tell her, did you?" she asked, getting to her feet to take the call.

"No. I knew you would want to tell her, yourself."

"Good. When Jo gets here, make sure to send her straight into the Boutique, okay?"

"Yeah. Sure."

"Wow," Ashley commented, "so much to do, but still no idea when."

"Yes," Renee groaned.

Just then, they heard voices out in the foyer, before seeing Jodi walk in.

"Well, here she is…!" Ashley cried, getting up to greet her.

"Jessi? Where is she?" Jodi asked.

"She's on the phone with your friend, Karen," Renee offered, while handing her a cup of coffee. "Come, take a seat. We're all dying to know just when this wedding is taking place!"

"Well," she began, seeing her cousin and Beth come walking in to join them.

"Hey, Cuz!" Jessi smiled. "I saw Jarred, and I sent him on out to talk to Alex."

"Yes, well he did say that he and Craig had things to do out back with Alex."

"Yes, now, when is all this going to take place?"

"Three weeks," she announced happily.

"What…?" two other women cried, walking in on their conversation.

Turning to look up, Jessi smiled at seeing Craig's mother. "Sue…, you're here!"

"Well, hearing my little brother was about to be married, I thought I should get Donna and get right over here to see what we could do to help!"

"Great! We could sure use the extra hands. Oh, and by the way," she turned to her cousin, "this is my cousin, Jodi, Jarred's fiancée. And Jodi," she smiled, "this is Sue, Craig's mom and Alex's sister."

"Hi!" Jodi smiled, as she was just about to get up.

"No. Sit!" Sue cried, while putting out a hand. "We have a lot of work to do, thanks to my nephew!"

"Yes, we do," she laughed, nervously. "I just wish my friend Karen would get here."

"Oh," Jessi announced, "she has a few phone calls to make. Something to do with the flowers."

"Do you already have them picked out?" Donna asked.

"Yes. I saw some in a catalogue Beth was looking at the other day, while looking for my wedding dress."

"Great! Now let's check into picking out a cake and invitations," Sue went on, while taking a seat and pulling out a few books she had brought with her.

Seeing one they liked, she went to make the call, when Karen walked in, looking glum.

"Karen," Jodi spoke up, when Lora walked in, with another chair for her friend, "what's wrong?"

"The flowers!" she cried. "I had called every shop I know, but only two of them had what you wanted. It's still not enough!"

Ending her phone call, Sue caught the tail end of their conversation. "What about the flowers?"

"We can't get in enough!" Jodi cried, disappointedly.

"I know someone who might have what you're wanting," she smiled, while turning to her phone again.

"Great!" they all cried happily, while waiting on word back from her.

"This is going to be one wedding to remember," Ashley laughed.

"No kidding!" Jessi agreed, shaking her head. "My cousin and Jarred, and now Alex and Beth! Who would have figured?"

"Yeah," Beth returned quietly.

"Beth...?" Jessi spoke up, hearing something in her voice.

"I..." she began timidly.

"Beth, what is it, dear?" Donna too asked. "Don't be shy! This is no time to be sad!"

"I... I don't have anyone to walk me down the aisle!" she explained, breaking down in tears.

"Oh... yes you do," Jessi returned, getting up to go and call the perfect man for the job.

Meanwhile, after a few more calls, Sue hung up and smiled. "Done."

"Really?" Jodi cried.

"Yep! Now let's go over the list of guests, shall we?"

"That'll be fun!" everyone laughed, while Jodi pulled out her note pad and pen.

"Beth…" Jessi called out from the doorway. "I have someone here who wants to talk to you."

"Oh? Who?" she asked, while getting up slowly to see.

Just as she did, Hank rounded the corner, smiling at her. "I hear you need a hand down the aisle!"

"You?"

"Yep! I had always thought fondly of you and the others. And I would be mighty proud to walk you down the aisle."

"Oh, my, gosh!" she cried, going up to give him a daughterly hug.

"Well, that takes care of that!" both Jessi and Jodi smiled at one another.

After hours of going over the guest lists, Annie walked in to announce dinner was served.

"Perfect timing!" Jessi returned, getting up. "Shall we go into the dining room now?"

"Sure!" everyone was in an agreement.

And with the men in getting cleaned up, the ladies walked into the dining room to take their plates over to the serving table.

"How are the plans going for the gazebo?" Sue asked.

"I'm not all that sure!" Jessi explained. "Craig won't tell me about it, and says it's a secret that he, Alex and Jarred won't share with us until it's time!"

"Yep!" Craig greeted, while walking in with the others to grab their plates of food, before joining the women at the table.

"Where are the girls?" Jodi asked.

"They're on their way," Jarred offered.

"They were just finishing up on a video game of Super Mario Brothers," Craig laughed.

"Great!" Jessi teased. "We won't have to worry about making sure they have a seat at the wedding. They'll be downstairs playing the whole time."

CHAPTER THIRTY

As for the rest of that evening, everyone talked up a storm, before it was time to call it a night, since Annie was having a special breakfast out on the back lawn, before everything got started.

Before they knew it, the day of the wedding was upon them, with both sets of brides and grooms vastly getting themselves ready. Or so Jessi thought, when coming upstairs from her quarters, looking for Jodi. "Where is she...?"

"Who?" Craig asked.

"That cousin of mine. She wasn't downstairs when I came out of the bathroom."

"Oh, she and Jarred went out earlier for a walk!" he returned, while coming downstairs from his uncle's room, shaking his head.

"Great..." she grumbled, heading for the family room, to look out over the backyard, where the ceremony was to take place, "we have so much, yet, that has to be done before they are ready to walk down the aisle."

"Hey, it'll all work out, you'll see! But for now, I am needed out at the gazebo," he smiled, while leaning down to give her a kiss, before excusing himself to go and talk to Hank, when Annie walked in just then to announce breakfast would be ready soon.

"Thanks, Annie," she replied, turning away from the patio doors to give her, her full attention.

"You look sad, dear! What's wrong?"

"Just thinking about my cousin walking down the aisle!" she turned, nodding sadly, out toward the gazebo.

"Oh, but you ought to see her."

"I know, she's beautiful."

"Yes, and how about that groom of hers? Isn't he looking fine for one who is about to be joined with his new bride?"

"Just as handsome as his cousin!" she smiled, looking out where Craig was standing, looking so tall next to Hank.

"Well, if you'll excuse me, I'll just be getting things set up now."

"All right."

Just as she left to go back into the kitchen, Craig came running up to the patio doors to ask what time his mom said they would be there.

"Soon. I told them about breakfast."

"What about Jodi's family?"

"They'll be here soon," she sighed. "It'll be great to have them all here again," she was saying, when looking out to see Jarred and Jodi walking up from the stable.

"Are you waiting on us?" Jarred teased, seeing the expression on her face, when the two walked up onto the patio.

"Yes…! So not to keep anyone waiting, why don't the two of you go and get cleaned up. The others should be here soon."

"Well, I'll see ya soon for breakfast?" Jodi asked, turning to her groom, while Jessi headed into the kitchen to see what she can do to help.

"Yep! Just as soon as I see about my uncle," he smiled down at her.

"Good. I had better be getting downstairs then," she gleamed, leaving the two of them to see about their uncle.

Looking over at his cousin, he asked, "Where's Alex?"

"He's up getting dressed, now," he laughed. "Heck, let's go see how's he's doing, since the last time I was up there."

"What so funny?" Jarred asked, on their way.

"Jessi. She won't let him see Beth, before the wedding, with the exception of breakfast of course. And man, you ought to count your lucky stars that you and Jodi's sisters got her out of here when you did," he continued laughing, when they reached his room.

"Hey there, Uncle!" Jarred laughed, when walking in to see his expression. "I heard you had to do without your lady!"

"Not for long!" he growled, seeing Jarred's enthusiasm. "How was your day?" he asked, grinning up at him from the bed, while putting on his boots.

"It was nice! I've got to know her sisters more! The things they told me about their growing up days," he laughed. "Interesting."

"Well, I'm glad to see one of us had a nice time!" he continued to grin, while getting up to head for the door.

Meanwhile, having read about the upcoming wedding of the well known Detective and his nephew, a man stopped off to deliver a few gifts for the two couples, while his boss remained out in the car that had been sitting outside Jarred's place a few weeks ago.

"Can I help you?" Ted asked the tall, bulky man, in his thirties, with sandy blond hair, thinking it was one of the brides' family or friends, coming by with a gift.

"These are for the two couples getting married today. Compliments of my boss," his voice was deep and mysterious, as he held his gaze on Ted, before turning to leave, when hearing Alex and the others coming out of his room, just then.

Caught off guard by the visitor, when setting the two fairly large gifts aside, Ted tried getting Alex's attention, while keeping an eye on where the stranger was going in such a hurry.

Upon reaching the foyer, the three were not only met up by Ted, but Marcose, too, when he came up from the side of the Inn, just in time to see the stranger making a hasty move for the car out in the parking lot.

"Alex…" Ted spoke up quickly, taking Alex's arm to pull him to the door, where he could see the dark sedan with its tented windows, about to pull out.

"What's going on?" he asked.

"We just had company," he pointed.

Seeing the car for himself, he asked, "Who was that?"

"At first I thought it was one of their family or friends dropping off a couple of gifts. But then just as soon as he heard you guys coming out of your room, he headed out before I could ask who they were from. He did, however, say they were from his 'boss'?" He turned to study Alex's expression. "His boss, Alex. And judging by his build, I would say…"

"Santose?"

"Yeah."

"Marcose, what about you? Were you here when he came in?"

"No," he returned, looking back at the two large gift boxes sitting on the front desk. "I was just coming around the corner, when I saw the guy hurry off to get back into the car, before taking off."

"For now let's just see what we have here!" Alex suggested, while walking over to the desk with the others, to check out the two nicely wrapped boxes.

"You don't think he would have sent a bomb, do you?" Jarred asked quietly.

"God, that would sure be the end of us all, wouldn't it?" Alex returned, grimly. "Never mind that! We have to get them in to be checked out, provided we have time to. Ted, call the bomb experts out here right away and have them run them through."

"Hold on a minute, Alex," Marcose spoke up, recalling a few of their buddies from the station. "Why not one of the K-9's our buddies brought with them? Like Zeus? He's one of the best. Not to mention, it would keep things quiet, until we know what we are up against!"

"Good. Go get him. For now, we will just put these out away from the Inn, until we know what we have here."

Doing that, he and Ted carried them out to where there were no cars parked nearby to be harmed, while Marcose hurried off to get the officer and his K-9.

Soon they had their answer.

"Thank, God," they were saying, when bringing them back inside.

"Yes, but still I have to wonder what his motive was for doing that. Was it some sick way of telling me it isn't over yet?" Alex growled, following them in.

Setting the gifts down on the reservation desk, Ted spotted the envelope that came with them. "Alex." He turned back to give it to him.

"What?" the others asked, curiously, while standing around to see what it was about.

Not wasting any time, he ripped open the envelope to read the card inside.

To My Worthy Adversary on yours and your nephew's wedding day, Just to congratulate you on a very prestigious occasion. And to let you know that you and your family will not be bothered again by any of my people. Please, consider this a gift, won't you?

Martin Santose

"Alex?" Jarred and Craig both spoke up, seeing his expression, when looking up from the card.

Handing them the card. "He's calling a truce! He's saying his people won't be bothering us or our family again!"

Reading it for themselves, Jarred commented, looking up from it, "He also refers to you as his Worthy Adversary."

"Yes, so I've read. But enough of this," he broke off, wanting to get back to his fiancée and the others. "Where is she?" he turned to Craig.

"Out back with the others, I would imagine. Oh, and I'm to tell you that Jessi and Annie have been working pretty hard on this breakfast ever since early this morning."

"So Beth was telling me, before Jessi separated us last night," he was saying, while they headed back to join the others, while leaving a man on the front door just to be on the safe side.

Catching the tail end of Beth's compliment to Jessi and Annie for how things looked, she was gladdened to feel Alex's arms come around her from behind, when giving her a squeeze. "Alex…!"

"Hello beautiful, did you miss me?"

"Yes. And you? How was your night?" she asked, turning to see that disgruntled look of his. "Not so good, huh?" she laughed, having heard all about it from the others.

"Yeah… laugh it up! You'll soon see how much, when I get you on our honeymoon!"

"Yes, well," Rose cleared her throat, hearing more than she wanted to, while the guys went to get their plate of food, "the Gazebo looks really nice too."

"We just want this day to be as special as it was for Craig and I," Jessi explained, with great restraint on her emotions, when turning to see Alex's guys mingling around with their own plates filled with food. *'Lord, so much has happened,'* she cried, quietly. *'And now it's finally over! We can all truly rest and get on with our lives. Though, I'm really going to miss seeing them here. Except for you, Alex, the pain in my backside. With Beth and Craig here, we will see you often,'* she smiled, just as he turned to look in her direction, while Jodi was going on about something.

"Jessi…?" Jodi asked, shaking her cousin's arm, while the guys were getting ready to return with their food.

"Yes?"

"I was saying, considering what you had gone through to be with Craig, no one could top that."

"Yes, you're right! I would have been lost without him!"

Just then, she felt Craig's thoughts reaching out to her, when closing the distance with his plate in hand. *"Hey! Are you all right?"* he asked, as she turned to see that all familiar smile of his.

"I am now…!" she cried telepathically, looking up at him, before going on to hug him. "I am… now…!"

After their special breakfast, it was time to get ready for the big moment.

Sitting in Jessi's living room, in front of a mirror, Beth cried, fumbling with her hair, "What am I going to do with this?"

"Here, let me help," came Ashley, walking in to lend a hand.

Meanwhile, pinning up her own hair in a loose bun, while leaving wisps of it hanging down at the nape of her neck, Jodi turned to see how they were doing. "Ashley, why not brush the sides back to show off how the dress bares her shoulders?"

"That's a great idea."

Doing so, soon Beth was ready, when Ashley stood back to give her room to get up. With her hair done, and makeup on, she looked absolutely radiant, as she turned in a circle to admire the gown picked out for her.

"Hey, girls… how are we doing down here?" Craig's mother asked, along with Rose, a family friend, when coming down to join them.

"We are just about ready here! How are the guys doing?" Jessi asked, while she and her cousins helped Jodi into her antique, white, wedding dress, with its high neckline, and trim fitted waist to show off her figure.

Turning at the sight of Jodi in her gown, Sue smiled warmly, before going on about the two grooms, upstairs, in the family room. "They're both a total basket case," she laughed. "Alex can't tie his tie, and Jarred can't find his cuff links."

Hearing that, they all laughed, just as there came a knock at the patio doors.

Turning, they saw Annie walking in to let Jodi know her father was on his way in to see how she was doing, then went over to help Beth on with her veil.

Seeing him walk in, she went up to give him a warm hug. "Hi, Dad…!" she cried, smiling like a little girl.

"Are you excited about today?" he asked, going over with her to have a seat on the sofa.

"Oh, yes, I am…!"

"I take it, then, this man is the one you are truly happy with?"

"Yes, he is. He loves the girls and I, and we love him!"

"Good! He seems like a very likable person!"

"Oh, he is, Dad! He… is!"

"Ladies…" Annie turned to announce. "It's nearly time now. Oh, and Jodi, before you go out, your mother would like to see you first."

"Now?"

"Yes. She's waiting on you up in the office. But you must hurry now. We can't keep the men waiting."

"All right," she replied, turning back to her father.

"Go! I'll be waiting for you here."

"All right!"

Leaving her father to go upstairs to her cousin's office, she had to sneak past the dining room doorway so not to be seen by the men, who were still waiting in the family room with the door open.

Meanwhile, just inside, she could hear Jarred's voice talking to Baker and Alex. "I have to admit," he was saying, "no doubt I'm nervous. I've waited for this day for as long as I can remember."

"You…?" Craig's voice then chimed in heartedly. "What about Alex?"

"First time?" Baker asked, grinning ear to ear.

"Yes, and she's worth the wait."

"Just like, Jodi!" Jarred smiled.

"Is it true?" Baker asked. "You waited all these years to be with her?"

"Had of I known that she had gotten a divorce all those years ago, I would have done gone after her and not waited so long."

'*Oh… Jarred, had I only known just how you felt about me…*' she cried, quietly, while leaning her head back against the doorframe, next to Annie.

"He's loved you for a long time!" she smiled, taking her hand.

"Yes, and now it's time to put the past behind us," she continued to cry, while going on into the office. "Mom…!" she called out, going over to give the matronly woman in her late sixties a hug, while Annie stood watch in the foyer.

"Hi, sweetie! I guess you have already talked with your father, and now it's my turn." Virginia replied, while going over to sit on the sofa with her daughter.

"Yes. So, what do you think of him?" she asked, holding her mother's hand.

"He's one fine gentleman, like his uncle and cousin. He had a lot to say however to your father and I. One of which is that he is madly in love with you."

"Oh, Mom, I love him, too. He is so much like…"

"Stephen, when he was alive?" she finished, when Jodi got up to go to the window.

Looking out, she went on sadly, "Mom… I miss him so… much!"

"I know you do. I wish your father and I would have handled things a little differently back then, but we didn't, and now…" She stopped sadly.

"How were you to know he was going to get killed?" she asked, turning back to face her.

"We didn't. What happened to him was…" She looked away.

"Yes, it was…" She cried, looking back out the window.

"You know that he would have wanted for you to go on with your life. Even if that meant marrying this Jarred, person."

"Yes, I know that now," she replied, when suddenly a feeling of joy washed over her, just as she looked up toward the Heavens. '*And I will always love you, too, Stephen,*' she thought to herself. '*I will always love you, too,*' she repeated, as her mother walked up behind her.

"Are you all right?" she asked, putting an arm around her daughter's shoulder.

"I'm fine!"

Just then, there came a knock at the door.

"Jodi!" Annie called out, sticking her head in. "It's time, dear! Your fiancé is waiting for you out near the gazebo."

"All right, Annie." Turning once again to her mother, she smiled brightly. "Well, it's time, and Jarred is waiting!"

"Yes, he sure is. Shall we?" she asked, turning to head for the door.

"Yes, just give me a moment. I'll be right out."

"All right."

Closing the door behind her, Jodi turned back to the window and closed her eyes to say a silent prayer, before heading downstairs to join her future husband. "Thank you, God, and you too, Stephen, for everything. For being there in my dream to rescue me and for letting me know that Jarred was the right one, motorcycle and all," she laughed, silently, ending her prayer.

Just before leaving the office, a feeling of warmth reached out and touched her shoulder from behind. Turning, she had thought that Jarred came in unexpectedly. Though to her surprise, she cried out covering her mouth.

"Hello, sweetness," he smiled brilliantly at her. "I just wanted to personally wish you well, before you walk down the aisle."

"I…I can't believe it. Is it really you?" she asked, looking fondly into his beautiful brown eyes. "S…Stephen?"

"Yes, and for what short time we have, I just wanted you to know that the dream was just my way of letting you know that I will always be nearby, but so will Jarred. Go to him, Jo. Love him with all your heart."

"I will. As I had…" She stopped.

"As you would have with me, if only you had known what you were feeling at the time…"

"Was love?" she finished, tearfully.

"Don't keep punishing yourself. Let it go, Jo. He's waiting for you, now. So, go."

Smiling back, she knew what he was telling her, as she wanted to hold him, but not sure it was possible to do in his state of being. But then chose to try anyway, knowing she would only have that one chance to find out. And find out she did, when she felt him, as her arms went around his shoulders. "I love you!" she cried.

"And I, you," he whispered softly in her hair, as he slowly began to fade away. *"And I, you…"*

Wiping her tears away, she hurried out of the office to join the others.

Once she had gotten back to Jessi's quarters, Beth was waiting along with the rest of the wedding party. Grabbing her veil with Karen's help, she put it on.

"Beth," Hank spoke up, just as he and Annie walked in. "Are you ready, dear?"

"Yes, I'm ready!" she returned, nervously, while taking his arm, as they went to stand in behind Jodi and her father, when Marcose opened the patio doors.

Hearing the music playing, the time had come for them to walk out.

"Jodi," Hank whispered, "you look wonderful. I hope Jarred knows just how lucky he is having you for a wife?"

"Oh, I think he knows," she returned, seeing him and his uncle, standing at the bottom step of the gazebo, in their black tuxes. "Oh… yes, I think he knows," she repeated, when looking back at Beth, as she reached over to squeezed her hand.

Just then, the music paused as the last of the guests had all arrived to take their seats, along with Ted, Marcose and Baker.

Now, for what everyone had been waiting for.

At the beginning of the wedding march, everyone stood to see Jodi and Beth walk out onto the back lawn with their escorts. It was then, Jarred and Alex's expression gladdened at the sight of the two women for whom they had fallen in love with, come walking out.

Turning to his nephew, while watching their brides walk down the aisle with the sun shining brightly down on them, he asked in awe as they got closer, "How does it feel marrying an angel?"

"Like I've died and gone to Heaven," he replied, when they joined hands with their future wives. "Like I've died… and gone… to Heaven."

EPILOGUE

A week after the wedding, Jessi and Craig ventured up to the attic to get it ready for when one of her daughters were to move up there. While there, they opened the hidden toy room and found all sorts of little girl things, including a little white wooden rocker that seemed to rock all on its own, but then stopped and never did it again. As if the little girl was saying thank you, and goodbye.

But was it goodbye for good_____?